I0654192

North
of the Rock

Ian Jones

Clink
Street

London | New York

Published by Clink Street Publishing 2019

Copyright © 2019

First edition.

ISBN:
978-1-912850-10-5 - paperback
978-1-912850-11-2 - ebook

Chapter One

Day 1

The rental car was a new Buick, perfect for the roads; heavy and wide, a big engine, all the gadgets and a full tank of petrol. He put his bag in the boot and drove out of El Paso International airport, heading south to pick up the 10. He loaded Gray Rock into the satnav. Stated time to destination was three hours and forty minutes. He yawned and settled into the drive, he had been travelling more than sixteen hours already. London Heathrow to Dallas, wait around the airport for a couple of hours, then Dallas to El Paso.

He hit the 10 and as he followed the road east out into the open space the familiar West Texas landscape surrounded him. Not familiar in he saw it every day, or even regularly but familiar in that he had done this journey about eleven years ago. This exact same journey, and in all that time it hadn't changed at all.

And now he was back. It had all started four days ago. It had been a quiet time for him, he had not accepted any work for a while, needing some solitude after taking on some difficult projects. He had been in town, buying groceries, wandering around, not really doing much at all and had eventually gone into a barber shop for a haircut. It had been fairly busy, but he was in no hurry so sat down to wait. There were newspapers and magazines scattered on a table and he had picked up a red top and flicked through it. There was nothing particularly newsworthy, a quiet day. But about ten or so pages in there was a 'World News' section, and there he was, staring out at him from the bottom of the page.

Anthony Collis. He hadn't laid eyes on him or even thought about him in close to eleven years. It was the mug shot picture, the same photograph that had been in every newspaper when the news broke all those years ago. The heading above the picture just said, 'Texan Assassin Will Be Freed.'

The article was brief and not particularly detailed. Texas had recently elected a new Chief Justice for the state Supreme Court, a man called Gregory Raymer, who had been a judge for many years, a proud Texan, viewed as a radical Republican with a controversial history. He was elected by a big margin, despite his extreme views. The case of Anthony Collis had been bouncing around in the Texas legal system ever since his incarceration over ten years ago, although it had quietened down a great deal after the initial furore. The original state governor had reacted very strongly when Collis had been found guilty, and there had been plenty of noise, rumoured pushes for the president to get involved. Reading the article John remembered it without much interest. Collis had murdered two men and a woman, and possibly others. He knew, because it was him that had made the arrest and handed him over to the FBI. But Texas was more than just a big state, it was practically a country in itself, and had rallied around its own. There had even been demonstrations and protests in several cities that it was a conspiracy, the wrong man had been convicted, the FBI had arrested an easy target. Now, Gregory Raymer had promised that one of the first things he would do in office would be to put this miscarriage of justice right, and was working to set an appeals courts hearing for as soon as possible.

Without reading any more, John turned over the page. This was a load of nonsense. Collis had done it, no question. Even the worst prosecutor in the world would have no problems making sure he stayed in prison where he belonged.

He got his hair cut, the usual number three all over and then drove home. It was autumn, late September. He loved this time of year, the air seemed fresher and it wasn't yet cold enough for a coat. He unpacked the shopping and then booted his laptop, idly opening his messaging service.

Despite choosing to take a break, he had been checking it fairly regularly over the past few days so there were only a couple of new entries, and one jumped out at him straight away.

Patrick Skelton – PLEASE CALL ME URGENTLY! – and then two landline and one mobile telephone numbers.

This was very unusual. Patrick was someone he knew who worked for the FBI, he was pretty senior there, his job was basically to investigate the investigators. There were plenty of people who were nervous of him. They had first met when John was working on a case in Atlanta, and then more recently when he had uncovered a mess in Las Vegas.

It was the 'urgently' in capital letters that made him think, this wasn't a word that he could picture Patrick using, everything had a specific place and time, well structured, there always had to be order.

Well ok, why the hell not, thought John and picked up his mobile. He liked Patrick, he was one of the good guys. It had been at least a couple of years since they last met, there was no harm in calling. Patrick was based in Washington, so he calculated it was about mid-morning over there. He called the mobile number as that was likely to be the easiest way to catch him.

Patrick answered quickly.

'Patrick Skelton, hello?'

'Patrick? It's John.'

'At last, some good news. How you doing?'

'I'm fine, what's up? Bit of a panicked message you left there Patrick.'

'Yeah, well panic doesn't really cover it. There's a lot of headless chickens over here right now if you get what I'm saying.'

John was surprised to hear it. Patrick led a well organised life.

'Why, what's going on?'

'It's not going to make the news over your side of the pond. But Anthony Collis, it looks like he's getting out.'

Patrick was looking for him to talk about that? Why?

'Actually Patrick, I just read about that today. By chance. Some new judge or something, but he won't get out, how can he? He was bang to rights.'

There was a sigh down the phone and some movement. Patrick sitting down probably. John could picture him; crisp shirt with sleeve creases that could cause an injury and a subtle tie. Shiny cufflinks.

'There was a lot of trouble over that whole thing John. The governor back then made out like Collis was Texas's favourite son. They claimed that we, and by that, I mean the FBI, set him up. At the time there was already some negative press about the FBI and this just made it worse. The CIA didn't want it, so everything was down to us; and as a result we ended up looking like we were only after the glory.'

John remembered. It was true, the CIA hadn't wanted it, even though it was an American citizen killing people in Europe. Which was why John had been asked to continue with it.

'Sorry Patrick, it's great talking with you but I don't see what I can do.'

'Right well, I've been given the job of going through everything and making sure that we are covered. The feeling is that this is going to become big news, and we will be dragged through it all over again. I've been told fairly bluntly that if we have screwed up anywhere at any point I got to get it sorted. Thing is, I wasn't involved in it at all back then, so it's all new to me. And trust me, I've got masses of files to wade through. And what's the first thing I see? Your name, right there in black and white, stamped all over it.'

'Yeah, well it kind of fell into my lap really. Came out of what we thought was nothing at all. I'd been working on something over here for a while and Collis's name came up. Like you said, the CIA didn't want it, they were no help but we had to do something so I went to the FBI with it, we had a good relationship with you guys. It was political at the time, all sorts of problems and your people were nervous about it, so

I offered to be on point. And it was no problem at all, we got the right man.'

'I'm sure you're right John. But there is another factor that you don't know about. You probably heard about all the protests down in Texas at the time?'

'Yeah, I kind of followed it because I'd been working with you but from memory it didn't do anything constructive though.'

'Right, but a year later Collis's younger brother Wayne walked into a public library in Austin with an assault rifle.'

'Shit. No, I didn't hear about that.'

'I never knew about it either. It can't have made headline news. Anyway, he barricaded the doors and demanded to speak to someone senior at the FBI. Said it was about his brother. If he didn't get what he wanted, then it's goodbye hostages. You know the score.'

'Jesus. What happened.'

'Austin PD were on the scene, and they had it pretty well secured, and they got their local SWAT team down there. Those guys know what they are doing. We sent in our local field officers, one of them starts claiming to be the section chief. Why the real chief didn't get his sorry ass down there I have no idea. It was a fuck up, that much is clear. Turns out, Wayne Collis was a crack dealer and also an addict, and had been taken down by this same agent in a sting operation along with the DEA just a couple of months before.'

'Ah.'

'Yep. So he starts shooting.'

'I can't believe I never heard about this, it must have been big news.'

'Well it would have been big news, no question. It happens too damned often over here. The rifle was an M16, stolen from a local gun club. But it was modified and re-chambered to take 9mm ammunition, as you know that's a lot cheaper.'

'Yeah. The original takes NATO rounds.'

'Right. Maybe he bought the gun off someone or he stole it himself we don't know, reading the notes we did an ok job of piecing it together but I guess there are a lot of unanswered questions. Ultimately, it looks like the gun was empty and didn't even have a magazine. Eventually we found out that he bought a clip fully loaded from an old soldier near San Antonio and well, you can guess.'

'The gun doesn't fire.'

This explained why it hadn't made the news.

'Yep, as you say the gun doesn't fire. Clip is full of 5.56 shells, it fits I guess but the round won't even get in the chamber, he would have had to force the magazine. So, there's no shots fired and the SWAT guys storm the building, total textbook stuff. No need to start shooting, nobody has to get hurt. Collis manages to get himself into a store room with a lady that worked in the library, he's got a handgun, which the PD didn't know about. So the situation is better, there were forty-odd hostages and now it's down to one. But that's one too many, and he could have any number of bullets sitting in there. Anyway, Collis is screaming through the door making all these demands about justice and the decision is made to wait him out.'

'Makes sense.'

'They get a negotiator down there and after a couple of hours Wayne Collis is crying his eyes out about how shit his life is. It's all looking good. By this time the real section chief has finally dragged his ass down there, probably to face the cameras saying what a wonderful job they are doing, it's all under control. The negotiator is doing really well, and after another hour or so the lady gets set free so all we have now is an inconvenience. We got a weeping crazy in a store room with a gun in a public place.'

'That's a happy ending right?'

'Should be, but it doesn't go that way. They talk to the lady to try and find out what gun it is, but she's upset and doesn't know, she can't really give us anything other than it looks old and is round. So the decision is that it's a revolver. Six shots, maybe get lucky and only five. The section chief, who was removed very soon after this episode by the way, he orders the SWAT team in. There is an argument. I kid you not, I have read right through this. The SWAT leader is not happy, he feels it is unnecessary and Collis does not present a real and present danger.'

'I have to say Patrick; with all due respect I would have agreed with him.'

'You know what John, if I had been on the scene I would too. But we weren't there. Anyway, there's a compromise. The store room is long and thin with the door at one end. They kick it in and tell Collis to come out.'

John thought he could guess how the story would end.

'And does he?'

'Not at first. He's still sobbing and then he ups and runs straight out the door waving the gun and one of our agents steps up and puts a bullet in him. Straight through the chest. Dies at the scene.'

'Ok, shit, well, that does happen. Heat of the moment.'

'It does happen. But Collis was carrying a toy gun. Made of plastic, and even worse witnesses said that he was holding the gun in the air by the side of it, he didn't even have his finger on the trigger.'

John felt for Patrick, the man was an out and out professional. It would have hurt him badly to have to read through all this.

'Well you can imagine what went on down in Texas after this John. It had just started to calm down and now the place went crazy again, for a time anyway. We were on everyone in the state's shit list, you can imagine how the FBI looked down there; we had a vendetta against the Collis family, and Texans in general. The FBI were no good. I actually do remember all this going down, it was a PR nightmare for the FBI. It took a long time but eventually, it calmed down. A new governor got elected, and he never said anything about the Collis brothers, well not in public anyway. Every now and then there would be something about Anthony in the local news, a new pressure group was formed to get him freed and all that happy crappy, but it never went anywhere and for the past six or seven years it's all been forgotten.'

'Until now.'

'Yep. Until now. And that's why I wanted to speak to you, as soon as I saw you were involved I figured you are the one man that could help out in all this.'

'Patrick, this was a long time ago. It was just a case assigned to me at the Department. I was actually undercover with these right-wing arseholes called One Race, and I met Anthony Collis through them. But I don't work for the government anymore, I haven't in years. You know that.'

'Yeah, I do. But we have a big problem. We can't be seen to be doing any work on this at all. The message to everybody from the top is clear as day: stay well the hell away from this. Then at the same fucking time I've got to get stuck in and look for the holes. We aren't even sending someone to the hearing, whenever that happens. It's politics John. We have to do what we are told, whether we agree with it or not. But of course it's never as easy as that. One thing gets said on one side, while something else totally different on the other. And all the time the FBI are not getting involved and publicly making sure everybody knows it. While all that's going on I've been told to do the exact opposite and make goddamn sure we're clean.

'I still don't see what the hell I can do Patrick.'

'Well, I have a request. And it's probably gonna piss you off. And I expect you to say no, by the way.'

John looked out of the window. Rain was coming in.

'So ask me Patrick. If I say no, then we will still be friends.'

'For sure. I want you to go and see Collis, and maybe go back to Gray Rock. If there is someone pulling strings like I think they are then I would like to know who. This shit doesn't happen by itself, you know that. Of course, we will pay any expenses, plus something in your pocket, that goes without saying.'

'I don't care about the money Patrick.'

'But?'

John sat still and stared out the window again, turning the mobile around in his hands. It wasn't that simple, what could he do? Gray Rock was just a small town, he had arrested Collis there and it was where the man had been born and bred. He had never met the brother. And what would he say to him in prison? Would Collis even see him?

Patrick had to be desperate.

There could be any number of individuals or agencies that the FBI could rely on to do jobs like this.

But Patrick had called him. And he had a lot of time for Patrick.

'Sure Patrick. I've got nothing on right now. Why not? I can spare a few days to go to Texas.'

He could almost hear the enormous relief in Patrick's voice.

'Thank Christ for you John. Seriously. Thank you.'

'Where is he being held?'

'Federal Penitentiary. Howarth.'

'Where's that, is it in Texas?'

'Yeah, in fact, it's not a million miles away from Gray Rock. It's up north of Odessa. Huge place apparently, the biggest in the state.'

That was saying something. Everything was bigger in Texas.

'But how will this work? I'm hardly going to be on his visitor list and it's not like I can just rock up and ring the bell.'

Patrick laughed.

'There's ways and means of getting that done John. That's the least thing I'm worried about.'

'What's on your mind?'

'To be honest John I don't know for sure what I'm sending you into. Now all this shit is back in the news feelings are gonna be running very high down there, and if anyone finds out who are you ain't gonna be popular.'

'Don't worry about that Patrick. I can do anonymous. Anyway, it sounds like a straightforward in and out. I can't see anyone would remember me in Gray Rock. I'll stay there before I go to the prison and then get the first flight out. It'll give me a chance to have a nose around, but I'm not sure if I will find anything. I mean it makes sense what you're saying, if there is anyone stirring this up then it's likely to be around there but the likelihood is I won't be able to find a thing.'

'Yeah, I do know that, but thank you very much old friend. Look, I'm sure you are thinking this is all bullshit and you know what? It probably is. But soon as I started looking at this alarm bells started ringing loud and clear and we are real exposed if this Raymer follows this through. Thank you for helping me out John, I have to say I am feeling a bit better. So when will you go?'

'I'll look into flights tonight, and then I'll let you know.'

'Perfect. Look John I am your backup. Store my numbers, I am available twenty-four hours a day, whatever you need. You find anything, come to me ok?'

'Yeah of course. Ok, I'll let you know the details later on tonight.'

'Thanks John, and one other thing?'

'What's that?'

'It's not just the bureau that's keeping this quiet. I'm not advertising this either ok? Reading through all this I think the agent down there is no good. Something stinks anyways. Speak only to me.'

John checked his watch; he was an hour into the drive. There were really only two roads into Gray Rock, and they both eventually led into the town from the north. He could head south down the 67, or carry on into Fort Stockton and take the 385. From memory there wasn't a lot of time difference, although the 385 was a better road. Either way it was along the 90 and then southeast to Gray Rock.

He thought about how Anthony Collis had come into his life.

Chapter Two

Eleven years ago, John was working in the Department, and considered one of the best agents in the team. He was always away somewhere around the world, working deep undercover, never knowing what would happen next.

He enjoyed his work, most of the time.

Out of nowhere a right-wing organisation called One Race suddenly appeared on the radar. Apparently, they had been making some noise for a couple of years but John had completely missed it as he was away so much. They had political aspirations but weren't really being taken any notice of, from time to time they would have someone pop up at a by-election somewhere who would normally come last and promptly be forgotten forever. But over time it was discovered that there were some alliances in unexpected places, even some senior members of the current government were found to be supporters, and a mosque was set of fire in Southall, with a One Race flag left at the scene. Suddenly they were taken a lot more seriously. They had several chapters around the UK; two in London, and then Bristol, Birmingham, Manchester, Hull and Glasgow. They were also present in other names and denominations around the world, France, Germany, Italy and particularly the USA where the movement had originally started.

It was decided that the Department should find out more, and John was sent in undercover. He joined one of the London chapters, which met every Tuesday evening upstairs in a pub in Victoria. He was John, unemployed from South London.

They were always looking for new members so were very pleased to accept him into the fold, and even more pleased at the fifty pound subscription that he paid. He very quickly discovered that this was not much more than a group of blokes who wanted to get pissed while complaining about how hard done by they all were. He went to six meetings, which varied in attendance. Some weeks there could be thirty or more, and others less than ten. John would just sit there while various men would stand up and rant, always the same thing, week in week out. 'Send them back,' 'No immigration,' 'Hitler had it right,' and so on. John learned very quickly to close his ears, and he became heartily sick of the job.

All the men were just right-wing stereotypes, Hitler had never been right, but even he would have been embarrassed to be surrounded by these idiots.

The morning after the sixth meeting he sat down at the office with his department head Neil. He tried to keep the moaning to a minimum but it was difficult. He wanted out, the job was a depressing waste of time. Neil sympathised, he would not want to be doing this either. They agreed that this was just a drinking club for racist losers, with some lucky individual getting fifty quid in his back pocket every time a new member started. There was no threat. The attack on the mosque had clearly been done by one or possibly more members, but likely to have been arranged by themselves rather than through the group. John had never heard any talk about any actions. There had been rumours of a demonstration outside the immigration office in Croydon but it quickly became obvious that actually nobody could be bothered.

Eventually after some persuasion it was agreed that John would attend three more meetings, and then a sign off report would be compiled covering everything that had been discovered. Which wasn't a lot, because there was nothing to find out. John had been very happy to agree to it, but the following Tuesday after spending a couple of hours in the gym and gearing up to go to Victoria he was annoyed with himself for not pushing it to be just one more rather than three.

It all changed that evening. When he got to the pub, the place was buzzing, practically full. There were many more people there than he had seen before, he didn't recognise pretty much any of them. There were even a couple of women there, the first time that had happened. John sought out a man he had spoken to a few times to find out what was going on. The man looked at him in amazement.

'Don't you read the bulletins then?' he asked.

John thought back. When he had joined up they had asked him for an email address which he had given, it was just a throw away one that he would use for this job and he had never once looked at it. He mumbled something about his computer being broken and the man looked at him pityingly.

'Martin Scanlon is here. Tonight!' he declared happily.

John had no idea at all who that was, so he excused himself and went and sat on the toilet. He Googled the name. Martin Scanlon was an American businessman from Iowa. He was one of the founding members of the movement that spawned One Race. There was a picture of him, a good looking man in his fifties with neatly parted grey hair and wearing an expensive suit.

John went back into the room and wondered what Scanlon would make of the great unwashed who were standing around here waiting for him. A small stage with a microphone had been hastily assembled at one end of the room and promptly at eight o'clock Scanlon stepped onto it.

He gave a pretty speech, how they were misunderstood, that they were not racist, but they were representing those that had become forgotten, the men and women of this country and many others who were searching for and deserved more. Devalued, and all they were looking for was a better, fairer world. It was politics at it's very worst, all they wanted was to make themselves heard. John had heard all this crap before, so stopped listening. Scanlon talked for nearly forty-five minutes, and when he ended it was to rapturous applause. He had not come alone, there another man standing on the stage, behind and to the left. He wasn't introduced, and looking at him John couldn't seriously believe he was there as any kind of a minder. He was younger, short, with brown hair and fluid eyes that were always moving around the room. Scanlon finished his speech and waving moved off the platform, and then the other man stepped up and lowered the microphone to mumble 'Sometimes a life has to be taken to improve your own.'

The gathering either didn't hear or took no notice, they had already stopped paying attention.

But John wondered who the man was and what he had meant.

Afterward it was clear that Scanlon was keen to get away but that was never going to be easy. Everyone wanted to shake his hand or talk to him and he had no choice other than to smile a lot and gradually edge closer to the door. The other man just stood to one side. John went to the bar and bought a pint of Guinness, and politely asked the man if he would like one. The man looked at John then silently gazed over at Scanlon for a while and then surprisingly said he would, he'd have the same.

John passed the drink over and the man looked at it doubtfully.

'It's good for you. Apparently. Lot of iron,' John told him.

The man took a sip and John introduced himself.

'Anthony Collis,' replied the man, and they shook hands. Collis's were limp and cold.

Up close Collis was unremarkable. Short and slim with a pot belly, and thinning hair. But it was his eyes that John found fascinating. They were so liquid it looked as if he was going to burst into tears at any moment, and they shifted constantly, never still for even a second.

It was disconcerting.

He said he was from Texas, and asked John if he had ever been there. Mesmerised by the eyes and momentarily forgetting he was unemployed John from South London he said yes.

Collis looked interested when he heard that, and asked where.

'Dallas,' John replied.

Collis shrugged.

'That's not Texas,' he said dismissively.

John asked him how long he was in London for and Collis told him just one night, they were flying to Germany in the morning to address the chapter in Dusseldorf. John didn't know there was a group there but Collis told him One Race backed a movement that was big in Germany.

At last discovering that there could be something worth knowing John tried to get more information out of Collis but it went nowhere. Small talk was obviously not something he did. By this time Scanlon had reached the door so Collis put down his barely touched pint and moved away and the two men were gone. John fleetingly wondered if he should take the glass for fingerprints but realised that it was most likely that Anthony Collis would be his real name, so he should be able to find information on him anyway.

The next morning John went through the previous evening with Neil, who was also very interested. He set to work finding out exactly who the two men were, and then came back to Neil with what he had discovered.

Martin Scanlon was born in Des Moines fifty-four years ago. His father started a successful printing business which Scanlon had taken over when he was still in his twenties, and the company was doing very well to this day. He had invested in several other local businesses and was something of an entrepreneur. He was regarded as a poster boy for Des Moines industry, and had no criminal record. He had become involved in starting up an equal rights movement (which was clearly nothing more than right-wing propaganda) after a company he was involved with had been fined for not hiring a black woman who was more than qualified for a job with them, instead they had taken on a white woman who had been sacked after a couple of months because she was so inept. It was then discovered that no business that Scanlon was part of, including the printing company employed a 'person of colour'. Scanlon had determined that he was an American first, and an employer second. He wanted America to be a great country again, and to that Americans had to be in charge, it was them who should have all the jobs. Soon after One

Race was born, with Scanlon as its flag waving leader. The initial reports they could find was that the group was well funded and grew quite quickly, at least in the early days.

Anthony Collis was twenty-three years younger. He was born and still lived in a small town called Gray Rock in West Texas. Once again, there was no criminal record, but there were some interesting things that had been discovered. Currently it appeared that he worked in a local internet café, but his employment history was strange reading. He had applied to join the FBI when he was nineteen, but his application was rejected forthwith; there were issues with his education. Then he didn't seem to work at all until he got a job aged twenty-three working on a support desk for an ISP. This meant he worked from home. However, when he applied for the job he stated that he had served in the army, and just come out that year. Following some complaints against him the company eventually did cursory background checks and discovered that this was a lie. There is a big army base about thirty miles from Gray Rock, so initially his story had been believed as it seemed a logical choice for a young man leaving school.

The company let him go, only to get a furious letter from the mayor of Gray Rock asking why he would be singled out in this way, claiming that Collis had worked for a secret division in the army which could never be admitted, hence his love of computers and why the army had denied his existence.

Rather than have to face any battles, the company re-employed him, but as second line support so he would never need to speak to any customers.

But very soon there was a new problem. Collis had a line manager, a black woman who had been with the company a long time. Collis was supposed to complete all sorts of online forms and documents as part of his job but never did so. They never had any idea of what he was doing, so the woman drove down to see him. He gave her such fierce abuse that she was so shocked she sat in her car for an hour in tears.

There was no other choice; Collis was sacked again.

He joined the local gun club and became a volunteer local deputy then started his own IT support business, fixing local people's computers, which failed quickly. Then he went to work at a local motel as the night clerk, before being fired following an altercation with a female resident.

Then there was one piece that John found very interesting. When he was twenty-six, and supposedly at the time acting as a deputy, he had shot a young man who was one of two attempting to rob a local petrol station. The man was seriously hurt, he had been hit in the upper back. However, there were two versions of the story; Collis's was that he was driving past at around eleven o'clock at night and noticed the two black men threatening the clerk in the petrol station, which had large glass windows right across the front. He had stopped, and the men had spotted him and run out. The victim had been carrying a gun, and fearing for his own life Collis had stated that he fired as the man turned to aim. But the second man, who was unhurt said that they had been driving and had gone into the petrol station hoping to buy a map. The clerk had been very rude and unhelpful, so there had been an argument. The two men were students at Houston University and were travelling to the National Park near the border and had got lost. He said despite the rudeness there were no threats made by either side, and they did not have a gun, neither man had ever owned one. Collis had walked into the station and approached them aggressively and they could see he was armed so walked straight out and when they had run for the car, Collis had shot his friend in the back. When the state police turned up no other gun was found. Collis then claimed there was a third man outside who had snatched it and run off. The clerk had not been able to give a statement claiming that he was under stress and taking medication so he couldn't remember the events clearly. There was a security camera, but it had been 'accidentally' switched off that day. The man who had been shot survived, and was able to provide a full statement, which completely matched the original his friend had given. Both men stated categorically that they had been on their own, there was no third man, there was no gun, no hold up. Collis' explanation regarding the circumstances that the man was shot in the back was that his victim had been running, twisting and turning and shooting which fortunately missed but Collis had fired because he had been very scared while trying to uphold the law. This meant it was one word against the other's. The state police washed their hands of it and handed everything over to the local sheriff, who said they would deal with it, as it was an internal matter.

Nothing further, and no mention of why a volunteer deputy would be carrying a gun in the first place. Case closed. No further action.

Then there was a list of small time, basic jobs leading up to now, when he was thirty-two years old. He was not married, and lived in the same house he always had, both his parents were deceased. He was still a member of the gun club in Gray Rock and had two guns registered to him. Both were .22s, one a Smith & Wesson revolver and the other a Ruger rifle.

John and Neil looked at each other.

'Bit of a fuck-up,' Neil said.

John agreed. The guy had been weird for sure. One to watch maybe.

Later that day John returned to his flat in St John's Wood. He was tired, he had been in the gym for a long session again and then gone for a run. He made some pasta and put the TV on.

Headline news; a German politician had been assassinated in Cologne. Helmut Romann was a good looking, clean cut and reasonably young man, thirty-seven years old and a member of the liberal Free Democratic Party. He was their spokesman for education and had been visiting the university in the town. He was shot in the head as he left the building to walk back to his car. As he wasn't regarded as being particularly high profile, his visit hadn't warranted any additional police presence and everyone was shocked.

John had no idea who the man was, but Cologne was at most an hour from Dusseldorf, which immediately seemed like more than a coincidence. But why kill Helmut Romann, what was the benefit? He checked Google again, to see what he could find out. Initially, there wasn't a lot. He had trained as a teacher but had taken a job working for the administration in Hanover and had just worked his way up, entering into politics. Nothing spectacular.

But then he stumbled upon something not well known about Romann. Four years previously he had been involved with Redefreiheit Jetzt, a part of the One Race movement in Germany, there had been an increase in right-wing candidates and it was part of a push to gain a parliamentary seat. He had made a televised speech which basically said that all One Race were doing was putting to words what everybody was thinking. Less than one month later he had renounced it, saying he was misguided and had been pressured into speaking publicly. He had completely misunderstood the manifesto as it had been presented to him by One Race because it had not been the version that was later released. He had honestly believed at the time that the party was looking to act in the best interests of the German people. He had realised his mistake and was now admitting it. Because he was so clean cut, and urbane, and carried himself well he was believed and forgiven, even by the media, and the Free Democratic Party leapt in for him immediately, and he continued his upward climb with them.

Defections between parliamentary parties were not that unusual, and it could easily be said that he was never really a full member of One Race anyway.

But John knew he was right, it had to be more than just a coincidence. Martin Scanlon had not mentioned visiting Germany once in his speech in the pub, and maybe Collis was not supposed to say anything either. But he had, and he owned a .22 rifle, which was not a calibre a sniper would use but was fine for target practice.

The next morning, he spoke with Neil who shared his concerns and they did further checks. Collis and Scanlon had flown back to the US into Chicago from Frankfurt the previous evening. John flew into Cologne that afternoon and met with an agent of the FIS called Dietmar. They looked around the university grounds and Dietmar took him to where the shot had been fired which was a window on a landing in a half occupied office building opposite. John looked carefully, it was less than three hundred yards which was meat and drink to a professional sniper, nothing at all. Dietmar was happy to talk, he seemed to be enjoying himself. He explained how they worked out where the shot had come from and John was impressed. He looked closely at the slight drag marks where the rifle barrel had been rested on the window frame. Romann had been killed by a 7.62 round which was a pretty standard bullet for a sniper rifle and told them next to nothing, but the FIS would hold onto it for ballistics checking. So far there were no suspects. They went for coffee and John asked Dietmar if there was any other information on Romann and explained that he knew about the One Race connection.

Dietmar nodded, they had also been looking into this but could find no link to anyone they were looking at currently. Romann had been due to marry a woman of Turkish descent, and there were no skeletons in the closet as far as they were concerned. Joining One Race appeared to be a blip on an otherwise spotless career path, they had been making a lot of noise at the time and it could have been regarded as an understandable attempt to build a higher profile. It was said that Romann was very reserved, he lacked a sense of humour and took himself a little too seriously but Dietmar had not heard of anyone being killed for those traits. John hadn't either.

He flew back that night and pondered the situation.

He was starting to believe that One Race did need to be looked at, that he was actually doing something worthwhile after all.

The next day the department began working in earnest. They started with the CIA, but as usual got no help at all. The FBI were better, One Race appeared to be very well funded, they had a network of rich donors. The majority of these were to be found in the south; Alabama, Mississippi, Texas. But nothing was read into this, they were strictly Republican states and possessed a large number of older ex-employees of the political world. It was noted that there were also several donors who wished to remain anonymous.

The FBI offered to examine this list more closely.

John continued his own research with his team and then uncovered something that on the face of it was even more incriminating. Just over six months previously, a French politician called Lucille Canour had been shot in the head as she watched a speech being made by her Socialist Party in the town square in Reims after they won a local election. Due to the increase in French right-wing support the One Race backed candidate had initially appeared to be doing fairly well in the polls, but then had fallen by the wayside massively. Canour had been very outspoken in her criticism of the party and had laughed when the low count for One Race had been read out. It turned out that One Race had a meeting of their chapter in Paris the night before, which had been attended by one of the founders from the USA. Not Scanlon this time, but a man called Norman Flint. Reims was no more than two hours' drive from Paris. The sniper was in a building which directly overlooked the square, the report read two hundred and fifty metres. They dug deeper. Anthony Collis had passed through immigration two days before and out again on the same day.

John spoke once more to the FBI, they were interested but powerless, the crimes had not taken place on USA soil but they were keen to help. John told them they would carry on digging, and then found a third one almost straight away. Italy, Tivoli. An elderly statesman by the name of Giovanni Trisi had been shot in the garden of his home in just outside Tivoli. This was just a year ago. One Race had run a series of commercials looking for new party members. Trisi had still been in local government at the time and had spoken out against them, declaring them to be Nazis. A chapter had started in Rome, and eventually it was discovered that there had been a representative from the USA the night before the killing, but this time they could find no trace of a name. It didn't matter, it was enough. Tivoli was an hour from Rome.

John picked up the phone and called the FBI, who looked into it and confirmed that Anthony Collis had passed through immigration back into the USA in Houston the following day.

He had seen all he needed to.

Chapter Three

Two hours in and John saw a road sign for Howarth Penitentiary. He had passed Van Horn and was close to Fort Stockton. The sign was high up on posts along with others pointing to Odessa and Midland. Patrick had emailed over a visit pass and other details; John was supposedly on an authorised visit from the UK government looking at wrongful arrests. Collis would remember him, there was no question of that but it would be too late by then. Fuck him if he can't take a joke.

Just over three hours had passed and John was finally approaching Gray Rock. He remembered the sharp climb uphill which led to an even steeper downhill and then the town would come into view on his right. But as he crested the hill he was shocked by what he saw and slowed to a crawl. There was now a huge building towering up between the town and the airfield which was further north, and on the opposite side of the road was now what appeared to be a business park. These had not been there before. He continued to slowly roll down the hill trying to take it all in. The town was there alright, but appeared to be more than twice as big as he remembered. The petrol station where Collis had shot the student was still there, just as he recalled immediately before the town limits. There was a big shiny new sign, which wasn't peppered with buckshot holes. It said 'Welcome to Gray Rock – Population 2611'. Which was well over a thousand more than when he was last here. There was a tatty poster cable tied to the pole that read 'Justice for Anthony'. He slowed even further to a stop and rolled onto the shoulder as he passed the plant, which looked brand new, it could only be a few years old. The main building was over five or six storeys high, a massive cube of concrete, glass and steel in a vast square of neatly cut grass and scrub with another big three-storey office block running at right angles and several smaller outbuildings and full car parks dotted all around. It was protected by a high steel mesh fence with razor wire across the top and John could even see a helicopter in the far rear corner. In front of him was a wide turning off the road which led onto a straight run down to a set of barriers with a guard house at the side. A massive white sign alongside said BRP Pharmaceuticals and this was also displayed across the top of the building. As he sat watching a big truck trundled past and turned in. A guard came out and checked over some paperwork and raised the barrier. As the truck disappeared around the side another came out, this one clean and shiny with the BRP logo on it. It went through the checkpoint and then followed the approach back to the main road and turned left, passing John on its way up the hill. It was all very impressive. He turned his head, looking back beyond the building toward the airfield and got another shock, there were several new buildings there too and a sign which said 'Gray Rock Airport'. Airport? It had been a small airfield eleven years ago, a hangover from the oil days. He pulled out and then turned left into the business park, prowling around to have a look. It was a rectangular shaped collection of single story buildings, identically finished in tan brick and mostly office units mixed in with some that looked like small warehouses. There were cars parked here and there. It looked like a lot of the buildings were occupied.

Times had really changed.

He pulled out back onto the road and continued down the hill, heading south.

He was driving on the original main road into Gray Rock, which was unchanged and came in from the north meeting the town in what was previously the northeast corner but everywhere had been built up since. The town sloped downward from north to south. Less than a mile later he saw the motel on his right, where he had stayed on his last visit and intended to stay now. It had been given a lick of paint but looked the same otherwise. Down the road further south on the left he was pleased to see the diner was still there. Past the diner it opened out, there was the crossing with the east west road which would eventually take him to the army base if he drove for long enough to the east, on the corner on the other side was the town hall.

He pulled into the motel parking lot, then got out of the car, stretching. It was starting to get dark and was warm and breezy. The motel was a two-storey building which had a short right angle turn behind on the left-hand side, like a stunted, inverted L shape. He glanced at the office and saw a woman inside staring out at him and talking on the phone. He collected his bag, locked the car and walked over.

Inside the woman was sitting behind the short counter, and glared at him malevolently as he approached. Her stance did not change when she heard his accent as he enquired about a room. There was a big sign that said vacancies so there really wasn't a great deal to discuss. He asked for two nights and she quoted him sixty bucks a night. Politely John pointed to the Vacancies sign, where underneath was written $40. She pursed her lips and said nothing, then took the eighty dollars he passed over without looking at him. Behind her was a board with a long row of keys, there were thirty-two rooms and twenty-eight keys, so business was slow.

She passed him the key for number sixteen, and then told him there was no parking directly outside his room, which was upstairs. He shrugged and picked up the key and his bag, then left the office.

He worked out his room was on the end of the L upstairs, so he turned right and began walking. He didn't get far. A Sheriff Chevrolet Impala came fast into the parking lot and stopped in the centre with its roof lights flashing. The driver's door opened and a short, fat sheriff climbed out with difficulty, then stood at the side leaning on the open door, breathing hard and staring at John, who looked deliberately at his watch and then continued the route around the motel.

'Now you stop right there boy. Stand still,' the sheriff barked.

John stopped and turned to look at the man properly. He was very overweight and his uniform was extremely tight around his belly. He had a big round head with a mop of greasy grey hair which was stuck to his forehead with sweat. As John watched, his dropped his hand and rested it on the butt of the Colt revolver he had on his right side.

He looked ridiculous.

'What can I do for you officer?' John asked politely.

'You can just step your skinny ass this way, is what you can do,' was the reply.

'I thought you wanted me to stand still?'

'Don't get smart with me, y'hear? I ain't got the time for any bullshit. Now get over here.'

John walked across to the car. He wasn't too surprised the sheriff hadn't wanted to make the short journey himself, he looked as if he ever took any exercise it would be the last thing he did. Up close he was even less impressive. He had on a grubby undershirt which was damp all around the neck and his gut was hanging down over his belt buckle. There was a dirty metal badge with the name 'Carter' on his left breast pocket.

John stopped and dropped his bag, waiting patiently. A Harley came down the road, grumbling and farting as it passed. There was a big man in a beaten up old brown leather jacket riding, he slowed and stared hard at the sheriff who conscientiously avoided looking at the man. He smiled, revved the bike and rode away.

The sheriff opened the rear door of the car.

'Right, get in. We need to have a talk.'

'Really? I just got here. Where are we headed?'

'Sheriff's office, I got some questions for you.'

'Sheriff's office? Isn't it quicker to walk?'

John looked pointedly down at the town hall. The sheriff's office was the next building, maybe a five minute walk at the very outside.

'Just get the hell in the car smart ass, I am done with this shit. Just get in.'

So John got in. Why not? It would be interesting to find out what this was all about. Carter threw John's bag onto the passenger seat and then walked back around. As he went to close the door John looked up at him.

'I think I'll make my phone call when we get there.'

Carter grunted and climbed back in the car, which sagged badly when he did so. John looked around, the Impala was way past it's best. Probably a brand new car in a smart precinct maybe twelve years ago, probably more. Maybe downtown in Chicago, or out in the bay in San Francisco. Then it had done its time there and been moved on to a more laidback police department, gratefully received, still working but with some miles on the clock. Then a few more years, and it had been moved on again, somewhere slower, more rural and then probably on again, to end up here. Inside it was very second hand. Tired and beaten up, there were screw holes all over the dashboard where various items of equipment had been fixed in place over the years. The rear seat was worn and filthy with a torn cover. The front seats were even worse, with a shotgun fixed between them in the centre just in front of the privacy screen, that was marked and scratched. The sheriff started the car and reversed back through a thick cloud of blue smoke, and then drove out. He followed the road past the diner, crossed over the east–west road and then turned in immediately after the town hall into the car park in front of the sheriff's office. Total driving time less than thirty seconds. There was one other cruiser parked there, equally ancient. Carter huffed and puffed getting out of the car, and finally opened the rear door which squeaked loudly. John swung his legs around and got out, then stood up. John wasn't a particularly tall man, a fraction over six feet but he towered over the sheriff.

He stood and looked around.

The sheriff grunted again.

'Let's go.'

They made their way over to the building, which was single-storey red brick construction and didn't look like much, more like a small office. They entered through a pair of glass doors on the right side. Inside was a basic reception area which led directly onto an open plan area behind, with a couple of open cells like tall cages in the back corner. The place was empty apart from an old man in a deputy uniform seated on a stool behind the counter. He looked at John curiously as they walked in. Carter gestured toward a short row of empty seats.

'Sit your ass down there while I get things sorted out. I got a lot of questions to ask you.'

John didn't move.

'I said, sit your ass down in there!' Carter barked.

John continued standing where he was.

'Thing is sheriff; I would like to make my phone call,' he said very politely, and dug his mobile out his front pocket.

'You do that when I say so, y'hear?'

Carter laid a hand face up on the counter.

'Gimme the cell keys will you Frank,' he asked.

The old man stooped down and came up with a heavy bunch of keys, which he laid in front of Carter, who swept them up and turned to face John.

But John had seen enough and looked at him levelly.

'I think you need to listen sheriff. Closely. Before you think about locking me in one of your cells. Firstly, I haven't been arrested. I haven't been told why I am being detained. Secondly, you put me in your car and you didn't cuff me, you didn't even search me. You didn't even look twice when I took my phone out my pocket. Thing is, I could have a gun on me right? But you know I don't, so I am getting interested now. How did you know I don't have a gun, and also to look out for me, and why was the woman in the motel told to call you? Why were you waiting for me?'

Carter stood looking up at him, mouth wide open.

'So, I'll just make my call,' John sat down without waiting for a reply and called Patrick.

Loudly he told him about Carter and all that had happened. Patrick reacted exactly as John had expected, and once the expletives had stopped told John to give him five minutes and then hung up. John relaxed, sat back and watched, waiting for the show to begin. The deputy was busy doing nothing at the counter and Carter had slumped uselessly in a chair in the main office. Both men had heard every word that John had said.

The office phone rang.

The deputy jumped and answered it, and then a stricken look crossed his face. He held the receiver away and looked behind.

'Ah … Joe. I got a call on one for you. It's the … Feds.'

Carter sat upright and stared out at John, then reached over to the phone on the desk in front of him and picked up the receiver. He pushed a button, and wasn't able to complete saying hello before the barrage hit him. Then, the office phone rang again, and once more the deputy answered it, looking nervously over at Carter who was still being grilled.

This time, the deputy rapidly became even more desperate, and then asked the caller to hold.

'Ah … Joe, I got another call!' he tried to interrupt. Carter looked at him, and was trying to speak at the same time. Eventually he nodded and spoke quietly and hung up. He looked at the deputy who indicated the phone so he picked it up again, and received exactly the same treatment but louder this time, whoever it was on the other end of the line was not holding back. John could pick up the odd word here and there, it wasn't Patrick. The sheriff was getting another bollocking from someone else altogether. Eventually the call ended and Carter sat back in the chair and rubbed his face.

John stood up.

'Right, well, I'll be off then,' he said brightly.

Carter got up out the chair and waddled into the reception area.

'So you got friends in high places. Well I'm the law down here, and I'll be seeing you again, you have my word on that.'

John walked over to him, and looked up at the clock on the wall.

'Fifteen minutes,' he announced.

'What?' Carter looked confused.

'That's how much of my time you have wasted. Fifteen minutes since you stopped me at the motel.'

He moved closer, so he was a couple of inches away and leaned in.

'Yeah, you will be seeing me again,' he said quietly.

Carter involuntarily took a step back.

John walked out, and over to the cruiser. It wasn't locked, so he recovered his bag and then crossed back over the road and on up to the motel. He waved at the woman when he got there. She just stared out at him, and he walked around and up some metal stairs at the end to his room.

It was facing backward on the end of the L. There was a metal walkway all around which ended just past his door. He turned and looked around. The change in the town was incredible, when he had last stayed here the northern area of the town had been pretty empty; just a few houses and the airfield in the distance. Now it was built up, with lines and lines of houses and some bigger buildings that were possibly schools further out. There was even some kind of stadium he could see. Looking across toward the horizon he saw that on the north-western edge there were some very big, grand houses that curled away up the steep hill. Immediately in front of him was a high wall with some kind of loading bay on the other side, he guessed that there were shops there, so there was a commercial district too.

All this done in eleven years?

Incredible.

It was full dark now, close to seven o'clock.

His phone rang, it was Patrick. John told him he was out again, no harm done and Patrick apologised down the phone, promising to keep Carter off his back if possible. John told him it wasn't a problem.

He unlocked and walked into the room, snapping the light on as he closed the door behind him. It was a standard motel room, which was all that could be said about it. Decorated in light brown with a dull orange carpet and curtains to match. The double bed was on the right, and a set of drawers with an elderly TV on top to the left. At the back of the room was a bathroom, with a wardrobe against the wall close to the doorway. Exactly the same as every motel room he had ever stayed in, he wondered if there was a motel designer somewhere who was now a very rich man.

He dropped the bag on the floor and sat on the bed. He was tired, but was wise to the fact that the trick to travelling to the USA was always the same. Stay awake as long as you can. It was two in the morning for him UK time plus he had been travelling and driving for hours but if he went to sleep now he would be awake at three and it would just fuel the jetlag.

He knew there was a roadhouse a couple of miles outside of the town to the west, and wondered if it was still there.

Probably he thought.

He considered walking, it was a nice night and maybe do him good but decided that if he did then all that would do would be to make even more tired when he got there. He stripped and had a shower, which was very feeble and dried himself with a threadbare towel, then cleaned his teeth and got dressed again.

He left the room and walked down the stairs and rounded the corner. There was nobody else about here, but at the front the lights were on in a couple of the motel windows. The woman was still sitting at the counter so he knocked on the window and waved, just to be annoying, and then got in the car and pulled out.

He went down to the crossroads and turned right, headed west.

He remembered that when he had first visited he had briefly wondered the name of the town and then promptly forgotten all about it until he had taken a look around; then he had immediately realised why it was called what it was, for there was a huge grey rock which sprouted up out of the earth. Previously, the town had grown out to the south of it, with a couple of lines of houses and hardly anything other than the airfield in the north. Now, it was in the centre, the north side had grown so much. The rock was roughly square, about four metres a side and a bit higher. It was surrounded by an egg-shaped patch of smaller rocks and scrub grass, with the town hall on its eastern side. As he made the turn he saw the rock, and could see that money had been spent here too. Now, in the space between the town hall and the rock a large paved square had been built, circled by flowerbeds and seats. In the centre of the square was a war memorial. It then led to a narrow strip of grass up to the rock, as he passed by there had been no change on the other side, and he could see the southern part, or the original town as he thought of it sloping away to his left. He would visit it tomorrow morning, have a look around. He was due at the prison at 3 pm, so he would have enough time, he just needed to make sure he got going before twelve.

To his right on the north side, he could see a couple of new roads leading away with a bar and family restaurant looking out to the rock and then to his great surprise there was now a Radisson hotel. A shiny new six-storey building. He carried on down the western road which he remembered was narrow, not a great road. If he followed it eventually he would hit the 67 and he could go south to the border, or north back toward Fort Stockton. As he cleared the town he saw a neon glow ahead and soon realised it was the roadhouse, still up and running, maybe some things weren't that different.

Chapter Four

It was still called Big Lil's and didn't seem to have changed at all looking at it from the outside. Still a mixture of concrete block and heavy wooden sidings, with wide shallow pitched sloping roofs on either side that raised to a peak in the middle. There were a few vehicles scattered around in the massive car park. He parked up and walked in, inside it had altered a bit, it had been updated. There were now TV screens everywhere all showing different sports, NFL, Basketball and other American Football matches being the most popular. There was a huge Lone Star Flag on the back wall, and a smaller Stars and Stripes fixed to the ceiling. Pool tables in the back and to the right, and a stage to the left. The bar was a wide rectangle right in the middle, with two young barmen behind it and another couple of pretty girls walking around taking orders. The menu was fixed to the walls in several places around the room, and John realised he was hungry. He walked across and sat down at the bar in the corner, which had a big wooden pillar from floor to ceiling on all four locations. To his right on the other side were a couple of young guys sitting next to each other, early twenties John thought. They were both big guys, in good shape, and covered in dirt. Probably builders at a guess. They were drinking Budweiser out the bottle and watching the football in front of them. John ordered a Miller and ribs, no coleslaw. He turned around and surveyed the room.

There were probably about thirty people there, mostly men, dotted around the room in ones and twos, chatting to the waitresses who were smiling and doing well at being the perfect hostesses. It was a typical roadhouse, and this is what they were all like in John's experience. On the occasions there was a band on the place would come alive, they would be good nights, worth coming to.

John sat there comfortably, just passing the time. He wondered what all the fuss was about earlier with that fat idiot of a sheriff, what the hell was the point? It did ask who was talking though, so far the only person that knew he would even be in Gray Rock was Patrick, and he would go to his grave before he said anything. So that just left the prison, somebody must be talking. It wasn't that much of a surprise, Texas is a huge state, bigger than the whole of the UK but West Texas is practically another state altogether. They had their own way of doing things out here that was for sure.

His food arrived, and he saw that the two young men had ordered chicken wings and they got theirs at the same time. He started eating, none of it was healthy, but it was very good. The ribs were coated in thick barbecue sauce and the chips were big and golden. He loved every morsel. As he ate he caught the eye of the nearest of the two young guys, who nodded to him.

'Should have had the ribs,' the guy said ruefully.

'Yeah, you should have,' John agreed cheerfully.

Both men looked at him, and the other one said:

'What accent is that? Australian?'

John laughed.

'No, much worse. British. From London, so yeah I'm speaking English but that means nobody else can understand me.'

The man chuckled.

'Nope, I can understand you speaking, but I sure as hell can't understand why you'd be sitting in here when you could be back home.'

John shrugged and carried on eating.

'Well, it's work. You know, I go where I get asked to go.'

He had given some thought about a cover story if he was ever put on the spot, and decided to try it out on these two. It couldn't do any harm, and he would be gone in a couple of days anyway.

'Oh yeah? What job is that then?' The guys were interested.

'Journalist. Just covering life down near the border. Nothing exciting.'

The one nearest looked at him carefully.

'Border is over thirty miles south you know.'

'Yeah, I do know, it's just a simple piece. Not particularly ground-breaking.'

The two men looked at him, measuring him up, then the further one wiped his hands on a napkin and reached over.

'Well, we don't get a whole lot of tourists down here. Good to meet you, I'm Danny, and this is Art.'

John carefully wiped and shook both their hands.

'I'm John.'

'So what do you think of our town then John?' Art asked as they carried on eating.

'I was here before, more than ten years ago. It's changed a lot.'

The two men looked at each other.

'Oh yeah,' Danny commented. 'It's changed a lot alright.'

John looked at them again. They were both big men, with thick arms under dirty t-shirts.

'So you two football players?' he asked.

Again the look.

'Back in high school,' Art told him. 'But Danny here played college ball. He could have gone all the way in my opinion.'

John didn't know much about American football, but he knew that not many players made it through to the NFL. No different from the football league at home. Soccer, to these two.

Danny looked embarrassed.

'He got injured,' Art explained.

'Sorry to hear that,' John replied. 'High school football is big round here right? Texas is famous for it I think.'

Art laughed.

'Oh yeah. It's a big deal.'

'Not in this town,' added Danny ruefully.

'Why's that? I thought you said you played?'

'Yeah, we did. But for the old high school.'

'There's two high schools here?'

Danny looked confused.

'Yeah of course. Gray Rock High is still there. But they opened the Gray Academy, what three, four years ago? And they get all the money. So, that's the team now, but me and Art used to play for the high school. It was all different back then.'

Art nodded.

'It sure was. We were a good side. Headed for State. Never made it of course, but we had a real good go.'

He held his hand up and Danny gave him a high five.

'You still gonna be here on Friday?' he asked John.

'Not sure. Maybe.'

'Get up to the game, see for yourself.'

'Watch them get beat,' Art said sullenly.

'No good then?'

'No, they are terrible. Like I got told in here once that I should be saying 'we', instead of 'they', but the truth is they aren't our football team. Me and Danny, we were the town, and every Friday in season everyone would come out to watch. That don't happen no more.'

'Why?'

'Because they lose. Week in, week out,' Danny replied. 'So every season it's like there's a new coach or they got the best quarterback or whatever bullshit they can think of to get people in the stadium. But it's always the same. The other teams are always better.'

John finished eating and took a drink. He liked these two.

'So go on then, you guys know much more than me, why are they losing so much.'

Art looked away. Danny leaned forward.

'Well that's real simple to answer John. Take a look around.'

John looked around the bar, it hadn't changed at all while he was talking, just men and he could count maybe two women sitting around drinking. He looked back at Danny, confused.

'What, I don't see anything.'

'Right. See any black faces? You see any colours at all apart from white?'

John sat upright and stared at him, and then carefully looked around. Everyone there was white. All the customers, the waitresses, the two guys behind the bar.

'I didn't notice,' he admitted.

'Well, that's how it is. And it's the same at the school. In the whole of the north side. Trust me,' Art told him defiantly, anger visible in his eyes.

John shook his head.

'That can't be right. It's not possible. This is America, there's no way it can happen.'

'It happened, and it happened right here. You said it yourself, the town has changed.'

'Well yeah, but I didn't mean …'

'Be a good story for you,' interrupted Art.

It would be an amazing story thought John. If I was really a journalist.

'So there you are. You see, all over the state there are high school football teams, and they have white, black, Hispanic, whatever. They field the best players that go to the school, that's how it works and how it has always worked. It's how it should be, of course it is. And a lot of these boys can really play. But the Academy they just put out a team in their shiny new uniforms made up of whoever is the right age that feels like playing and they get hammered. All white boys, every one. It's bullshit.'

Art was obviously upset. He drained his beer and got off the stool.

'I gotta go. I gotta work tomorrow.'

'Where do you work?' asked John.

'Up at the quarry. We both do.'

'Quarry? I don't remember a quarry, where's that?'

'Just follow the road past here about three miles. You'll see the concrete works, and it's right next to that.'

Concrete works made sense with all the construction, and he supposed the quarry did too.

Danny also slid of his stool.

At that point another man entered, and walked across the room to sit on a stool at the bar a couple down from John. It was the big man who had been riding the Harley earlier, John recognised the jacket. As he got comfortable he glanced over at the two young men and nodded.

'Hey Gilbey,' Danny said as a greeting.

The man nodded again.

Danny and Art walked around the bar and shook John's hand again.

'Gilbey, this is John. He's visiting the town. We were just explaining that things are different here.'

The man turned slowly and looked at John carefully.

He was a big man, in good shape but a lot older, maybe even in his seventies. He had flyaway grey hair and a craggy face, with bright blue eyes.

'Things are different here alright,' he replied.

'Yeah, we were just saying. He was here before, he's noticed the changes,' Art told him.

'Oh yeah? That could be a long list,' he commented. He had a deep and gravelly voice, which was perfect for him.

Danny slapped him on the back and told him he would see him later then the two young men walked out. A barman put a bottle of Budweiser on the bar in front of Gilbey without asking.

Gilbey took a drink gratefully, then set the bottle down carefully on the bar in front of him.

John also took a drink. He saw in the clock behind the bar it was nearly nine, he could safely go to bed soon. He was aware of Gilbey looking at him, so he turned to face him.

'So what brings you here?' Gilbey asked.

'Oh I'm a journalist, just writing about life near the border.'

'Journalist, are you? Lot to write about in this town, if you care to take a look. A close look.'

'Really? Well, ok. So, where should I start?' John asked him curiously.

'Go and see the three wise men , that's as good a place as any.'

'The three wise men?'

'Yeah. It's not difficult to find them.'

'Who are they?'

'Just the three wise men.'

'So why would they be worth talking to?'

Gilbey's eyes narrowed, and John guessed he had said the wrong thing.

'There's a cancer in this town. It needs cutting out. Talk to them, see for yourself. You're the journalist, so you say.'

Gilbey said nothing else, just turned to face the bar. End of conversation. John finished his drink and with a muted goodbye and a nod to the barman dropped some dollars on the bar and walked out.

Abel hung up the call on his mobile with a shake of his head. What the hell were they paying for? It wasn't the first time he had wondered about this. It was a good job there was always a Plan B. He called Barlow, who answered quickly. Abel walked over to the window and looked out into the dark, the lights of the town spread out in front and below of him.

Barlow spoke first.

'Don't tell me. There has been a screw-up.'

Abel was just glad it was nothing to do with him.

'Yeah. That fat asshole Carter dropped the ball. As usual I might add. He gave the guy his phone call! Believe that?'

There was a loud exhale of air from the other end. Abel smiled, he could picture Barlow stalking around his living room, head swivelling from side to side on his long neck.

'I swear to God, I really do. Can that fucking guy do anything right?' Barlow breathed down the phone.

'Yeah, I hear you. But I guess we'll just do it the hard way.'

'I guess so.'

'Right then, I'll make the call, organise it now.'

'Do that. But make sure Cane fully understands that this has to go away, this guy needs to understand not to make any more calls and just get the hell out.'

'I'll tell him. Do you want me to call Hunter myself too?'

'No, let Cane do his job. He can make amends. He's supposed to looking after these things, making sure the work gets done. It's like we're forever cleaning up.'

'Yeah I know. Goodnight.'

'Goodnight, see you in the morning.'

Abel killed the call and dialled another number.

John drove back to the motel, but diverted off the east–west road to go through to the south side, to see what he remembered. The street that had the shops and restaurants was still there, but now with a few boarded-up fronts. The bar he remembered called Pinto was open, as was the restaurant on the corner. But it was quiet, not many people about. He parked up in the street and got out the car. This had been a vibrant, busy place, with the bar, a couple of restaurants and some shops. Now there was a large pawnbroker right next to the bar, and not a lot else.

What had happened here?

He walked from one end of the street to the other. Off to the south were two roads that led into the residential area, which was a happy hotchpotch mixture of houses and streets. He walked down one, but everywhere was quiet. He could see the lights on in most of the houses but there was nobody around. He turned and walked up and then followed the road out to the town hall and looked back. In the dark it really looked like two completely separate towns, but close together. The south side sloping gently away and the north climbing up.

It didn't make any sense at all.

Wearily he walked back to the car and climbed in, then drove past the rock and turned, crossing the road and parking up at the motel again. He got out and breathed in deeply, it was still warm. He locked the car and as he walked across the car park a man walked out of the office and moved quickly across to stand in front of him.

John stopped and looked at him closely. Probably a few years younger, pumped up, spent a lot of time in the gym. He was wearing a polo shirt, some kind of vague colour impossible to make out at night. The man was standing with his hands on his hips. Now he had John's attention he moved over and leant heavily against the wall on his left side, legs sticking out at an angle.

'Evening,' John said casually.

The man didn't answer, instead he put his hand in his pocket and drew out a quarter, and then flicked it up in the air. It spun lazily over and over and then fell to the dusty ground between the two men with a soft clink.

'Heads or tails?' the man asked.

'What do I win?' John countered.

'Well asshole, that's real simple. If it's heads, then I just let you go on up to your room and get all your shit, and you can get the fuck out of here and don't look back. But if it's tails …'

'Please, go on.'

The man put his hand in his pocket again and this time produced a flick knife. He popped the button and the blade sprung out, glinting in the dark.

'If it's tails, then I guess we'll be calling a doctor.'

John nodded, and took a step forward. The man didn't move. Then John leaned down as if looking at the coin and then swept his right leg around, hard and fast. It connected with the man's ankles and he crashed down heavily onto the ground. John jumped in and rabbit punched him hard, right in the centre of the face, busting his nose and sending his head banging heavily against the wall behind him. The hand holding the knife was down to the right and John stamped down hard on it several times, grinding his heel down. The man cried out in agony and stared up, wondering what the hell had gone so wrong. John punched him again, right in the mouth, and picked up the knife and forced it against the wall, snapping the blade off, then stood back and collected the coin, and looked down at the man. He was a mess; his face and top half of his shirt were already soaked in blood. He was cradling his wrecked right hand and had tears of pain welling up in his eyes. John checked his pockets; no wallet, a few crumpled notes, which he took.

'I'm not going to ask who sent you, I'm going to guess I'll be finding out soon enough.' John told him and looked at the coin.

'It was a tails. Lucky me.'

John grabbed the man's hair and banged his head solidly off the wall behind, then set off across the front of the motel. He walked up the stairs and went into his room. He checked the time, just before ten. He carefully positioned the curtain so there was a gap and then cleaned his teeth and then laid down on the bed fully dressed. He reckoned he should be able to get a couple of hours rest before he had another visit.

Chapter Five

In the end the arrest eleven years before had been almost ridiculously simple. The Department liaised with the FBI, and it was ascertained that Collis was at home in Gray Rock, in fact he never appeared to leave there. What was the next step? There were several back and forth discussions and then John was invited over to make the arrest, in appearance as a courtesy but the reality was different. He would hand Collis straight over to the FBI, but by doing it this way it would mean that they would not appear to be directly responsible for his capture. The Department agreed, and so a couple of days later John walked out of El Paso airport.

The town has an FBI office, and he was collected and taken straight there. Everyone seemed genuinely pleased to meet him. The case officer in charge was a wide man called Duncan Fairhead, who had massive shoulders, a red face and a shiny bald head. He also had a knack for always saying the wrong thing and John liked him immediately. Fairhead had flown in not long ago himself, he was based in Virginia.

They sat down around the table in a small conference room and discussed the plan, Fairhead had it pretty much worked out.

'Ok then, so we keep this simple. We give you a car, and you get yourself down to Gray Rock, it's a long drive and I'm sorry about that. There's a motel in the town. Me and my team will also get down there, but we are gonna hole up in another motel about thirty or so miles away, out near the army base. We ain't gonna alert the sheriffs, we are not sure about them at all. The nearest police department is in a town called Carline, but it's the best part of seventy miles away and the road is not great, so we are gonna use the state police. We will make sure they collect you from the motel at nine in the morning. Sound good so far?'

John nodded.

'Good, well, we will be mobile before then, but keeping a low profile. You go with the state cops and make the arrest, and we come straight in behind you. We search his place; we should find what we need but we got enough to hold him while we do it.'

John nodded again. Simple, but effective.

'Right, now, I got some stuff for you.'

He handed over a mobile phone with a car charger and a Glock 17 in a holster.

'We checked you out, we know you can handle a gun but it is only there to protect yourself ok? We don't believe he will come out shooting but I can't risk it. For all we know he could have an RPG in the house. Listen, please, I really don't want to have to try and explain why you shot somebody. That's more paperwork than you could ever imagine.'

'I get it, no problem.'

'That's good. Now we planned on it all going down tomorrow, but I couldn't get a search team in time, they don't have one here, it's no problem San Antonio are sending theirs. They will stay with us at the motel. So it will be the day after, I got no choice in this, is that ok with you?'

'Yeah, that's fine.'

'Great. I have had people watching him for the past couple of weeks. He's a loner, doesn't really leave the house much.'

'I thought he worked in an internet café?'

'It's part time, or so we think. He's in and out of there occasionally but fact is, he doesn't really do anything. Most days he just stays at home. Buys groceries sometimes, but that's it. Never goes to a bar. There's a roadhouse outside town that's supposed to be good, there's been a couple of bands on but he's not interested in that either. My guys say he's got a bunch of computers set up, and he seems happy to sit in front of them all day.'

John thought back to meeting Collis. Both he and Neil had decided he was an oddball, a bit of a fuck-up they had said. He hoped it wasn't worse than that.

'Ok.'

'We checked out his finances, he's got some put away, his parents died and left quite a chunk of money, split with his brother. He ain't rich but seems to have enough to live, there's some kind of complex trust fund he gets a regular transfer in from.'

'That could easily be a cover up, it's a good way to hide money.'

'Well, yeah, and it probably is. We've tried, it's held at First Texas Bank, they tell us it's managed by some attorneys down in Austin, so we spoke to them and all they will say is it's a family trust, non-resident, and not US citizens. So we could spend a year and not get any further forward.'

Fairhead looked at him.

'Listen John, the thing that bothers me is that we have got no real idea what we are dealing with. We got all your intel and there seems to be nothing missing there, but he could have anything inside the house. I know, I know I am going on about this but maybe it's ringed by hand grenades or Claymores, I know it ain't likely but I would prefer to get you on the plane home in one piece. So, no heroics. I need your word on that.'

John smiled.

'You got it.'

'And one final thing. When you go in the house, try and get him outside, at the least make sure he stays in one room, and try to do the same yourself if you can. I know how these things go down sometimes, but I need to do a proper search and I don't want any confusion on the forensics. The team always do a great job, but we got a lot to try and find and sometimes this can all go to hell once it gets in the court.'

'I understand, don't worry.'

'Thank God. Now there's a lot more up here than there is in Gray Rock, do you want me to get you a hotel room?

John considered.

'No thanks Duncan, I think I'll get down to Gray Rock so I can see it for myself, check it out a bit. Can't hurt.'

'Ok, if that's what you want. Leave the cell on, I will be in touch.'

'Right.'

'Give me five minutes, I'll get you a car.'

It was a recent Ford Crown Victoria, dark blue with 'I am a government vehicle' stamped all over it. But it didn't matter. It had a full tank so he borrowed a map and set off.

Fairhead had been right, it was a long drive, but eventually after coasting the top of a steep incline there was an even steeper downhill, and there was Gray Rock. The town was over to his right as he entered, mostly scattered behind a big grey rock, which explained the name, but he found the motel straight away after passing a petrol station and pulled in. He got a room right above the office, and then walked out to look around the town. He ate in a small restaurant which was on the corner at the rock end, looking out at the town hall and the sheriff's office next door, and then walked around for a while until he got too tired and went to bed.

Next day he had a good breakfast in the diner which was just a short distance down the road from the motel, and then decided he would go and have a look at Collis's house for himself. He would have to be careful, he didn't want to bump into him just in case Collis remembered who he was. He called Fairhead and advised him what he was doing, so whoever was watching the house could be alerted. He checked the address and asked his waitress if she knew the road, which she did and gave him clear instructions with a big smile. He walked across the town, Collis lived in a small development which was to the west and north of the rock. He followed the east–west road to the turning which didn't take very long, it was basically two roads which led off the one heading west out of the town. All the houses were identical, wide but shallow single-storey with small porches, and scrub grass front gardens, well spaced out so they weren't all on top of one another. There were about thirty houses in all. Both roads were cul-de-sacs, so only one way in and back out again. He was glad he had walked; his borrowed car might have looked suspicious. Collis's house was at the top of the northern road, facing south. There was no sign of activity, and the garage in place to the left was closed. Behind the house was scrubland, with scattered rocks and berms heading up the slope leading to the steep rise behind. He back tracked, and then found he could easily get into the land behind, so followed the line back around the houses. Just a simple wire fence separated them. He was careful not to walk too close to Collis's house, just in case he was looking out the back window, but again, there was no sign of anyone at all.

In fact, every house appeared empty, he wondered if everybody was at work, but where the hell would that be? Gray Rock was literally in the middle of nowhere, pretty much in the wilderness. He stood very still and looked all around him. Away up the hill he could see a couple of pick-up trucks, and a group of men measuring and knocking in poles into the ground, tape between them. Some kind of building project soon to start he guessed.

There was nothing more to look at, and he knew that the longer he stayed around in the area the more noticeable he would become so he turned and walked back the way he had entered to the east–west road, and headed south past the rock. He took another walk around the town, had a coffee in a cafe and learned a bit about its history. It had been around since 1868 originally, when some French settlers who were mining precious stones had decided their fortunes lay under the rock. It hadn't proved correct, so they had moved on a year or two after, naming the place Derriere. Some time passed and then some ranchers moved in, renaming the town Gray Rock after one of the men, a schoolteacher, had explained what derriere meant. It was originally right on the Mexican border before everything got settled to how it is today, and for a while was a busy trading post to the south. Then, in 1930, oil was discovered in the area, and the place went crazy. Then it went bust, and then boom again throughout the seventies and eighties, before bust again. And since then, the town had been pretty much limping along as best it could.

Fairhead checked in during the afternoon and told him everything was still set for the morning, expect the state police at nine.

As the day moved into evening he walked out to the roadhouse, which was a couple of miles outside town to the west. He followed the road that led past where Collis lived. He ate some barbecue chicken and drank a few beers. There was a raucous crowd, a loud band with an old guy playing the steel guitar on the stage and John enjoyed it, the place was busy and everyone was having a good time. He didn't stay too late and set off back to the motel around ten.

Next morning he was showered, out the room and in the diner for eight, and had yet another good breakfast, looking out the windows up the street for the state cops. They arrived early in two cars, so John paid the bill and walked up to meet them. There were three men in total, the lead was an older cop called Milner, who had big grey mutton chop sideburns and with him two quiet younger men. Milner was in the first car on his own, and was friendly enough. John offered them coffee in the diner, but Milner wanted to get into position so John climbed in the car with him and they set off. John called Fairhead and was told that they were all grouped on the eastern edge of Gray Rock and waiting.

They drove across town and moved off the east–west road onto the development where Collis lived. John told Milner what he had seen the day before. Under Milner's directions the second car with the two young cops pulled in right after the turning and Milner stopped just in front. He got out the car and walked back to speak to the two men behind, who started walking over the scrub toward the rear of the houses. Milner got back into the car.

'Right, so they are going to cover the rear. Me and you will walk right up to the front door. Nice and easy, if he decides to run he's got nowhere to go, all agreed?'

'Yes, perfect,' John said, and then they continued up the slope to park right in front of Collis's house. It looked the same as the day before, the curtains were open, but there was no sign of anyone inside.

'Ok, so I will have to read the Miranda, I guess you got some other script,' Milner said, half smiling.

'Actually, I'm not a cop, so no I don't,' John told him.

'Yeah, I forgot that. It don't matter, it's your arrest, we have the Fifth Amendment and I got to stick to the rules. This is a new one to us and we were a bit unclear how it worked, so I'm just gonna do what I'm told.'

'Fine.'

'And I don't know where you got that Glock, but I can guess. I'd appreciate it if you can keep it holstered, at least unless it all goes wrong and we got no other choice.'

'Yeah, I get that. Don't worry.'

The two men climbed out the car and walked up to the house. John recalled what Fairhead had said to him about Claymores and hand grenades so checked the front yard carefully. No trip wires, and nowhere to hide a Claymore anyway. Any hand grenades would have to be thrown from inside, in the unlikely event there was any. John had been through this many times before anyway and knew the drill. Milner indicated for John to stand behind him and knocked loudly on the door with his left hand, his right on the fat HK45 which was in the holster on his belt.

John stepped back so he could watch the windows, but nobody looked out.

Instead there was a rattle and the door opened, and Collis was standing there looking out at them. He was dressed almost in a make-believe paramilitary uniform, a camouflage t-shirt, jungle pattern trousers and a pseudo-German army jacket. With slippers on his feet. He looked bemused to see them, and then surprised when he spotted John. It was clear he was trying to place him.

Milner moved in fast and pushed Collis back hard against the open door, pinning him with his left hand and grabbing handcuffs off his belt, then spun him around, forcefully pulling his arms behind his back.

John wasn't needed, he just watched. Milner was a pro.

But Collis offered no resistance, and the cuffs were snapped on, then Milner pulled him backwards out the house making him stumble. John called Fairhead and was told the FBI were rolling.

Milner stood back and looked at Collis then read him his rights, the short version, automatically.

'You have the right to remain silent. Anything you say can and will be used against you in a court of law. You have the right to an attorney, and to have one present during any questioning.'

Collis nodded dumbly, still trying to work out who John was, it was clear he remembered him from somewhere, but where?

Milner looked at John and nodded.

'Anthony Collis, you are arrested on three counts of murder, the FBI are on their way and will be handling this investigation,' John told him.

'The British guy. I remember you now,' Collis said. 'But who am I supposed to have murdered?'

'Helmut Romann, Lucille Canour and Giovanni Trisi. That we know about.'

'Who the hell are they? You got the wrong guy, you're gonna ...'

John held up his hand interrupting him.

'Save it. No point saying anything to us. Tell the Feds.'

Milner pushed Collis so he was sitting on the ground, and then got on his radio to tell the other officers the situation. The door was still standing open into the house.

'Anyone else inside?' Milner asked.

Collis shook his head.

'It won't be a woman anyway,' John said and Milner laughed.

Two cars approached, moving fast, and screeched to a stop in the middle of the road. Two more dark blue Ford Crown Victoria's identical to his loan. Fairhead jumped out beaming. A van pulled in close behind and three people climbed out and started pulling on paper suits and shoes.

Fairhead joined them by the front door and looked down at Collis, who gave him a sullen glance.

'Been inside?' he asked.

Both John and Milner shook their heads.

'We don't know if there is anyone else in there, he says not,' Milner said.

'Right, thanks.'

Fairhead took out a sheet of paper from an inside pocket and dropped it in Collis's lap.

'Warrant. That's for you,' he told him.

There were now two more agents standing there with Fairhead and behind them the search team; two men and a woman.

Fairhead pulled out his Glock and indicated to the other agents who did the same.

'Stay behind me,' he told John, and they entered the house.

The front door opened straight into the living room, which led into an open plan kitchen at the rear and a short hallway to the right. The room felt cluttered, there was a long sofa all the way down the left wall, and a big TV in the right corner next to the window, which was playing cartoons with the sound turned all the way down. Then there was the hallway, and on the other side a long trestle table covered in computer hardware. John could see a laptop, two desktop PC's and a big black server under the table. There were monitors, mice, keyboards and miles of cables everywhere along with a couple of boxes with flashing LED's on them. The kitchen was simple, old fashioned units down one wall and a small table with one chair. Down the hallway the bathroom was first on the right, and a tiny box room opposite. The master bedroom was down at the front of the house, and a smaller second bedroom to the rear. The house was clear, there was nobody else there.

Collis was taken to one of the FBI cars and put in the back, then was driven off and the search began.

John walked around carefully staying out the way, trying to get a sense of who Collis was and how he lived. There were no photographs anywhere, nothing personal at all. The house wasn't particularly untidy but was dusty and uncared for. In the kitchen, there was a dirty bowl in the sink, presumably from breakfast but not much else, only really some basic food and plates and cups for one person. The search team methodically went through everything, carefully packing up the computers which would be taken away for analysis. The box room was literally that; filled with boxes. The team went through each one and here, there was evidence of family life, ornaments, pictures, even cartons of clothing. Collis had obviously packed it all away once the house was his and just stacked it out the way. The master bedroom had a wardrobe less than a quarter full of clothes, and a chest of drawers the same. Collis's passport was taken away, but there was no other documentation anywhere. The bed sheets were grubby and there was a pile of dirty clothes in one corner. Everywhere was searched.

The second bedroom had a single bed in it, unmade and nothing else.

John walked outside and looked in the garage, which contained a fourteen-year-old beige Ford Taurus that looked as if it hadn't moved for a while. The car was locked. There wasn't much else to see, a tired lawn mower, a few ancient gardening tools and a battered, old-fashioned washing machine. He left the door open and went back into the house.

There was some excitement, the guns had been found. The Smith & Wesson revolver and the Ruger rifle. The .22 weapons. They were in a wooden box under the bed in the master bedroom, along with three cartons of ammunition. Fairhead had gloves on and was looking at them carefully, John crouched down next to him.

'The rifle has been recently fired,' Fairhead told him.

John looked at the gun; it was an early model Scout with a worn wooden body and fitted with a Hawke sight.

'Not the murder weapon,' Fairhead said.

'No,' John agreed. 'We knew about these two guns, I'm guessing he just uses them for target practice. Collis is in some local gun club.'

Fairhead nodded.

'Yeah, we saw that. I think we need to talk to them next. See if he keeps anything there.'

The guns were bagged up and the search continued. John stepped outside. He looked around at the other houses in the street. They were no more than thirty or so years old, give or take and were all the same design. A couple of them had been through some improvements over the years, there was an extension here and there, and a few had smart gardens. Nobody had come out to watch what was going on, which was unusual in John's experience.

Fairhead came out behind him and walked over to the state cops, who were standing beside the car parked out the front. He spoke to them for a while, and they got ready to move out. John walked over and shook their hands and thanked them, and they drove off.

Fairhead stretched and looked at the house.

'Let's leave them to it, go and check out this gun club, see if they can be of any help.'

He walked over to the car and John got in beside him. It was a complicated manoeuvre to get back out of the road because of all the vehicles parked in the centre, but he did it finally, and they set off heading east.

'We passed the club on the way in,' Fairhead told him.

It was about five miles out of town, they drove through a massive expanse of nothing, then there was a simple fence on the left and finally a couple of buildings came into view. Then there was a turning, with a sign that said 'The Rock Gun Club' and another underneath that read 'MEMBERS ONLY' in bright red, and then finally a third that said 'DANGER! KEEP OUT'.

The gates were open so Fairhead made the turn and drove down the track to a square of beaten earth which had several vehicles parked on it, mostly pick-ups. They could hear the sounds of shots being fired, rifle and hand guns. There was an insignificant low building with the word 'Office' written above the door and next to it a barn which stretched away behind.

They walked into the office, which was nothing more than a small cabin with a counter at the back. A man in his sixties with his grey hair shaved in a buzz cut stood behind it wearing a faded green t-shirt. He was writing something on a pad and looked up when they entered.

'Members only,' he said automatically.

Fairhead produced his ID, and the man seemed to shrink back.

'What the hell do you want?' he asked. 'I am legal you know, nothing in this goddamn place there shouldn't be. And nobody does any shooting here I don't know.'

'Yeah I bet,' thought John, but he said nothing, instead walked over to the counter and turned around the register that was laid there. It was a thick book of dates, times and names.

'You see?' the man said. 'Everybody has to sign in and out, and I ain't at all sure you're allowed to read that.'

John shrugged and closed the book, sliding it back over the counter. Fairhead scratched his head.

'We're not here to close you down. We just need to ask you some questions about one of your members and would appreciate your help.'

'What's your setup here?' John asked suddenly.

The man looked at him sharply, confused by the accent, wondering who he was.

'Nothing fancy. Handgun range indoors, two rifle ranges outside, one two hundred and the other four hundred yards.'

They could still hear the shots firing.

'What can you tell me about Anthony Collis?' Fairhead asked.

The man looked at them, still trying to work out who John was and why he was there.

'Who's he?' he asked, talking to Fairhead and nodding over at John.

'John is someone working with us. Please answer the question.'

The man moved behind the counter and dragged a stool across then sat down heavily.

'I ain't got nothing to say. I hardly know him.'

'But he's a member here?'

'Yeah, but it's not like we stand around shooting the shit or nothing. He don't say much.'

The man clammed up and looked at his nails.

John glanced at Fairhead.

'You keep guns here?' he asked.

The man looked up.

'Some, but only ours. For competitions mainly. So not really, members bring their own. We got rules.' He looked hopefully at Fairhead.

'Can I see them?' John asked.

'What, the rules?' the man asked, confused.

'No, we're not interested in the regulations.' John replied. 'We'd like to see the guns you have here.'

The man looked at Fairhead again.

'Please,' Fairhead said pleasantly.

The man sighed and stood up and went to a door set into the right wall behind the counter. John and Fairhead climbed over and followed him in. Better safe than sorry. Inside was a narrow room with a toilet at one end and a locked steel cabinet at the other. The man unlocked and opened it and then stood back.

There were three rifles inside, in a line pointing upwards. Two Remingtons and a Winchester. They were all old model, but looked in reasonable condition. There was a shelf toward the bottom loaded with boxes of ammo, and below several handguns. John looked closely at the rifles and then back at Fairhead.

'.308s' he told him.

Fairhead nodded and began writing down the serial numbers on all the guns.

The man was standing very still watching uneasily. He didn't look worried, but unsure what he was supposed to be doing. John looked at him carefully, and then took out the Glock Fairhead had loaned him from the holster.

'Would you mind?' he asked, holding the gun up.

The man looked at both of them then shrugged and led the way back out. He opened a hatch in the counter top and they filed out the front of the office and then over to the barn.

Inside was a long sectioned off counter, with ten clearly numbered shooting bays set into it. Two men were standing at the far end and they looked over.

'Number one,' the man said and reached up and yanked on a rope to one side. He attached a simple target and then pulled on the rope again and the target was sent to the back of the range. He put on a set of ear defenders and handed another to Fairhead then stood to one side. John stepped up to the counter and looked down to the bottom.

Handguns are not known for their accuracy, especially over distance. The range was fairly standard fifty yards, but the man had pulled the target all the way back past the marker point so it was a fair length longer now. But John was a good shot, and well trained. He knew the gun would be good, the FBI wouldn't make mistakes like that. He pulled on ear defenders.

He moved forward and worked the slide on the top then took up the stance, holding the gun two-handed and relaxed, breathing slowly, then lined up the foresight with the target, which seemed a long way away now.

No matter.

No safety on the Glock, just a clever release mechanism, he squeezed the trigger, and let loose. One after the other, unmoving, solid, almost rapid fire, despite ear defenders the gun loud and blasting away in the confined space. One, two, three, he fired off ten rounds and then raised the gun up and stepped back. The two men at the end had moved closer and were staring down the range. The club man looked stunned and reached up to winch in the target.

Ian Jones

The centre was completely destroyed, but only the centre, a dime sized hole.

The man held the target out, unsure.

'Shit. That is good fucking shooting,' one of the men standing nearby said and the other whistled, long and low.

'Let's go outside,' John said, and they walked back out again.

In the car park John turned to the man.

'Right. So, let's start again. You're army I reckon?'

'Yeah.'

'Ok, what branch?'

'Fourth infantry.'

'Rank?'

'I was a sergeant, an E-8.'

'So you knew your stuff then, you were a good soldier.'

'I did ok.'

'Gulf?'

'Yeah, 1990.'

'Same here.'

Fairhead looked at him surprised, but the man visibly changed immediately. He smiled and reached out a hand.

'I knew there was something. Sergeant Thomas Clancy, US Army, pleased to meet you.'

John shook his hand and smiled back.

'John Smith. British Army, once upon a time.'

'What branch were you?'

'First Para,' John replied cautiously, he didn't like to talk about his past.

The man nodded and smiled again.

'I remember you guys, hardcore.'

'So now, let's start again. What can you tell me about Anthony Collis?'

Clancy shrugged.

'Ok, look, I'm real sorry I was being a smartass, but I weren't bullshitting. I don't really know him at all. He only comes here once in a while these days, it used to be a lot, but he never says much, and he's always on his own, brings his old

Ruger down. Mostly.'

'Has he got another rifle, not his Smith & Wesson?' asked Fairhead.

Clancy nodded.

'Yeah he has. Maybe more than a year ago, he came down here with a Mossberg, a Predator, looked new. He brought it back here a couple of times.'

Fairhead looked at John questioningly who nodded back.

'Yeah, it's a 7.62, we need to find it. What range did he use?' John asked.

'Normally he was always on the two hundred, but sometimes he used the four for the Mossberg. I asked him about it, it's a real nice gun but he didn't say much. He told me he bought it cheap on the internet, but I'd say that was bullshit. Like I said, the thing was new. And that is a good gun.'

'Yeah, it is,' John agreed.

'Is he a good shot?' Fairhead asked.

Clancy laughed.

'No, not really. About average I'd say. No, worse than that. Barely even hits the target on the four hundred. But he loves his guns.'

'One more question,' John looked seriously at Clancy.

'What?'

'Who told you not to say anything? You were desperate when we came in, I'll bet you even thought the FBI badge was a fake.'

Clancy looked around him and his shoulders sagged.

'Look, when he first turned up with the Mossberg, he had a couple of other fellas with him, older guys, one of them a mean guy with a bad beat up face. The other one was this real military lifer pain in the ass. They made it clear to me, that they weren't there. I ain't seen them. None of them, and the beat up guy puts down this bit of paper with my address on it. Right on the counter. I got a family. I ain't the greatest dad, or husband, but …'

John nodded.

'I understand. You see those guys ever again?'

Clancy shook his head.

'No. And Anthony never said nothing about it, but I remember he was acting all proud that day, like he'd been given the gold key or something. But I never saw them before, didn't know them at all.'

'Ok. Thanks for your time.' John shook Clancy's hand, who looked at him seriously.

'Do I got to be worried?' he asked.

John patted him on the shoulder, shook his head and they left, Fairhead drove back to Collis's house.

'What was that all about back there, you showing off?' he asked as they followed the road back into the town.

John shook his head.

'No, I know the type. Army right through, the only way to get him to open up is if he talks to one of his brothers. He was nervous, straight away. He didn't believe you were FBI, I could see that. He thought we were checking him out, he was asking himself why some British guy is there asking about Anthony Collis?'

'You believed him, about his family and the guys turning up?'

'Yeah I did, I reckon it's been on his mind.'

'So it was true then? You were in the Gulf?'

'Unfortunately.'

The arrived back at the house and an agent came sprinting across to them holding a mobile phone.

'I was just about to call, quick, check this out! They found it in the attic'

They got out the car and walked quickly across to the house. The agents were standing in a circle inside.

In an open flight case on the living room floor was a rifle. A Mossberg Predator. It was packed inside a shaped foam insert, with a Leica sight and a square black plastic box. One of the agents opened the lid on the box, it was full of NATO rounds, full metal jacket.

Chapter Six

He was brought back to the present from his thoughts, in the end they gave him over three hours, which John thought was generous.

John had a skill, something which he had learned to do a long time ago, from frequent hours spent in potentially hostile situations. He could shut down, effectively go to sleep while he was still able to remain aware of his surroundings. So when the first quiet, grating footstep occurred on the bottom of the metal staircase a little after one in the morning he was instantly wide awake.

He jumped out of bed and moved across the room with his back to the wall next to the window, then edged closer and peered through. With the gap in the curtain he could see outside and across the landing to the top of the stairway. A man appeared, moving slowly and staring at the window. There was a light for the landing shining down immediately above the door so John knew he couldn't be seen and he continued to watch. The man reached the top and then waited, and a second man appeared, shorter than the first but wider. Two big men, both wearing identical polo shirts similar to the man earlier, some kind of uniform. The short one seemed to find something funny, and was grinning like the Cheshire Cat. The big man took up station at the door, and then indicated for the other to go to the railing opposite, which he did, still with a stupid grin on his face.

John watched them.

First mistake; not taking the job seriously.

Second mistake; bad positioning. If John was armed he could easily take them both out, the better option would be for the second man to be against the wall on the other side of the door.

John wasn't armed. No matter. Two on one, they weren't terrible odds, John could manage that, he had been here before. The trick was simple; speed and surprise. Three on one, things got tricky and despite his skills he was likely to lose. He wouldn't be lining up like he was now, he would be looking for a way out of the room.

He crouched down and moved under the window to stand behind the door. As he did so a shadow passed over and he guessed the tall man was still trying to look in through the window. He reached up and silently undid the lock.

There was no noise at all, and then a gentle knock on the door. One, two, three quick raps.

John waited.

Again, silence. There would be a debate in the men's heads, was he even there? Maybe the guy earlier had scared him off after all.

Another rap on the door, followed by a hard knock.

John timed it, as the man's fist came back to knock again he yanked the door open and launched himself outside, his right arm swinging in hard. It went better than expected, as the big man knocking had his head lowered, maybe he was going to try and look in the peephole. John's fist crashed full pelt straight onto the bridge of his nose, shattering it and rendering him temporarily blind. He went down on his side with a howl but John had already forgotten him and was moving fast over the landing to other man, who's grin was slipping and he was raising his arms. John grabbed him by the crotch, got a real tight handful pulling upward and squeezing, his left hand gripping the stunned man by the throat and lifting, then twisting forward with his shoulder he barged him up and over the railing. With a shriek the man fell down headfirst landing on his back on a couple of plastic chairs outside the room below. John turned and kicked the big man hard in the side of the head then grabbed his foot and ran down the stairs pulling the man behind him.

The short man was dazed and trying to get up, John lashed out and kicked him hard in the face, he collapsed back onto the ground and John beat his head backwards until his eyes rolled up and he was out.

He glanced over at the tall man, who was rolling trying to get into a kneeling position. John kicked him hard in the kidneys, and booted him in the side of the face then turned back. He stamped down hard onto both the short man's hands, splintering all the bones, and broke his right arm. He searched him, tucked into the waistband was a gun, a Beretta M9FS, John checked it was loaded and pushed it down the back of his own jeans along with the couple of hundred dollars he found then moved onto the second man. He was lying on his front, John rolled him over and searched him. Another couple of hundred dollars and another Beretta, the same gun. Also loaded, but neither gun had one in the chamber. Amateurs.

John looked around quickly, they couldn't be seen from the front of the motel here and he knew the room below his was empty. Safe enough. He crouched next to the man who was staring up at him, he was covered in blood and dazed.

'Right, question time. Who sent you?'

The man shook his head.

John held the Beretta out in front of his face.

'Yeah, I got your gun. Both guns actually. What are you, the reserve team?'

The man blinked slowly.

'I can't say, I'll be hunted,' he whispered thickly.

John looked at him carefully. Hunted? No idea what that meant but the man wasn't going to tell him anything. Here wasn't the time and the place for a lengthy interrogation.

'Right, so here's a warning, and listen to me good. You are fucking with the wrong guy,' John said the last part slowly.

'So far I am three–nil up, and look at me, not a scratch. I got a message for you to pass on; I'll be waiting. And now I'm armed, both these guns are going to be close by. And I can't be prosecuted for anything by the way, because I'm not here. So I don't care who I have to hurt or kill, it means nothing to me. You tell whoever it is that I am not going anywhere, so they should expect to lose more like you.'

He reached down and slammed the man's head off the ground hard, then stamped down to smash both his hands. Then he rolled both men on their sides and checked they were breathing.

As with the first man, neither was carrying a wallet so had no ID at all. Three men, sent by someone to get him out of town. Or worse. He walked around and looked through the window into the office. The woman wasn't working which was good, now there was a young man sitting there, reading a magazine. John tried the door but it was locked, so he knocked sharply on the window and the man looked up, bemused, and didn't move. John waved at him and pointed to the side.

Ponderously the man put on a thick pair of glasses and stood up, then slowly made his way over to the door. He unlocked it and opened it a tiny amount and looked at John through the gap, pointlessly as it was all glass and had a window at the side.

'Rooms are forty bucks,' he said.

John sighed.

'I don't need a room; I've already got one. There's a couple of guys lying in your car park, they look like they're hurt to me,' John told him, and went to walk away.

'What, again! Wait, Jesus, look wait there,' the man grumbled, and locked the door again. He made his way back to the counter and ferreted around behind it, emerging with a big old torch and a bunch of keys. He walked back over to the door and unlocked it, then walked outside and locked it again with a key and then stood there looking at John.

'Good job I'm not in a rush,' John told him.

'What?'

'Never mind. This way.'

They walked back across the front of the motel to the corner. The men were still lying there, the shorter one was moving his legs and moaning.

The man from reception gasped and switched on the torch, which was unnecessary as there was a bright white light above them.

'I don't believe it,' the man said. 'There was another one of these earlier, what's going on?'

'No idea. Perhaps there has been a misunderstanding,' John replied.

'But …'

'Right, I'll leave it with you,' John interrupted and headed around the corner and up the stairs. He let himself into his room and sat on the bed and took his boots off, then quietly went back out onto the landing and looked down. The young man was talking rapidly on his cell phone, worried.

John smiled and went back inside, stripped down to his boxers and laid down. He fell asleep easily, he wouldn't be bothered again tonight.

Chapter Seven

Eleven years previously Fairhead offered to drive John back to El Paso, one of the other agents would take his car instead. They stopped for coffee at the diner and then set off.

They discussed the case as they travelled along; Fairhead mentally storing all the information away for later. He asked a lot of questions, particularly about the intelligence gathering.

'I'm impressed,' he said with a wry smile.

It was a long drive, but they had a lot to talk about so it passed reasonably quickly.

Once they got to the office there was another conference before the first interview took place. Collis was being held in the basement; there were two detaining rooms there. Fairhead had a deputy; an agent called Bianca. John was unable to work out if it was her first or last name, but everybody called her that. She was about his age, an attractive Hispanic woman with long, thick black hair and an attitude that oozed 'I will break anyone's arm who touches me' from every pore. She was undoubtedly Fairhead's ace in the hole, she had consolidated all the data, every photograph, every statement, every single detail into ordered files, and would be conducting the first interview alongside Fairhead. This was another genius idea. Collis would not have any idea how to react to a woman, especially a Hispanic one.

Bianca had organised everything into folders, there was even one for John. Collis was brought upstairs from his temporary accommodation in the basement. He had become rude and aggressive, brusquely waiving his right to an attorney at this stage but had made his phone call, it was to a mobile phone number which was currently being traced. They discussed everything they had so far, and what more they could expect from the search team.

As the meeting ended Fairhead held John back gently by the arm.

'Listen John, I feel bad about this but I can't let you in the interview. I'm real sorry, you done a lot of work on this. But we got rules, well, you know I guess.'

'I understand,' John replied, who had been expecting to hear that anyway.

'But look, you'll be watching, we got a smart setup here. And we wear earpieces, so if we miss something or you got a question for him then just hit the button and let me know ok?'

John was shown into a room which was surprisingly comfortable with armchairs and a coffee machine. It had a long window set low in the wall which looked down into the interview room. Fairhead explained that there were mirror panels all around the top of the room which had a high ceiling, and it was possible for him to hear as everything was recorded and there were loudspeakers and TV monitors positioned on either side of the viewing window. There were microphones set into the wall above the window with buttons labelled 'Talk' next to them.

He made himself a cup of coffee and took a seat in one of the armchairs. He was joined by another couple of agents he vaguely recognised from earlier in the day, plus another smartly dressed man who introduced himself as Ingram, the local section head. They sat in a rough semi-circle around the window.

Collis was brought in a few minutes later, led inside by a young agent who took a seat just inside the door watching Collis impassively. He walked around the room staring up at the mirrored panels wondering where the watchers would be. He was now wearing paper shoes and constantly hitching his trousers up as his belt had been taken. He had a defiant look on his face and was clenching and unclenching his fingers. Finally, he sat down and placed his hands flat on the table in front of him.

After a short time Bianca appeared; wandering in casually without speaking, deliberately not looking at him. Collis stared at her and started cursing but she said nothing. She placed a folder down and opened it to the first page.

Then Fairhead entered the room, walking briskly over to the table and threw his own folder onto it with a loud thump. He didn't sit down, instead he stood leaning on a chair back staring down at Collis, who looked anywhere else.

The room stayed this way for what seemed like an age, and then Fairhead sighed heavily and stood up straight with his hands in his pockets.

'You see Mr Collis; this is all a waste of everyone's time. And money. Shit you would not believe what you have cost us.'

Collis looked up at him confused.

Fairhead grinned and pulled out the chair and sat down.

'Sorry, I should explain Mr Collis. You see, I've been doing this job a long time. And you know what? I have never had anyone in front of me as guilty as you are. Never. We could have just got your local sheriff to pull you in. Would have been a lot cheaper.'

Collis recovered. 'I don't even know what I'm supposed to have done.'

Very patiently, Fairhead went through everything, going through the evidence so far. Collis said nothing of any value, other than to repeatedly say that he was being set up by the British guy, and the FBI were assholes as they were falling for it. Fairhead got to the Mossberg rifle and showed photographs.

'That ain't mine,' Collis said smugly.

'Really? Well we found it in the attic of your house. It was hidden, although not very well. It was under some loose insulation,' Bianca told him.

'Bullshit. You planted it. You won't find my fingerprints on it. I never seen it before. I know what you people are like.'

'My people?' Bianca asked.

'Yeah. You people.'

'You mean FBI people?'

'I mean all you people. That's what I mean.'

Fairhead stepped in. 'You are right. Your fingerprints aren't on it, in fact there are no fingerprints on it at all. It's been wiped clean. Which seems very suspicious to me. An expensive, high power rifle, hidden in your attic, wiped of any fingerprints. What do you think Bianca?'

'I think this guy is a jerk.'

Collis reacted to that.

'Don't you speak to me like that! You need to show me respect. I'm better than you.'

Bianca laughed and Collis raised his eyebrows.

'I think I'd be hard pressed to find anyone that you're better than.'

Collis stood up angrily.

'We know what you all think,' he shouted.

'We?' asked Bianca.

'Us. Texans. You all think we are stupid rednecks, just some hillbillies but we are smarter than you, and one day you'll see. You all will. One day, and we'll all be sitting back laughing.'

'Yeah, yeah,' Fairhead commented. 'Sit your ass down. I've heard all this shit before. White power, am I right? God bless America.'

Collis went into a rambling rant, reciting crime figures and prison numbers for young black men and drug arrests for Mexican cartels, who was really to blame for 9-11 and why Hitler had been in the right. All of it just variations of the exact same stuff that John had been forced to listen to relentlessly on far too many Tuesday evenings in a crappy run down pub in London.

Fairhead and Bianca sat and listened in stony silence, and then Fairhead stood up.

'Right, I'm ending this. We'll pick it up later. Forensics will be coming in thick and fast and in no time, we can just lock you up with all your other Aryan buddies, and they are going to love you. You're gonna be very special to them.'

Complaining loudly Collis was led from the room.

Then there was another conference back in the meeting room, with Fairhead and Bianca and they were joined by Ingram who polished his glasses and looked all around the room.

'So, have we got enough?' he asked.

'I've requested all the forensics and ballistics on express, and I should get everything from Germany, France and Italy latest tomorrow morning,' Fairhead told him.

'I'll get you a hotel room,' Ingram told John.

'Thank you. Can we get anything from Martin Scanlon or that other guy Norman Flint now we've got Collis?' John asked.

'Scanlon is with the Des Moines office right now, apparently being real helpful, but it does look as if he genuinely was unaware of Collis's reasons for travelling. Apparently, these overseas trips are always driven from Texas, but as far as he knows it's all about recruitment. He was just told that Collis would be there on this occasion but he didn't really know why, apparently Scanlon didn't take to him and they didn't speak a whole lot on the London trip. He had never met him before or seen him since. In Germany, Scanlon had been told beforehand that Collis had to go to talk to a politician but he wasn't to go with him. Flint is retired, lives in Florida. He's known to the local PD for spouting all the same crap Collis just let loose with. They've pulled him in, and an agent is on their way but it seems unlikely he will be able to add anything even if he wanted to,' Fairhead told him.

'Right. So, what's next?' Ingram asked.

'Me and Bianca will go again tonight, we'll go in heavier this time. I'm praying we get all the results back before tomorrow afternoon and we can just put this to bed.'

'He does seem like an asshole,' Ingram agreed.

The second interview kicked off a couple of hours later, and immediately there was a change. It was clear that Fairhead and Bianca had done it before, they operated like clockwork. Bianca tore into Collis, destroying everything; who he was, his way of life, his history. She didn't mention his views once.

But Fairhead did. He told Collis he would make sure he was locked up in Arizona, there was a federal penitentiary there that was over ninety percent black and Hispanic, and Collis would be in there sharing a cell with at least three other inmates.

Collis just sat there, shaking his head, clearly scared now. The smug look was off his face but to John it felt like there was still a long way to go.

In the end, it was all but over the following morning. The data from the computers was back; Collis ran the One Race website from the server they found, and they had retrieved a long history of conversations where Collis had bragged about the shootings. There was also pages and pages of racist propaganda, copies of Hitler speeches, even Mein Kampf.

But even better was the fingerprint. Forensics hadn't given up and had continued with the rifle and had discovered a thumbprint on the base of the stock. One hundred percent Anthony Collis's right hand thumb. The assumption was that the gun had been meticulously wiped and put back in the case. Then later Collis had gone to close everything up but the rifle had not been seated properly in the foam, so automatically he had pushed it in with his thumb. Ballistics were matched with those from Germany, France and Italy and also were identical, the bullets recovered were on their way over right now in readiness for court.

They had everything.

As soon as the interview started Fairhead laid it all on the line, one piece of confirmed evidence after the other, and then he sat back, staring at Collis silently.

Collis sat there shell-shocked. He said nothing, just gaped at Fairhead. He closed his eyes and sat back, then gave a bitter smile and leaned over to the microphone set at the edge of the table.

'Er … Houston? We have a problem,' was all he said.

The team were celebrating. Collis now wanted an attorney but insisted on his own, so asked to make another phone call. Fairhead happily told him that he had already made one, but they would call on his behalf. This totally flummoxed Collis, who in the end gave a number to call, which was the same as the previous day.

The phone was answered by a man called Paul Hunter, whom Collis claimed was an 'associate'. Hunter was clearly unhappy with receiving the call from the FBI and would only confirm that an attorney would be sent.

John wondered if Paul Hunter was one of the old guys that Clancy had seen, and he was found out to be a former soldier living close to Gray Rock, had no criminal record other than a complaint of harassment from an ex-wife and was a few years older than John.

The wheels were in motion, Collis was guilty and they had more than they needed, so John booked his flight and set off for home.

Chapter Eight

The three wise men sat around the table having breakfast. They were in the Country Club, which was the latest addition to their empire. Abel and Cane had finished their meals, and Abel was watching Barlow still eating methodically, small mouthfuls, chewing carefully and precisely. Cane was staring out the window pensively, looking at the golf course that was under construction. Nobody was working yet as it was still early. The contractor, who had been chosen due to some wonder turf that would apparently grow anywhere, had told them it would take two years, but they were four months in already and barely seemed to have started yet. He would probably get the blame for that too. He shook his head slowly and pushed the remains of a sausage around his plate.

This was their regular meeting. Originally, it had been every morning, often including Saturdays and Sundays but now the town had grown and they were on top of everything it had been reduced to twice a week. They used to meet in Barlow's house, but had switched to the Country Club once it opened. As usual, they were the only people in the restaurant. Membership numbers were low, very low, but they had anticipated that, currently there really wasn't a lot here for the guests to do. But the swimming pool would be finished within six months, and the tennis and squash courts were well on their way too. And once the golf course was completed people would fall over themselves to join. Abel and Barlow were very confident of that. They were always confident of everything, but they could afford to be, and so far, they had largely been proved right.

Finally, Barlow finished eating and sat back. He looked around the room, and a young girl came scurrying over. She cleared the table and Abel ordered another pot of coffee, then produced his agenda. There was always an agenda, Abel liked them. These days, it was at best a couple of neatly handwritten lines, Barlow believed it to be a waste of time but allowed it, in deference to Abel he let it be, he supposed there was no harm in it.

They went through the two items, not much to say really, the prison contract was agreed, land had been acquired and they should begin breaking the ground within the next few months. There was an offer on one of the remaining grand houses and the hopeful buyer had passed all the initial checks. Barlow added that the big project that he insisted should not be written down anywhere and as usual they opted not to discuss openly would soon be agreed. Abel wrote some ambiguous comments neatly on the sheet of paper then cleared his throat.

'Now, any other business?' he asked, staring at Cane.

Barlow immediately turned and looked the same way.

Cane reddened and bristled indignantly, he had known it would be his fault, everything always was. But as ever, he would just sit there, taking it.

'Look,' he started but Barlow interrupted.

'No dammit, you look. This is a mess. It's one man, and he's laughing at us.'

'I don't think he knows who we are actually,' Abel commented mildly.

'Well that's one good thing, at least make sure it stays that way,' Barlow retorted, shaking his head. Then he sat upright angrily. 'No, actually, that's wrong, he should know exactly who we are, who the hell he is dealing with. So, who wants to explain this to me?' He continued staring at Cane.

Abel poured out three cups of coffee carefully.

'Firstly, I did what I was asked to do. Abel called me and then I called Hunter. This is what I always do. I only found out there was a problem this morning,' Cane said, attempting to sound forceful.

'A problem? I don't think it was just one,' Abel said, as calm as ever.

'That's not what I meant. We sat here and you told me that Carter would deal with it, I wasn't involved in that decision, and then you rang me when that failed and I spoke to Hunter. That's it.'

Barlow rubbed his face with his hand.

'Well maybe you should get Hunter here to explain then,' he retorted.

'I already did that. He's on his way,' Cane replied.

Abel took out his mobile phone and laid it on the table, positioning it carefully in line with his sheet of notepaper.

'I think I have an idea,' he said.

'Good,' Barlow said, and took a drink of coffee.

Abel picked up the phone with a flourish and swiped the screen up and down and then selected a number. He sat back in his chair staring up at the ceiling. It was a while before it was answered, but Abel had expected that. He listened and then spoke quietly and deliberately.

'We need something done. As much time as you can give us, but it has to be this morning and it is important.'

He listened again.

'I am aware of that. We have been let down by a local resource, and unfortunately our resultant attempts at resolution have also failed. Which is why I am calling you.'

The voice on the end of the phone became louder. Abel raised his own in return.

'Of course, of course. You will be well compensated.'

Pause.

'Thank you, I will expect a call back very soon.'

He hung up the phone and placed it back on the table.

A middle-aged man walked into the restaurant wearing a green bomber jacket and black jeans. He was stocky, solid, with a shaved head. He came stalking over to the table and didn't look at all happy to be there.

'Good morning Mister Hunter, care for some coffee?' Abel asked him.

Hunter pulled out a chair and sat down without being invited. He was the only one who would act this way with the three wise men. He reached across to the empty table next to them and picked up a cup and pushed it across to Abel, who poured out the coffee.

'Care to tell me what went wrong Hunter?' Barlow asked, cleaning a finger nail with a fork.

Hunter looked at Cane, who immediately resumed staring out of the window. Hunter scared him.

'Firstly, it would have made everybody's life easier if I had been given some useful intel on this guy, because I got next to nothing at all, and that's not right,' he stated angrily.

Barlow raised a hand.

'Well, in fairness, when we discussed this last week, we told you what we knew.'

'Yeah, and you told me that Carter would deal with it. And I told you that the fat useless ass could barely issue a fucking parking ticket. And I was right.'

Abel nodded patiently.

'Yes, you were. And it has been noted. But you are normally so reliable.'

'It seems to me like I was given a job to do at short notice, that I had to arrange quickly without being told any proper information. Now my guys are all good, but they went in blind also and got sucker punched, and I ain't happy about it. I'm down three fucking guys here, thanks to this bullshit.'

'What? Three?' Barlow asked, beaky nose quivering indignantly.

'Yeah, three,' Hunter confirmed. 'I sent Gary first, because, as you know he ain't someone who fucks around. He always gets the job done. But the English guy cold-cocked him when he wasn't expecting it; Gary said he had just asked to speak to him and he got taken out. I had to go pick him up. He was a mess, I knew straight away we had more of a problem than anyone had told me, so I had a think about it and I got Stevie and Rimmer to go knock on the target's door. I ain't got much out of Rimmer but Stevie says the guy was waiting for them. Expecting them, he says. He made a whole bunch of threats at the end apparently.'

'Gary and Rimmer? Are they hurt?' Abel asked.

Hunter stared across the table.

'Oh yeah. They are fucked up. Out of action. Arms broken, hands all busted up. That goes for all three of them. This guy knows what he is doing. Like I said it would have been avoided if I had known what I was dealing with.'

'He made threats? What threats? Against who?' Barlow was even more annoyed to hear that.

'Yeah, he said he would take on everyone and will make sure he finds out who's driving. Basically that's what the motherfucker said, anyways,' Hunter explained.

Barlow and Abel looked at each other. Nobody threatened them, and this was bad news, Gary was a genuine hard case; the most professional of all the Regulators, and Rimmer was a big, useful man, two men they used a lot and would leave a hole behind.

'Are we going to have enough now? Should we get outside help?' Barlow asked.

Hunter shook his head.

'This close? No, it will just get outta hand if we do that. I don't want to have to deal with a whole load of fresh unknowns. No, I still got seven guys, plus me. Ok, so losing Rimmer and Gary is gonna look bad to the others but I will have to deal with that. Meantime you better find out just who the fuck this guy is, we can't have any more surprises.'

'Yes, you are right. I will deal with that,' said Abel.

'And there's another thing I guess you don't know,' Hunter announced.

'What?' asked Barlow.

'He took Rimmer and Stevie's guns.'

Barlow visibly blanched and Abel grimaced.

'Right Paul, we need a new plan and quick,' he said urgently.

'Well, I got an idea, but it will mean he leaves town permanently. Back to basics.'

Barlow shook his head vehemently.

'No. We said all along that this is a bad idea, it will bring the FBI down here in droves and we can't have them anywhere near us right now. It's not long to go. In less than a week they can do what they want and not get near us but now I can't risk it.'

Hunter nodded slowly.

'If you are sure about this then I hear you. Ok. But I just want to say right now I don't agree, it would be the simplest solution. I guess maybe there are other ways. I'm watching him.'

'Good. I have given this matter a lot of thought, it is my decision. We trust you, you know that.'

At that moment Abel's mobile phone rang, loud and shrill in the silent room. He glanced at the number calling and swept it up, then listened carefully, head cocked on one side.

'Good, thank you,' was all he said and then hung up looking pleased with himself.

'I've got us twenty-four hours, hopefully more.'

Barlow nodded and then sat back in his chair, pointing his long fingers under his chin.

'You find out what you can about him, and I think we should invite him to come and have a chat, let him see who he is dealing with,' he said thoughtfully.

'What?' asked Cane, but Barlow ignored him.

'I got to say that sounds like a bad idea,' Hunter countered. 'Better he doesn't know about you at all.'

'I disagree, and we know who he has been talking to, right? People will be telling him about us anyway. Once Mr Abel has got the information we will be forewarned, and what better way to get an understanding than to speak face to face?'

Hunter looked annoyed but said nothing further.

'Meet here?' Abel asked, surprised by the decision.

'No, let's invite him to the office. This morning. Please get that done now Mr Cane.'

Hunter stood up to leave, but Barlow stopped him.

'Mr Hunter please ask Jamie to stop by the office, say in a couple of hours,' he asked.

'Jamie? He ain't on the team.'

'I know that, but he has been useful in the past, and it means that we aren't putting any more of your people at risk.'

'Fine,' Hunter said abruptly and left the room.

'I better make some calls,' Abel told the other two and picked up his mobile.

Chapter Nine

John slept later than usual, the journey the day before and the night activities had taken its toll so it was after nine in the morning when he woke. He sat up and stretched, and then padded across to the door and pulled it open. As expected there was no sign of the two men on the ground below. He closed the door and then had a long, hot shower. He cleaned his teeth thoroughly then got dressed, and decided to go for breakfast.

As he went to leave the room he spotted something on the floor and looked down in surprise, there was a white card that had been pushed under his door. He was sure it hadn't been there when he had looked out earlier. He picked it up, there was just a simple message printed neatly in capital letters:

'WELCOME TO GRAY ROCK! THE COUNCIL WOULD LIKE TO MEET YOU!'

Underneath there was an address and a time written; 11 am, presumably today. He tapped the card on his teeth and considered. What the hell was this about? It would be tight; he would need to leave here no later than twelve to drive out to the prison. But did he want to go to meet this council anyway? Why would he be interested in meeting anyone? He put it down to it being a reaction to the sheriff's pointless activities yesterday and decided not to bother going, he wasn't interested.

He had a thought and looked at the two Berettas, both new. He didn't want to leave them in the room. He picked them up and walked out and down the steps into the square area at the bottom. There wasn't much to see, the high wall in front and a lower one to his left, the motel to his right and then the car park behind. Under the landing to his room door was an overhead light for the room below. It was bolted to a wide board that was fixed to the metal edge of the framework, and open at the sides. He glanced around, then reached up and slid the guns on top of the board until they were out of sight. Perfect hiding place.

He jogged back upstairs and locked his room, then walked down the hill to the diner, and sat in a booth by the window. The breakfast rush was nearly over now, but there were still a few people in there. There were two waitresses, one middle-aged and one older, wearing the same light blue smocks. Behind the counter were a couple of short order cooks; one old and one young. He ordered the American classic breakfast and a milky coffee from the ever smiling waitress and then looked out the window. From his position he looked up the hill and could see the motel, and beyond it the plant towering up, gleaming in the sunlight. The place was huge, he wondered how many people worked there. It would be a lot, there was the office block too.

His phone rang. Patrick.

'Hey Patrick,' he said cheerily, he wanted to speak to him anyway for any last minute advice on how he should go about the meeting at the prison. He still had no idea what he would say to Collis or if he would even get to see him.

'Hey John, listen I got some news I hope this isn't a massive pain in the ass.'

'Why, what's up?'

'The visit is off, I just got a call. The prison is in lockdown, they've lost one.'

'Ah.'

'It happens. He won't have got out, he'll be hiding someplace, but they have to find him, so no visits today.'

'Ok.'

'I'm sorry John, can you stay one more night?'

'Yeah, why not? It's no problem.'

'So how is it down there?'

John told him about the men from the night before. Patrick whistled.

'Who the hell are these guys I wonder?' Patrick asked.

'No idea, but listen this place has changed. I mean really changed, in the last ten years there's a whole new town sprung up in the north. And there's a huge factory here, BRP Pharmaceuticals.'

'BRP? Those guys are massive. Pretty much the biggest in the world. You go buy a packet of aspirin and it's probably made by them.'

'I thought I knew the name, it may be worth checking out, what do you think?'

'Sure, let me look into it. Probably nothing.'

'Yeah.'

They rang off, and John's breakfast arrived. Outside there was a loud rumble and the Harley pulled into the car park, ridden by the big man, Gilbey. He climbed off, pulled the helmet from his head and laid it on the seat, then walked up the steps into the diner. The older waitress went straight over and planted a kiss on his cheek, he had to bend down low to get it. He gave a smile and looked around, and then to John's surprise he dropped into the seat opposite. He was wearing the same beaten up old brown leather jacket, which he took off revealing an old faded Whitesnake t-shirt. He was tanned and his arms were thick and strong, as John had thought the previous night he had to be in his seventies but was in amazing shape.

'Morning,' he said with a slight smile.

'Good morning,' John replied.

Gilbey picked up and looked at the menu, which was obviously pointless as he had to go there all the time. The waitress brought over a black coffee and didn't bother asking what he wanted to eat.

'So how do you like the town?' Gilbey asked.

'I've been here before. About eleven years ago or so, it's changed a lot.'

'Yeah, that's for sure.'

John could feel Gilbey studying him, which made him uneasy after the events of the previous night, he could be part of all this. It could have been him that tipped them off. The waitress arrived with a plate of bacon and eggs and set it down in front of Gilbey, who looked up at her and smiled.

'Thanks Carrie,' he told her.

'Got to look after you Gilbey,' she replied and bustled off to another table.

'So, you a journalist, right?' Gilbey asked John.

'Er, yeah,' John replied, wondering where this was going.

'Bullshit. I know who you are. I recognised you last night.'

Gilbey said it mildly, and started eating. He didn't look up.

John had been worried about this, and had said so to Patrick who had believed it was very unlikely that anyone would know who he was. But Gilbey hadn't said it as a challenge or an accusation, more like a casual comment. He took a mouthful himself and didn't answer straight away.

'Oh yeah? You got a good memory. It was a long time ago.'

He looked steadily at Gilbey who returned it, calm blue eyes. Gilbey smiled.

'Not really. It's become a habit of mine.'

'What has?'

'Just trying to work out what the fuck is wrong with this town, and what is going on.'

It dawned on John that he had only just arrived, others had been living here and been watching all the changes first hand from the inside.

'Well, ok. So, what is going on?'

Gilbey drank some coffee and looked around the diner.

'I was born here. Right here in Gray Rock. Now that was a long time ago. But I've been away, almost as long and I came back here with my wife maybe a bit more than ten years ago. When all the changes started, so I have seen everything.'

'Well, like I said, a lot has changed since I was last here. It's only eleven years. In fact I can't believe it if I'm honest,' John replied.

Gilbey finished eating and sat back, eyeing John critically.

'So why are you here?' he asked directly.

John considered a lie, but couldn't see the point. Gilbey obviously knew the history.

'I've got to have a conversation with Anthony Collis. In Howarth prison.'

'Long way to come to say hello to that dumbass.'

'Yeah, well, things seem to be changing. Suddenly there's all sorts of things getting said in the press. I got asked to get over here and find out what's kicked it all off, if I can. I was supposed to go there this afternoon but it's been cancelled.'

Gilbey looked surprised.

'That fucking ape ain't gonna speak you anyways.'

'No, well actually, I think the same. But the feeling is that he might be gloating, may be feeling victorious somehow, he might want to tell me that he's won. Be full of himself now it looks like he's getting out. So that's why I'm here.'

'Ten years in jail isn't winning to me.'

'It isn't to me either.'

Gilbey waved a hand at the waitress who came over and refilled his cup and looked enquiringly at John, who decided he could learn a lot by just sitting there so he asked for another milky coffee.

'I came back here for my wife, I always promised her I would,' Gilbey told him.

'How long were you away for?'

'More than forty years. Seriously.'

'Forty years? Jesus. In the service, I'm guessing.'

'Yep. Marine. And you too I'd say. Special Forces, you got the look.'

John smiled and stuck out his hand, and Gilbey shook it. Strong grip.

'You said there was a cancer in the town, and mentioned the three wise men, who are they?'

'They're the guys that did all this. The town, the plant, the airport, the hospital, schools, business park, everything.'

'There's a hospital?'

'Oh yeah, had to, it was a condition of the plant setting up.'

'But who are they?'

'Nobody really knows, I've been trying to find out but apart from a few basics there isn't much to know. Names are Barlow, Abel and Cane. Three very rich men. Barlow is something to do with BRP and the plant, and I know Abel is in construction. So they've been a happy combination coming here I guess.'

'They didn't live here?'

'No. Abel and Barlow showed up about what, probably the same time you took Collis down. I came back here and they were just suddenly around. The town had already started changing by then. They built those real big houses first, you seen the ones up on the hill?'

'Yeah.'

'Barlow lives in the biggest, and Abel's got one too. Then the construction started, I mean it was just like that. The plant got built, it was non-stop for ten years. Crazy. It's slowed down a piece in the last few months but it's still happening.'

'But what about building permits, planning, stuff like that? You have all that over here right?'

'Oh yeah, but money talks. That'll get you whatever you want.'

John made a decision. Something was definitely wrong in this town, and he was here now. It could all be connected back to Collis anyway, as it seemed to have all started when he had been taken in, although it could just as easily already have been happening, but behind the scenes. He could tell that Gilbey was being honest, and opted to trust him. He reached into his back pocket and withdrew the invitation he had received that morning and laid it on the table. Gilbey picked it up and read it, then nodded.

'Yeah, this is them. But I never heard of this before. I wonder what's on their minds.'

John told him all about what had happened last night with the men at the motel.

Gilbey whistled.

'You just met the Regulators,' he announced.

'Regulators?'

'Oh yeah. They are the guys that put pressure on people who don't toe the line, they turn up and someone gets hurt. People are pretty scared of them around here, nobody knows who they are or when they will be knocking on the door.'

'They are something to do with the three wise men?'

'For sure, but unofficially. Nothing ever gets said, nobody talks. See, I've been putting together a file on all this shit, I started a couple of years ago. They lean on people. It's what happens. All the white folks up in the north and the brown down in the south. That's why they built the plant. Cheap labour. Gray Rock was bust, there were no jobs here. Now they run busses out to the plant every morning, and all the managers and the office staff live on the other side of the rock. Everybody's happy.'

'Apart from they aren't at a guess ,' John said flatly.

'Too fucking right they ain't. That's why I started making all the notes. This place is fucked up. People just disappear. Nobody does anything. The mayor, the sheriff, all in the three wise men's pockets.'

'I'd like to see that file. But listen, you can look after yourself, it's obvious, how come you haven't done anything?'

Gilbey sighed deeply and ran his finger along the edge of the table.

'Oh I did. They used to have these town meetings. Nobody ever went apart from the people from the north. I turned up this one time. The three wise men were there along with the mayor. They knew who I was, and I told them straight I was going to find out what was going on.'

'What happened?'

'Two days later I got this put through my door.'

Gilbey reached into his jacket and pulled out an old well stuffed wallet, and withdrew a folded photograph. There was a blonde woman with a pretty young girl, smiling and happy in a sunlit park somewhere.

'That's my daughter, and my granddaughter,' Gilbey told him.
John understood.

'I get it.'

'John I was a Marine a long time. I served all over the world, always moving on, and my family would pack up and come with me. Often with no notice at all. I did it for far too long. My daughter got married to a good man, and lives in California. They found her. I tried but I wasn't around as much as I would have liked when she was growing up, and I can't risk anything now.'

John looked at him.

'You know, this is the second time I heard this story. Or one very like it, at least. The first was eleven years ago, right here in Gray Rock.'

John told him what had happened all those years ago at the gun club.

'That's something else I didn't know, something for the file. But I do know Clancy, he's army, but I don't hold it against him,' mused Gilbey. 'So maybe the three wise men knew Collis?'

'I think so. I think they own him, along with everything else round here by the sounds of it,' John replied.

Gilbey nodded slowly without saying anything. He was watching the waitress, and then smiled.

'That's my wife. My Carrie,' he said.

John smiled back.

'I thought there was a connection.'

'I got to look after her too you know. But I was on my own, and now I ain't. You took out three of the Regulators last night like it was nothing. We could do some real damage here, if we work together.'

'I don't know Gilbey, I was just defending myself. I'm not here to get involved in any wars.'

'It ain't a war John. It's right versus wrong. Look, you are here, and now we're talking. Hell I haven't spoken this much in like, well I never spoke this much.'

John considered. He liked Gilbey, and understood the man completely. He thought of his own daughter, and the lengths he would go to just so he could protect her. And he wasn't at all scared of the Regulators, although he understood why the townsfolk would be.

'Ok,' he replied simply.

'Thank God for that. Jeez, I've been waiting for this for too long, I can't point the finger but nobody wants to stand up. Look, why don't you go meet the three wise men, you can make your own mind up but you will see that I'm right.'

John nodded.

'Yeah, I may as well I suppose. You told me about Abel and Barlow but what about Cane?'

'I don't really know him at all. He never says anything, he just turned up. I can't find out anything about him anyplace, and you can believe I have tried. I have no idea who he is. Or what he is.'

'Right. You've convinced me, I can try and help but I ain't making any promises. This could all be in your head, and I'm not saying that to be an arsehole. Ok, I'll go and meet them. Shall we hook up later?'

'Yeah, let's have a beer at the roadhouse. Lil's. There is someone there we should talk to, she has been on the inside and will probably know something. I've spoken to her about all this shit before.'

'Good. I want to have a proper look around this town. Let's say about seven, is that ok?'

'Perfect.'

John checked his watch, it was nearly half past ten. The day was passing quickly. He dug out some cash but Gilbey insisted on paying, and told him where the three wise men's office was.

Chapter Ten

John left the diner, crossed over the road and turned back the way he had just walked then looked around. To his left up the hill was the motel and further up the plant and the road to the airfield. To his right over the east–west road was the town hall and next door the sheriff's office. In front of that was the new plaza that led to the rock. He turned around again. There was another street which ran parallel to the east–west road just along from where he was standing, which was where Gilbey had said he would find the office so he set off that way.

Once he had moved a short way down he realised it was just a normal high street. As he walked along there was a small shopping mall on his right which he worked out must have the loading bay area that backed onto the motel. He wandered around in it, there were a few shoppers milling about and the usual shops, none of them busy, the place was small. He went back on the high street, more shops, a couple of restaurants, two banks, a bar and a coffee shop, with a couple of roads than ran off to the right in between, heading away up the slope. Then there was another bank that covered about half a block, which had a single street door to the right. He checked the number, this was the office. He was early so he carried on walking along the street right to the end, where it opened out into a square seating area at a T-junction with the Radisson hotel opposite. If he turned left he would end up back on the east–west road, if he turned right it sloped up and all he could see were houses. He sat down on a seat and called Patrick, who answered immediately, as usual.

He asked for all the information available on Barlow, Abel and Cane, residents of Gray Rock, and then as an afterthought for whatever he could find on an ex-Marine called Gilbey. He explained that he had just met Gilbey who had some interesting stories and he would be meeting the so-called three wise men in twenty minutes so any information that could be found beforehand would be very useful.

He watched the few shoppers then got a call back in ten minutes.

Patrick was his usual no-nonsense self.

'Right, so let's start with William Harold Barlow. He is sixty-seven, and this guy is beyond rich. His daddy was an oil man down in Dallas and did very well. Barlow was born in Fort Worth into a pile of money. You wanted to know about the BRP plant? Well, he is the B., Barlow Rainer Pharmaceuticals. Founded in 1975, it went public in 1983 but he still retains the controlling interest. I mean there is wealthy, and there is Barlow. I looked into the company and the plant over in Gray Rock, it opened six years ago. Took nearly three to build and is the biggest of its kind in the world. BRP are insanely rich, they're making millions every day.'

'Wow! So who is Rainer?'

'Ah, now that's a good question. But easy answered. His first wife. He's actually been married four times according to this. Anne Rebecca Rainer, and she was also very rich, from a ranch family close to Austin.'

'You said "was".'

'Yeah, she died in a car wreck in 1984.'

'Hmmm ok, what about the others.'

'Well, Abel is also straightforward, again rich but not in Barlow's league. Dennis Arthur Abel. He is sixty-four. Born in Houston. Took over his father's construction business in 1975 and got into commercial buildings. Now he is one of the biggest in the whole of Texas, actually more like THE biggest. He moved to Gray Rock just over ten years ago, as did Barlow. In fact, his company built the plant, and pretty much all of the town as far as I can see.

'And Cane?'

'This is a lot more interesting. Cane is not his real name. He changed it ten years ago, right when he moved to Gray Rock. He was born William Franklin Cage in Philadelphia. He's a bit younger, only just sixty. No rich family, he's a banker by trade.'

John pondered the information.

'So he's not a Texan then? What's the connection? And what's with the name change?'

'Well there's no law against it, so long as you go through the proper channels, which he did in this case. Connection is he started working for BRP in the nineties, some chief of finance or something like that. Reading this I think he must have been Barlow's banker for some time, then he must have been given the job. He moved to Dallas, which is where BRP's corporate headquarters are.'

'So what's he doing here in Gray Rock?'

'Well, here's the big news. He was released from prison ten years ago. He changed his name and moved to the town straight after. But it's not like he is a wealthy man by any means, so it isn't clear at all why he's around.'

'That is interesting. What was he jailed for?'

'I've got to do some digging here, it looks like several offences, first look underage sex and child abuse among them, but it's a separate file. I can find out, but it will take longer.'

'Thanks, please get what you can. So they all live here, any families?'

'Barlow is listed as married, but his wife is in a medical facility in Austin, again I can get more information on that. Abel was married, but divorced fifteen years ago. Cage, sorry Cane, never married. No children showing for any of them.'

'Ok.'

'And I will need more time on Mr Gilbey, military are a different procedure.'

John stood up.

'Right, thanks Patrick. I'll go and say hello then.'

'You should take care John, from what you are telling me they seem to be the centre, of what I don't know. But the town would never have happened without Barlow and Abel it seems. And to me it sounds like they are running things.'

'Yeah, they are, and I will be bringing that up with them. Got to be a connection with Collis, I will be asking him too.'

'Yeah, about that. Should be all clear for tomorrow.'

'Fine, get digging and I'll talk to you later.'

'Right.'

John walked the short distance back down past the bank, the street door he had seen was now standing open. A man with a shaved head walked out wearing a green bomber jacket and stalked off up the street in the opposite direction. Inside there was a corridor which ran to the back of the building with stairs on the left. He walked up to a short hallway with an open door on his right. Sitting just inside the door was a man. John had never seen anyone like it before. He had a big round head on massive shoulders, and was probably around fifty or so. But it was his face; it was completely covered in battle scars. It was all lumps and bumps, the nose was swollen and twisted and pointing in the wrong direction, and the ears were tattered and misshapen. The face and the head were crisscrossed with scars and old lacerations. The man looked out at John through tiny eyes that were set back far in the ruined face as he walked in.

'Morning,' John said pleasantly.

The man stood up, barring the way. He wasn't tall, but very wide. He said nothing in return, just stared.

John looked back at him impassively.

'Please Mr Smith, do come in,' a voice rang out from inside the room, and the man in front of him moved slowly aside, staring at him all the time. John gave him a beaming smile and walked in as the man sat down again.

The room was a simple large square, with windows running along the front and back walls, the doorway was in the right hand corner at the front. Running across the back was a long table, and sitting behind it were three men. There was a single wooden chair centred in front of the table.

The three men watched him curiously as he approached. They were evenly spaced behind the table, and John returned their gaze. The man on the left was slightly overweight, with grey hair coiffured into an elaborate style that reminded John of the KFC colonel, he was wearing an open light blue shirt with a thick thatch of grey fur visible and was smiling amiably. The centre man was tall, that was obvious even with him sitting down. He was acutely thin, with a long neck, huge pointed nose and a very prominent Adam's apple. What little hair he had left was combed back severely. He was wearing a dark grey suit, white shirt and a blue tie done up tight. He was staring at John with narrowed eyes. The final man on the right had a battered, careworn look. His wispy hair was untidy and the check shirt he wore was creased. He watched John walking forwards but wouldn't meet his eye.

John stopped by the chair.

'Please Mr Smith, sit down,' the man on the left said, still smiling.

'I'm fine standing thanks,' John replied.

'As you wish. Now, thank you so much for coming to see us. We do appreciate that you can spare us your time. My name is Mr Abel, and next to me on my left is Mr Barlow, and finally on the other end is Mr Cane.'

'A, B, C. Very nice,' John replied casually.

Barlow flushed slightly, still staring. The man was angry, it was obvious. Watch him. But Abel continued to speak, still smiling.

'Ha ha, yes, ABC indeed. That is amusing, nobody ever mentioned that before.'

His voice was without the usual Texan twang, it was cultured, soft.

'So what can I do for you?' John asked patiently looking at the three men in turn. Cane still wouldn't meet his eye.

'Well Mr Smith, we were just interested in you, we're a small town, people like to know what's going on, they ask questions, and hey, you know how it is,' Abel replied.

'Not really.'

Abel produced a notepad and an expensive fountain pen and wrote a heading and underlined it.

'We know who you are Mr Smith!' Barlow snapped, eyes flashing.

'Do you?'

'Yes, we do. And we want to know why you have come back, considering all the trouble you caused the last time you were here.'

'Trouble I caused? I don't recall causing any problems. And it's funny, I don't remember you. Any of you,' John told him.

'Oh we were around. We were working hard on making this town what it is and what it soon will be even back then,' Barlow replied.

'I can't see the connection. Between you and Anthony Collis I mean. I would have thought you'd have been pleased to get a murderer out the way,' John said, looking directly at Barlow.

'Not a lot of people believe he is guilty,' Abel told him.

'Not a lot of people around here maybe. But out in the real world it's a different story. And like I said, how are you connected to Collis anyway?' John asked.

'We knew Anthony, but we have no connection,' Abel replied smoothly.

'Why don't I believe that I wonder? Seems a major coincidence to me considering. This town springing up out of nothing within ten years.'

'Mr Smith, this is a busy town. For decent, hard-working folk. There is virtually no unemployment here, something I am sure you will understand we are immensely proud of. We have the plant, and soon we will have the prison, and we are also very close to finalising another huge project. What's in the past is in the past. So, we don't need someone coming along causing trouble, digging up ancient history, upsetting people and their way of life,' Barlow told him, speaking quietly.

'Yeah, I got that, it's not exactly open arms here is it. I'm guessing tourism isn't much of an industry considering the welcome I received,' John said.

'Really? Please, let me know what occurred. We always welcome newcomers,' Abel said and took the cap off his pen again with a flourish and pressed the nib against the paper, looking at him expectantly.

John stood up very straight and looked at him with interest.

'I see. Well, OK, then let's just pretend you have no idea. I didn't even make it into my motel room before I was picked up by that fat idiot of a sheriff, who took me to the station with no mention of why, he just appeared to believe he could throw me in a cell without any particular reason. But I was able to resolve that very quickly. That would have been enough, but then later that same day, and this is just last night by the way, a couple of gentlemen wanted to discuss me leaving town. But again, they changed their minds. And I get the feeling you men know all about these occurrences.'

Abel had been preparing to make a list, froze, and then looked at Barlow.

'I think you need to be careful what you say, what you are accusing me of. Us of,' Barlow told him.

Abel put the cap back on his pen and began to toss it up in his right hand a few inches, it landed back in his podgy open palm with a soft plop, and he repeated it, over and over again.

John stepped forward. Immediately he heard the man behind him at the door get out of his chair. He leaned deliberately on the table.

'Just to be completely clear, none of this shit intimidates me. None of it. I don't care who you are, or should I say who you think you are and I really don't care what you think about me. I also can't be bothered working out why you would invite me along here today. But I would bet a substantial sum on you all knowing what went down last night. Abel, Barlow, Cane. ABC? Cane and Abel? I'd say very clever but it isn't. We all know if I start taking a close look then I'll find the connection to Anthony Collis, plus a whole lot more I'm sure.'

The pen was still being tossed in the air; throw, plop, throw, plop.

He stepped back and gave a quick glance behind. The man from the doorway was now standing in front of the chair in the middle of the room. John took another step back, and then whirled around, pushing the man hard with both hands at the top of his chest using all his strength. With a loud gasp the man fell backwards over the chair and crashed onto the floor, striking his head hard. John jumped over and stood solidly on the man's throat with his right foot and reached into the jacket, withdrawing yet another new Beretta. He flicked out the clip and checked the chamber which was empty. He looked down at the man on the floor who was staring at the table and struggling to breathe while vainly trying to push John's leg away.

John pushed the magazine into the pocket of his jeans, worked the slide pulling it off the gun and putting that in with the clip and then threw the Beretta onto the table, where it slid between Barlow and Cane and onto the floor behind them with a crash. He lifted his foot off the man on the floor and moved back.

'So you think this scares me? You're looking to intimidate me? Jesus, look at this guy. This is a hard man? Sure, I bet he's had a whole lot of fights in his life, but it looks to me he never won a single fucking one of them. You three have fucked up. The three wise men? Don't make me laugh. I am only warning you once. Don't make an enemy out of me. Leave me in peace and I will do the same.'

Without waiting for an answer, he walked out of the room.

The three men behind the table watched him leave while the one on the floor dazedly struggled to sit up. Cane turned in his seat and picked the gun up off the floor and laid it on the table.

'Jesus Christ,' he said wearily.

'Who the hell is this guy?' Abel asked.

'That's what you were supposed to be telling me!' rasped Barlow. 'All you found out is he used to be, and that is "used to be" some government guy, and before that a soldier. You told me nothing else. I asked you to find out before we met him. You got nothing, and that isn't very helpful. I mean what is he doing now?'

'It's not easy, I can't just call Downing Street. I don't have any idea who he is. Nobody seems to know.'

'Find out,' Barlow ordered. 'I want to know everything there is to know about him and fast. And get Hunter back in here. In a couple of days, we get the paperwork signed and we are set for life. Nobody will ever dare to fuck with us again. A couple of days, that is all we have to go and this guy could undo everything if we don't keep him in check. I suggest you call Thomas, if you haven't already. It's about time he earned his money.'

'Thomas?' Abel asked. 'But I thought you wanted to steer clear of the FBI.'

'They just pay his salary. The FBI don't own Thomas. I do. We do.'

'But he's saying he needs to be careful, things have changed, they are watching him.'

'Why would I be interested in that? We've paid him a lot of cash over the years, now he needs to do some real work.'

He got to his feet. His tall angular frame stooping as he walked around the table pushing past Cane.

'I want this resolved. I mean it.'

He looked at the man on the floor.

'Pathetic Jamie, I am very disappointed. He made you look ridiculous.'

He walked across the room and stopped by the door and looked back at Abel and Cane.

'This ends. He cannot go to see Collis, he is not to talk to anyone, I want him gone. This goes no further, he is not allowed to start digging around in my town. Am I understood?'

Abel nodded and Barlow glared at the two men then walked from the room.

Outside, John stretched in the sunshine and walked back along the street towards the motel, dropping the clip into a bin then doing the same thing with the slide along the way. He felt good, in his mind the sheriff was round one, the men the previous night round two, and the meeting round three and he had won them all. He knew that there would be further action, but he would be waiting.

He stopped at the coffee shop, which was a clone of every big brand variant he had ever been in and sat down in the window with a latte. A large well-polished black Cadillac rolled past, Barlow sitting bolt upright in the back.

John had a lot of questions. There was definitely something going on here.

He took his time and then finished up and left, walking back down the street. He had got to the corner opposite the diner when his phone rang; it was Patrick.

'Hi Patrick.'

'Hey John, well I done some digging, you may want to take a seat.'

'Ok.'

John walked quickly back to the motel and up to his room, then sat on the bed.

'Ok, so I'm gonna start with Mr Gilbey. I think you may be interested in this.'

'What did you find out?'

'Well, it ain't easy finding anything out about military personnel. There's a lot of them and they don't like sharing, but Gilbey is a reasonably uncommon name I figured, and I found him.'

'That's good, it would be handy to know.'

'Well John, Gilbey wasn't a Marine.'

'Shit,' said John. He had liked the man, and had wanted to believe him.

'Hang on. I said he wasn't *a* Marine, he was *the* Marine. Seriously. His record is ridiculous, He has won every medal including the Medal of Honour, also the Navy Cross, Silver and Bronze Stars all over the place plus four Purple Hearts. Commendations going back to day one. He joined up when he was seventeen and went straight to Vietnam after just a few weeks basic training, in fact he did three tours out there. That's where he got the Silver Star, plus two Purple Hearts. He served in Beirut, Liberia, Mogadishu, Albania, Bosnia, Iraq, Somalia and Afghanistan. He finally retired twelve years ago when he was sixty.'

'Sixty? He was in, what, forty-something years?'

'Yep. Look, I don't have access to every detail, the military don't work like that. But this is impressive. It looks like he was kept on just because of who he was, but he was there in the thick of it alright. The guy stayed at sergeant major, I'm guessing he didn't want to be an officer but they must have convinced him at the end. He mustered out at major. My guess is he was an inspiration, and they wanted to keep him.'

'That sounds about right,' John commented. He could definitely see Sergeant Gilbey, out in the bullets with his men, getting his hands dirty.

'Listen, this guy is the real deal. He is commander in chief of the Texas national guard for Christ's sakes. At Fort Blunt, which is just down the road from you. So what I don't get is why he is sitting on his hands down there? If these assholes are doing whatever they feel like.'

'I asked him the same. Listen, he served all over the world. He's got family, and they went with him. Six months in the Philippines, and then off to South Korea or Cuba, whatever. Anywhere he got posted. They did this for years and years, always moving on. He made a deal with his wife. They are both from Gray Rock so he came back here once he was out. He didn't like what was going on and made some noise and they threatened his family, and I reckon he took that seriously. I think me being here has given him some incentive.'

'Well, to me he looks like a useful guy to have onside. Now the next thing you are gonna find interesting is all about your Mr Cane.'

'He's not mine, but go on.'

'The big news is William Franklin Cage served eleven years in Leavenworth, close to the Military prison. Actually got sentenced to fifteen but got out due to good behavior and a cancer scare. It's all on record.'

'Fifteen years? What the hell did he do?'

'Right, well I got everything there is. Right in front of me. Cage got busted after the Dallas PD raided a house in Highland Park one evening.'

'What the fuck is this about? Drugs?'

'Oh no, this is a whole lot worse. The house was basically a brothel, for clientele with particular tastes. Namely not legal age. It is shocking stuff to read, really shocking. The place was run by a couple of guys who were already on the radar, PD found thirteen girls aged between twelve and fifteen and four boys about the same age. They arrested nineteen men and Cage was one of them.'

'Jesus.'

'There's more. Barlow was also there, and also arrested.'

'Ok.'

'Now I got all the original statements here. Cage stated it was his first time, he was invited to come along but he wasn't told what the club was. He had expected it to be an upmarket strip joint. He didn't take up what was on offer, he wanted to get out of there. And Barlow made the exact same statement. Identical.'

'But they would have been separated, right? In custody, I mean. Kept apart? Made to give their statements individually.'

'Yeah, I guess so. Both statements have different officer names on the documents, and Barlow's was taken nearly two hours before Cage's.'

'So who was supposed to have invited them?'

'Again, I think there's something there. Remember this is all new to me, I am reading this for the first time but I can see there are a lot of procedural holes all over it. The main guy who ran the place was called Seaton, he has a record of various offences and he was arrested on the same night. Barlow claimed that Seaton was the guy who invited him, reading between the lines he actually went to some lengths to name him and make sure it was on record. My guess is that he knew that Seaton was going down whatever happened, so why not use it. And of course, Dallas PD already knew all about Seaton, and Barlow would have guessed that. But Cage refused to say anything, he wouldn't name any names, he would just say it was someone he met and then nothing else.'

'That's strange. So maybe somebody else other than this Seaton invited him.'

'Yeah, and there's more, and this where it really starts to stink, but this was all PD, FBI weren't involved at all. I'm not trying to duck out of anything here, but this is bad.'

'I hear you. Jesus.'

'Sorry! Anyways Dallas PD went to town on the house, like you'd expect. Forensics read perfect to me. They took like a million prints, everywhere, they had skin samples, DNA, the lot. And now, it gets weird. Barlow, he got sent home. In fact, he was back in work the next day, along with a couple of others. Cage, Seaton, and most of the rest got held in Hutchins while the evidence was being gathered. This is normal for cases like this, they can't risk anybody disappearing.'

'So how in hell did Barlow get to go home?'

'Barlow, and four others. All high fliers, rich men. Pharmaceuticals, oil, finance. They all got released, papers were sent to the judge for review as normal and these guys all walk out free as a bird. In fact, Barlow was detained for less than three hours after being picked up. The other fourteen are all sent to Hutchins. The forensics come back, and guess what. Barlow's prints are all over the house. Everywhere, in fact all five of the free men are the same. But Cage, only prints for him are the living room, which was some sort of social space it seems. Nowhere else.'

'Hmmm this really stinks, so maybe Cage was telling the truth, it was his first time. But Barlow was a regular, maybe he made the invite.'

'That's what I think. But it gets worse. The judge steps in, case thrown out for the five, plus eventually a couple of the others. No case to answer, no charges.'

'Shit!'

'Right. Which explains all the procedural problems that are evident all over it. The cops were getting pushed and pulled all over the goddamn place. It would have been a total nightmare. They were basically being told who to leave well alone. And the judge's name? Gregory Raymer.'

'Fuck. The same one that's stirring all this shit up now.'

'The very same. Two weeks before the trial, Seaton and another man arrested with them called Greaves are murdered in Hutchins. Seaton is found stabbed in the showers and Greaves is beaten to death in the yard. And of course at this stage they aren't in the main prison, they are still in the holding area in the jail. Now Seaton was about to be moved, it seems like he had things he wanted to say. There was a protection order raised against him, copy in the file. Greaves, well it seems he was just like Cage. No prints anywhere in the house in Highland Park other than in the living room, very vague statement, seemed scared and confused. Apparently, him and Cage shared a cell. Barlow visited Cage a day or two before it happened. Rest is history.'

John thought hard.

'Cage did the time for Barlow. So, are you saying Cage, who is now Cane, is here because Barlow owes him?'

'I'm not sure, but Cage was left with nothing other than the fact he's still breathing. Greaves getting murdered would have been a big warning. Maybe Greaves got the short straw, or maybe there was a reason for keeping Cage alive. Either way, Cage said nothing at the trial. His prison record is good, he didn't need any protective custody, kept himself to himself. Treated for a melanoma on his tongue. Gets out, and next thing is he is in this town council or whatever it is.'

'Yeah, whatever it is. I just met them, Barlow is one up tight prick. Abel seems to be the voice, Cane didn't say a word. But they are up to something for sure.'

'John, you need to take care. We still haven't heard back from Howarth.'

'What does that mean? I won't be able to go tomorrow?'

'It's your choice I think. I don't speak to them personally we have a liaison department, and they pass on the message, but I'm moving all the time now, heading toward you. Communication isn't always great.'

'Right. I'll get up there tomorrow.'

'Ok, I will be based in San Antonio, I will keep in touch.'

'Yeah, you do that.'

Chapter Eleven

John decided he would take a proper look around the north side of the town, and walked all the way up the hill past the plant, then turned off down the road that led to the airport. There was a wide gap of rocky scrubland to the edge of the airport grounds, which were enclosed by a chain link fence. After the hill the land around was relatively flat, the runway less than a couple of hundred metres from the road. John carried on walking, and then came to the main entrance which was just a short drive off the road. There were low buildings on either side, the left with a large sign displaying 'Gray Rock Passenger Terminal'. Beyond that, on the far side of the runway were other buildings, two large hangars and a line of storage sheds. He carried on, past the passenger terminal and then a long car park. He couldn't really remember how this had been before, he had never seen it up close, but the buildings all looked new. The place wasn't busy, there were a couple of men working by one of the hangars and a truck moving about but that was it.

The road ended just past the airport at a couple of old rusty tin clad warehouses which were set back behind a tatty square concrete apron, again no sign of life. He stood, looking around then walked across the scrub until he was looking down the hill. The town was laid out in front of him. Closest were the big houses beyond and to the right of the massive plant. Some kind of landscaping had been done behind the houses, there were growing cypress trees presumably to act as a barrier to the plant and also the airport, but the trees were new and it was still possible to see through. The houses were close to the top of the hill in a long curve, and John could see another development out to the west. This was a large white building, and he could see groups of men working all around it. Heading downward, there were more houses, these were smaller and grouped together, and got denser as they reached the bottom. He could see the rock far away in the distance right at the very bottom of the hill, there was a road which ran south between the houses and the streets joining the east–west road which ran across in a straight line. He considered walking down past the plant across the scrub but decided all he was likely to do was end up looking at someone's garden fence so turned and set off back the way he had come.

The going was warm and dusty, and when he reached the bottom of the hill he bought a cold can of Coke from the diner, then set off back down the high street, this time turning off to head up the hill again on one of the side roads. There was a neat red brick church, and then it was all houses with turnings off on both sides that led to basically the same streets and cul-de-sacs, which were all laid out in an ordered pattern, everywhere was generally identical, the places just got a bit bigger and the gaps between a bit wider the further out he walked.

As the houses started to thin out he turned left and followed a long road round. He saw the hospital, a two-storey building to his right. On impulse he walked over and in through the main entrance. There was a lobby with some vending machines and a low counter opposite, an elderly lady in a starched uniform sitting behind it. John told her he was staying in the motel and had found a couple of men passed out in the car park, so he had called in to see how they were. The woman looked confused. There had been no admissions at all for over a week. John nodded, apologised, and left; that was no real surprise. He walked back to the long road and followed it to see where it took him. There was a junior school, and then more houses, and finally a high school. All new and shiny. Further out he could turn left again and head back down into the town. On his right there was the turning to the road with the big houses, so he decided to follow that. They were very grand, with double and triple garages and huge gardens, none of which were established yet. At the end of the road there was another turning, with an elegant green and gold sign which read 'Gray Rock Country Club'. That had to be the white building he had seen with all the men working to the west. It didn't interest him so he walked back and then down the road into town. More houses, and there was a football stadium with a big car park on the right. This would have surprised John had he not seen it from the motel, or spoken to the two young men the night before as he knew there was already a football stadium on the south side, next to the original high school. He walked around it, not much to see other than a banner with 'Go Dragons' written on it. He realised it had been built on the land behind the house that Anthony Collis lived in, and decided to walk round to have a look. Nothing had changed, it was just as he remembered it, but now the land was covered in buildings. He wondered idly if someone else lived in the house now.

It was a strange town; he had been walking around for more than a couple of hours and had hardly seen anyone. Nobody really out and about, there had been a few shoppers in the high street but that was it. And only a few cars driving around. He had seen some street sweepers, and a garbage collection truck moving slowly around. He knew a lot of people would be at work but he had never been anywhere so soulless in his life. Here and there he had seen the same 'Justice for Anthony' posters fixed up, but there was no sign at all of any excitement over the news of Collis's impending release. It looked like the FBI had got that wrong, perhaps people genuinely didn't care anymore.

He walked back into the town, ended up at the square at the bottom end of the high street by the Radisson hotel and followed it back toward the diner end, past the office door which was now closed. He went into a café and had a chicken sandwich and sat eating it, again wondering at the lack of people. Once he had finished he left and walked along to turn right opposite the diner and down to the east–west road. He crossed it and walked onto the plaza. The rock sat there glowing in the sun. He saw the fat sheriff come out and get into his car, then went to drive out but stopped, staring out the windscreen at him. John gave him a cheery wave and then walked across to enter the south side.

The difference was immediate.

Here, there were people. The remaining shops were smaller and scruffier, and there were nowhere near as many but the place felt alive. He walked along the street, which had changed a lot but everyone was getting on with their lives. He walked past a small park on his left with a children's playground close to the road. It was immaculate, with all the apparatus shiny and brightly painted. And the streets were clean, no rubbish anywhere. John guessed that they did all this for themselves, the town's focus was the north, so here in the south they didn't look anywhere else for help.

He walked the full length of the main street among the shoppers, a mix of colours, and nobody looked at him twice. The majority of the people were Hispanic or black, and mostly women. The restaurant that he remembered looking over the rock, the town hall and the sheriff's office was still there. In the park some kind of event was taking place, kids were running races and proud parents were watching. It was a happy place, a million miles away from what had been built less than a hundred metres on the other side of the rock. John walked back to the centre of the street and then turned and followed the road to the south, walking through the houses. He passed a big old wooden church, that was listing slightly but in tidy grounds. Here, it wasn't the uniform grid that the north had, the road meandered and there were many turnings off on each side. The houses were all different, a wide mix of small and smaller, some with gardens, most close to their neighbours. As he walked he passed a workshop, guys working on cars, a hardware store, another church, a busy Mexican restaurant, and the old high school with the stadium behind. But as he got further south he started to see the impact on the old town. On one side were some small warehouses in a line, now all boarded up, then a closed down petrol station and all the few remaining houses here were in disrepair. It was like the town had shrunk in on itself and headed up toward the main street. He reached the edge and saw the road veered off to the left, a little more than a gravel and dirt track that joined up with another headed south. The border was maybe thirty or so miles away give or take.

He sighed.

How had this happened? How could a whole new town be built almost on top of another, in a little over ten years?

Disheartened, he continued to follow the road until he reached the point where it linked up with the other, which was a similar surface, only wider and then he turned north. It became tarmac again shortly after, and he followed it along, the old town to his left. Eventually, he arrived back at the sheriff's office and town hall.

He had seen all he needed to.

He headed back to the motel and laid down, deciding to take a nap before meeting with Gilbey. Sleep when you can, he believed in that.

He woke up just after six, and felt refreshed. He had a shower and decided to drive to Big Lil's, he had been walking all day, and he couldn't see that Gilbey was expecting a big night out.

Outside the sun was setting, and it felt a bit cooler. He climbed into the car and reversed out, there weren't many other cars parked, the motel still wasn't busy. He drove onto the road, down past the diner and turned right at the east–west road, passing the now glowing orange rock on his left and followed the road out of town.

The car park outside Big Lil's was busier than last night, with a line of Harleys right outside the front doors. John parked up and got out the car and walked across toward the entrance. He was about half way over when he heard the now familiar rumbling farting noise and Gilbey appeared, turning off the road and bumping across the uneven surface without really slowing down much. He ignored the other motorbikes and drifted into a spot, almost exactly where he had parked previously and killed the engine. Silence now, apart from a low bass thump coming from inside the bar. He pulled off his helmet and dropped it on the seat and grinned over at John. As he did so he glanced behind and nodded sharply. John turned to see what Gilbey was looking at. On the rear edge of the car park was a new red pick-up truck facing out. There were two men inside, both wearing pale polo shirts. Just sitting, watching.

Gilbey shook his head and raised a middle finger high in the air, then he and John walked inside.

They went over to the bar and John looked around. The bikers had pulled a couple of tables together and were sitting in the centre of the room, pitchers of beer in front of them. One called out 'Hey big dog!' at Gilbey as he passed, who flapped a hand in response and sat down in his usual space. Elsewhere the place was pretty much as it had been at his last visit, small knots of white men sitting around, some playing pool. Very few women, a couple of young and pretty waitresses darting around with trays of beer, ribs and fried food. John sat down on a stool next to Gilbey, and two bottles of Budweiser were placed in front of them without anyone asking. Gilbey took a long drink and burped quietly.

'Wonder what those assholes are doing sitting out there watching this place,' he commented, not showing any sign of real concern.

John shrugged.

'No idea. I don't recognise them. Neither of them were the guys from last night. I'm not surprised about that though.'

'Me neither. Sounds like you fucked those assholes up,' Gilbey smiled, and tapped his bottle against John's.

'So you don't normally see them here then?' John asked.

'Don't normally see them period. They're like a rumour, but everyone knows they exist. I ain't bothered about them, if any started something with me I'd hurt them like you did. But nobody knows who they are, or how many of them there are. The two outside ain't familiar to me neither, I'd say they ain't from the town, but it's possible. I guess you stirred 'em up, brother.'

'It wasn't my intention. Anyone leaves me alone, then no problem. Happy days. But if they don't then I'm likely to be the arsehole.'

'I get that. But you're the reason they're sitting there.'

'Maybe.'

Outside in the car park the two Regulators sat silently, waiting. They had made the phone call as requested so now they needed directions. They would get their orders.

No mistakes, they had been told. There has been enough go wrong already.

Both men were relatively new to the job, and anxious to move up the ladder where the money and rewards were better for sure. And respect. They didn't get a lot of that. They had heard things had gone wrong the previous night, and that Gary had been badly hurt. Gary, he was the best as far as they were concerned, a hard, hard man. Nobody ever messed with him.

But he was out of action, and they didn't know why or what had happened, nobody was talking about it.

Headlights appeared, and moved into the car park, circling around and then heading straight for them. The car pulled alongside and the driver's window dropped down, they did the same.

Hunter looked up at them.

They hadn't expected to see him, and both men asked themselves why was he here? And now they were wary.

'So, he's inside?' Hunter asked looking out at the Roadhouse.

'Yeah, yeah he came in with that fucker Gilbey. Maybe half an hour ago,' the driver told him.

'Ok then. So tell me, what's the plan?'

Hunter stared at the two men unblinking. The Regulator sitting in the driver seat looked down at him and swallowed.

'Well, we were told to wait here.'

'Ok, and then what?'

'We jump him. Then the sheriff takes him in.'

'Carter takes him in? How is this gonna work?'

'He's on his way, he's gonna wait in the corner. Out the back. Then we jump the motherfucker when he comes out, he gets a beating then the sheriff locks him up for disturbing the peace.'

'That's your plan?'

'That's what we were told.'

'By who?'

'By the sheriff. He said the guy made him look like an asshole.'

'Jesus Christ. That's because he is an asshole. And so are you two for having any part of this bullshit. This guy is connected for Christ's sakes. To the fucking FBI. Nobody tell you that? You jump him, two against one and that fat prick Carter takes him in? More wasted fucking time and effort. And more busted arms is my guess. Get the fuck out of here. Now. And from now on I give the fucking orders.'

'Yeah, but …'

'Shut the fuck up. It's lucky someone got the brains to call me, or you two would be all busted up and Carter would be in an ever deeper pool of shit. Get going.'

The Regulator started the pick-up and rolled out. Hunter reversed, turned and followed them. As they got back on the road the sheriff's cruiser pulled up and Hunter waved it down. He stuck his head out the window and glared at Carter, who looked anywhere else. He too was scared of Hunter.

'You really are a prick, you know that right?' Hunter snarled.

'What? I was just doing what was needed,' Carter replied indignantly. He had hastily put all this together and was proud to be doing what needed to be done.

'No, you were going to get those boys hurt and leave me another two down you asshole. Then one phone call and you got the Feds breathing down your fat neck again. Jesus Christ. If I was you I'd get back to counting paperclips or whatever the fuck you waste your time doing in the evenings.'

'I'm the sheriff and …'

Hunter interrupted and pointed out the window.

'Listen to me. You are who we say you are. You do what we say. You pull shit like this again and I swear you will be sorry.'

Hunter rolled the window up and powered away fast, leaving Carter to wonder what he had done wrong this time.

Back inside Gilbey looked around, his eyes following a waitress as she scooted back into the kitchen behind the bar.

'So I'm gonna introduce you to Rita, she's kind of my niece, but not really. Her dad was an old friend of Carrie's, she was like a big sister to him. He ain't around no more.'

John nodded and looked around again.

'Not many women in here, which one is Rita?'

The waitress barrelled out of the kitchen again, tray piled high with food that she placed on the biker's table; skilfully dodging the hands that were reaching out at her backside from all directions.

'That's Rita,' Gilbey told him with a big smile. 'She did the day shift, so she'll be off soon, I'll get her to join us.'

They sat and sipped their beers for a while, and then Rita appeared next to them. She was still in her uniform, such as it was; frayed denim miniskirt and a short sleeve check shirt tied up at the waist. Gilbey ordered three Budweisers then slid off his stool and John followed them over to a booth at the side, sitting down next to Gilbey with Rita opposite. She stared at John openly and he looked back. She was slim and pretty in an unconventional sense, long dark hair with some bright red streaks in, and emerald green eyes. A little older than he had originally thought, early twenties he realised. She was smiling, showing small white teeth. The bartender placed the bottles on the table and she picked one up, nodding.

'Thanks Gary,' she said and the bartender nodded back.

'No sweat,' he told her, walking away.

'Can we get some chicken maybe?' Gilbey asked, and the bartender nodded again.

Rita switched her attention to Gilbey, looking at him affectionately.

'So?' she asked.

'So,' Gilbey replied. 'This is my friend John. There has been some interesting shit gone down since he set foot in the town, and I think you can fill in some gaps.'

'When did you get here?' she asked John.

'Just yesterday. I haven't been here long at all.'

Rita laughed delightedly.

'I love that accent! Where you from, sugar?'

'London. England.'

Rita sighed and looked around wistfully.

'I'd love to go to London. I really would.'

'So what's stopping you?'

She raised her eyebrows.

'What do you think? Money. I heard it's real expensive in Europe.'

'Nah, you can do it cheap. The flight is the killer, but once you're there stay clear of the West End and the tourist spots. It's like any city, just like New York.'

'I ain't never been there neither.'

John looked at her, seeing the small town girl that she really was, and liking her immediately.

'You always lived here?' he asked her.

'Pretty much. I was about five I think, when we moved. I was born in Fort Stockton. My daddy used to work up at the airfield. Which is the airport now.'

Gilbey raised his bottle and touched it gently on hers.

'To your daddy. He was a real good man.'

Sadness washed over Rita and she looked down. John felt he should say something.

'Hey, look I can help you with a trip to London if you really want to go. I know a few people, some cheap hotels, that sort of stuff. If you want to, you should go.'

She looked up, and smiled again.

'Thank you. Hell, I'm going to be twenty-four in six months, and I ain't never been out of Texas!'

'Shit girl is that right?' Gilbey asked. 'Yeah, you need to do something about that.'

'I got plans Gilbey, trust me. I ain't staying around here. My friend Shelley lives out in Tucson now, and she can get me a job there in the bar she works at. I just need a bit more cash saved and I'm out of here.'

'Aim high girl,' Gilbey told her, smiling.

'Always,' she replied, smiling widely back. 'Like I said, I got plans.'

Gilbey got down to business.

'Now John here seems to be the centre of attention for some folks around here, and looks like your buddies the three wise men are involved.'

Rita shuddered.

'Hell, they are NOT my buddies. Jesus. I work for them sometimes is all.'

'That's why we wanted to have a word with you. I thought you might be able to explain a couple of things.'

'Sure, ask away. I don't know nothing about them, but I got no problem talking.'

'So what do you do for them?' John asked.

'It's no big deal. They throw these parties, they invite some guys and they hang out, and I go and pour drinks and be nice to them.'

'How nice?' Gilbey asked, concerned.

'It ain't what you think Gilbey. Jesus. I mean that shit goes down for sure, there are these other women there, always. But me and Katy have been the last couple of times. It's easy. In fact, they want me for one this Friday.'

'So what happens at these parties?' John wanted to know.

'Well, they have them out at the Country Club. They have these rooms there, all nice. And I think the men they invite stay out there. So me and Katy got to wear these little like maid outfits, you know. And we just do what we are asked. But there are these other women, like they are older than us? And yeah, I reckon they are hookers alright. They disappear with the men. Sometimes a couple go with one guy. Hell I ain't stupid, I know how the world works. I seen these guys taking these blue pills, I know what those things are.'

'But you don't have to do that shit?' Gilbey looked annoyed.

'No, least nobody asked me. But last time, one of them asked Katy though. He was all over her. It was like it was expected, but the guy was a sleaze, and Katy avoided him. But her rack's much bigger than mine.'

She looked down at her chest.

'And Katy's real pretty too. So nobody looks at me.'

John shook his head.

'No, you're real pretty. Don't do yourself down, and you don't want to be doing that stuff anyway.'

Rita looked at him, green eyes glowing.

'You think I'm pretty?' she asked.

Gilbey gave John a sideways glance and sighed.

'So, back to business. Where are the three wise men while this goes on? How many guys are you talking about?'

'First time there was two, last time only one. Yeah Mr Barlow and Mr Abel are there, they run the show, I think the women give them freebies, but I don't know, I mean it's hard to tell what they do. They leave us alone. Like Mr Abel, he can be ok, kinda funny sometimes. Mr Barlow is a real prick all the time to everyone.'

'What about Cane?'

'Oh yeah, I forgot all about him! I seen him there, I think the first time, at the Country Club. But he wasn't in the room with us. Never. Not sure where he goes. And he wasn't there last time at all, least I didn't see him.'

'How do they get in touch with you?'

'They just call my cell. Tiffany, she's one of the women who is at the parties, like she's in charge of us, she calls. I think she organises everything. They pay me, and hell I need it, I'd be happy to do more if they asked me. Actually, I'm at the plant tomorrow, but it ain't the same thing. Like I've done that a few times too, they have these guests there, show them around and shit. I have to make the coffee and bring out the sandwiches. It's not like the parties. It's pretty boring, but at least I don't have to wear the maid uniform. But look; it's all cash for me. I'm getting outta here, I need the dough.'

'So these other women, they aren't at the plant when you're there?'

'No, never. I don't ever see them except at the parties, and I never seen them in the town neither. The plant thing, they call it meet and greet, some shit like that. I've been doing that for a while now, I think that's how I got asked to work at the parties.'

'Do you know any of these men who are at the parties? Ever seen them before?' John asked.

'Not really. I seen one of them at the plant once, and then he was at a party that night, the first time. I get the feeling they are like, VIPs or something.'

John and Gilbey looked at each other. Who was coming to these parties?

'Can I ask a question?' John wanted to know, talking to both Gilbey and Rita.

'Fire away, ask me anything,' Rita replied quickly.

John smiled. 'How come there aren't any soldiers here?'

'What do you mean?'

'Well, you got an army base, what thirty-odd miles from here. Normally any town near a base is real busy in the evenings with soldiers out spending money. But not here, and I hear it's a big base.'

'It's fucking huge,' Gilbey stated.

'I don't know,' Rita replied. 'Like Gary, he's worked here forever. It's funny you ask me that question, cos he told me a while back that they used to get loads of soldiers in here, every night. But not now. I don't know why.'

'It's weird,' John said.

'Now you mention it, it is weird, I never thought about it,' Gilbey agreed.

The other waitress appeared with a tray of chicken and chips. It looked good, and they dug in, chatting about the town in general, Rita adamant that she would get out as soon as she could. It was clear that Gilbey had a paternal instinct, he encouraged her at the same time as warning her to be careful. They finished eating and sat back.

Rita looked at her watch.

'Thanks Rita,' Gilbey told her.

'No sweat.'

She drank the last of her beer.

'You boys staying?'

'Maybe have one more,' Gilbey told her.

Rita stood up, and blew him a kiss.

'I'm off, I can get a lift with Stacy, nice talking to you,' she said and walked out, the bikers all watched her go.

John laughed.

'Interesting. There's like a whole other world here.'

'Right,' Gilbey replied seriously. 'I sure would like to know who gets invited to these parties. Like, why would they come, I guess the drinks and hookers are a sweetener right? There has to be a reason.'

John shrugged.

'So let's find out.'

They had another beer, and Gilbey wanted to get home and see Carrie. John paid the bill then patted him on the back and they walked out together. The red pick-up had gone. John got back in the car and headed off, the streets were deserted, and it was only nine in the evening. He parked up at the motel and walked up to his room, unlocked the door and walked in.

Rita was sitting up in bed with the sheet pulled up.

'Hello again,' she said with a wide smile.

John glanced outside quickly and then closed the door.

'Rita, you really shouldn't be here,' he said.

'Why not? I'm old enough, and you are the nicest and most interesting guy I met recently. In fact ever.'

'Look that's very sweet of you and all that, but I am way older than you, and Gilbey would not be happy.'

'Gilbey wouldn't care. He likes you, and anyways, it ain't none of his business. Look, I don't have much excitement in my life ok? I live with my mom, and she is, well, let's just say she ain't easy. I like you. And you said I was pretty.'

'I meant it. You are pretty, but I'm not going to be here long. I will be gone, and soon, I'm not a dependable guy in things like this.'

'Fuck. I ain't waiting for you to ask me to marry you! It's what adults do right? You married?'

'No.'

'Thought not. Got a girlfriend?'

'Not really no.'

'Well then. Consider this two people who met and thought what the hell. We ain't doing nobody any harm.'

John was struggling, and knew it. She really was pretty, and he liked her.

'Jesus Rita, how the hell did you get in here anyway?'

'Let's just say Randy Andy downstairs now thinks I owe him a favour. In his dreams.'

'I still don't think …'

But Rita interrupted him. She stood up and walked naked over to him, and put her arms around his neck.

'Then don't think,' she told him quietly, and just like that the last of his resistance was gone.

Chapter Twelve

John woke up and looked over guiltily. Rita was fast asleep facing him, long dark lashes down over closed eyes. He smiled to himself ruefully. He had no regrets, but he didn't want any complications.

He got out of bed cautiously and had a shower and cleaned his teeth, then dressed in clean clothes which were basically the same as his outgoing ones. He moved around carefully and quietly, but Rita woke up anyway, and watched him with one eye open.

'Good morning,' John said cheerfully.

'Morning.'

'You can use the shower if you want.'

'What time is it?'

'Early, just after seven.'

Rita jumped out of bed.

'I got to be at the plant by eight-thirty.'

John heard the shower running, and went outside. He stood on the landing and looked out over Gray Rock. A bus appeared coming around the corner from the east–west road and lumbered past slowly going up the hill. He wondered if that was how Rita would get to the plant, she had told him she didn't have a car. The door opened and there she was, wearing her Big Lil's uniform but looking worryingly young without makeup on.

He sighed.

'Come on,' he said, 'let's get some breakfast.'

They went to the diner, John remembering Carrie worked there only after they had walked in. So it would get back to Gilbey anyway. Nothing he could do about that now. Idiot. Carrie gave them a knowing smile. The radio played country music. John ordered an egg and bacon muffin and Rita wanted the same. They both drank milky coffee.

'So where do you live?' John asked.

'Just along from the stadium.'

'Oh yeah? Which one?'

'The new one.'

'Right. North side then.'

'Yeah, but only for a couple of years. We lived down in the south before.'

'Why did you move?'

'They went to see Mom, and offered her a new place, cheap to rent or something. By then most of the people we knew had already moved. I don't really know but they said they wanted the housing in the south for the plant workers.'

'Hmmm, that doesn't really make sense, why didn't they just put them in the north?'

Rita shrugged indifferently.

'No idea. I wasn't asked about it. Mom jumped at it of course.'

John finished his muffin and watched Rita eating hers.

'So you really gonna get out of Gray Rock. Really move away?' he asked.

'Fuck yeah! Sorry! I mean yeah, definitely. I hate it here. Place is full of creeps, there is always some bad shit happening to someone.'

'What do you mean?'

'Oh you know, how they talk. Sometimes people just disappear. Just like that. Well, it's what they say anyway.'

'What people?'

'From the south. I don't know them. It could be bullshit I guess. But yeah, I am outta here. I just need a few hundred more, probably a thousand.'

'Did you mean what you said? You never been out of Texas.'
She looked at him.

'No, never. My daddy died when I was ten, he was the dreamer. He always used to tell me where he was going to take me. He said I had to get school out the way first. We used to sit in the kitchen and talk about it, he had this big old atlas, it was the best time, we would make all these plans for hours sometimes. I used to love it. He would talk about all these countries with crazy names like he'd been to every one of them. Of course, he never had but he would tell me all the things we could do there. But life ain't like that, that's for sure. Sometimes he would have to go somewhere for his work in a truck, and I went with him on the long trips when I could. We went to Dallas, and Houston. It was great. We were going to go to New Orleans and Miami he said. But he got sick and that was that. My mom never thinks of doing anything like that. She just tells me I should be thankful. She wants me to marry and live here.'

'I'm sorry about your dad.'

'He was a real good man. Yeah, well. It was quick, one day there, the next gone near enough. I miss him, every day.'

She sat and sipped her coffee, the same faraway look in her face he remembered from the previous evening when Gilbey had mentioned her father. The radio started playing a track with a heavy, grinding bass line. Rita looked up, eyes shining.

'Man I love this fucking song! Reminds me of my daddy, he always used to sing it, always.'

John recognised the track. Black Velvet, he couldn't remember the name of female singer. Rita sang along and then slid out the seat and began to dance to it, squirming and weaving while she sang. Every single male eye in the place was watching, mesmerised. The track finished and she sat down. John clapped and laughed.

'Well I would have paid to watch that,' he told her.

Rita blushed. 'Stop it.'

'How are you getting to the plant, do you walk there?'
She jumped up.

'Shit I forgot. Damn I got to get changed I can't turn up wearing this.'

'You look great.'

'Thank you, but that's not what I meant. They wouldn't like it. Damn.'

'Don't worry, I'll drive you. You need to go home first?'

'Thank you.'

John dropped a twenty on the table and they left, moving quickly back to the motel and getting into the Buick. Rita directed John down the high street, as they turned in they heard Gilbey getting to the diner. It took just a couple of minutes and John pulled up outside a small single storey ranch style house, in a street of all the same. Rita ran inside and was back out again five minutes later, now wearing a smart black skirt and doing up a white blouse. She looked great. As he pulled away she dug some make up out her bag and put it on using the mirror in the visor.

'So, I ain't working tonight. You want to do something?' she asked him.

Try and stop me, John thought to himself.

'Yeah, I do. I got an appointment near Odessa this afternoon, but I will be back later. Fancy going for a meal? My treat.'

She stopped applying lipstick and looked at him.

'Really?'

'Yeah, of course really. Why not? Where's a good place to go?'

'Hey, I never got taken out for dinner before. I thought you'd just say go to Lil's.'

'I wouldn't do that. I like the place but you work there, so it's not really a meal out for you. Any of the other bars or restaurants in this town any good?'

'God no. But there's some nice places in Carline, or anyways there used to be. My daddy used to take me there on my birthday.'

'Where's Carline?'

'It's a ways. About sixty, maybe seventy-odd miles, past the army base.'

'Fine, let's do that, it's not much more than an hour.'

They reached the plant and John pulled in close to the barrier. The clock said 8:25.

'Good timing,' he told her. 'What time will I pick you up?'

'I'll come to the motel, about seven ok?'

'Perfect. I should be back by then. Here, this is my mobile number. If I'm not at the motel call me.'

John wrote down the number on the inside of the hire car map, tore it off and passed it over. They kissed quickly, and then she sprang out the car, always full of energy. John watched the guard at the gate make some comment and she gave him the finger in return then walked off toward the main building. She turned and waved, and he waved back.

Oh dear.

He liked her.

He drove back to the motel and parked up, wondering what to do before he left for the prison.

The three wise men were back sitting around their normal table, the breakfast dishes cleared away. Barlow had been short and abrasive all morning, particularly with Cane but even Abel had felt it too. There was no news, which Abel insisted was a good sign.

Barlow leaned his bony elbows on the table.

'I only want to say this once. Friday is our most important yet. It must go without a hitch. Can I at least be assured that this is the case?'

'Everything is arranged, there will be no problems,' Abel assured him.

His mobile rang and he grabbed it up, glad of the distraction.

'Right, thank you, I will find out,' was all he said after listening for a while and he hung up.

'That was Hunter. He has come up with a plan and it will be in effect today. He wants to know that the prison is still locked down. I'll make the call.'

Barlow pursed his lips and nodded. Cane looked out of the window. As usual.

Abel's second call was equally brief.

'Right. Well they haven't made any contact with the FBI that the lockdown is lifted,' Abel said with a smile.

'What the hell does that mean?' Barlow demanded.

'Well, I am no expert, but I imagine that the FBI will be waiting to be advised that the lockdown is over, don't you?'

'What's to stop the FBI just making the call?'

'They say it doesn't work that way.'

'Humph. I sincerely hope so. Where does Hunter say Smith is now?'

'He is back at the motel. He spent the day yesterday walking around the town as we know. Hunter believes he is waiting for the FBI to give him the go ahead, so he is just wasting time.'

'Right. Well he can't do us any damage if that's the case.'

'Exactly. He also asked me to get Carter under control.'

'What? Jesus, what's he done now.'

'He cooked up some idea, Hunter's upset. He says he could have ended up down more guys.'

'Ok. Speak to him. Remind him who the hell he works for.'

John really was just wasting time, so in the end he called Patrick, who was now even closer, having set up in San Antonio. Patrick had heard nothing regarding the prison.

'You know what Patrick? I'm just going to get up there. I'll chance it.'

'It's up to you. We filed your clearance anyway, so you only have to report in. Make sure you take your passport.'

'Yeah, I'll have it. But I'm going to let you down, I know it. This is going to be a waste of time. I still don't think he'll say anything.'

'Maybe, maybe not. I'm hoping that he will feel it's his victory, that he's got one over on us, and you especially. People like to gloat you know. He might say something. I know he'll never come right out and tell you who's getting it done but something might slip, you never know.'

'I'm sorry Patrick I can't see it. He's been inside for ten years. Not much to gloat about even if he's getting out next week.'

'No way it's gonna be that quick, but yeah, I do know what you mean. I just feel that it's a chance to try and find out what's going on and why now.'

'I'm gonna ask him about Barlow and Abel, that's for sure. See what effect that has.'

'Yeah? I guess so, can't hurt.'

'Right, well I'll call you.'

'Ok.'

John hung up the call and checked his watch. Close to ten. He didn't need to leave for a while. He decided he would walk into the town and get a coffee from the shop he had seen. He left the motel heading for the high street, and then into the coffee shop. Like everywhere it was quiet. There was a young girl behind the counter grinning away at something she was typing in her mobile phone. She glanced up and did a double take, and then smiled even wider.

'Hi!' she said eagerly.

'Hi. Can I get a latte please?'

'Sure. Coming right up.'

The girl busied herself behind the counter, giving him sideways looks. John wondered what it was with the young women in the town. Maybe he should move here. The girl's phone beeped so she grabbed it and typed something rapidly, then finished John's drink. Her phone beeped again. The girl laughed.

She pushed the coffee across the counter. John dug a five out his pocket.

'No, no, Rita says I can't charge you,' the girl said.

Ah.

'Er right, well, thank you.'

'I'm Katy by the way.'

The girl stuck her hand out, and John shook it. She was another pretty girl, probably the same age as Rita with black hair in a short bob.

'Nice to meet you Katy. But, how do you know who I am?'

'You kidding? Rita was texting me telling me all about you.

She likes you John. This is a small town, how many British strangers do you think we have here?'

'Right! Well, it's great to meet you Katy. She told me about you too.'

'I bet. You make sure you look after her tonight you dog.'

'Er … yeah, I will.'

'You break her heart I'll hunt you down, believe it,' she told him with a wicked smile and a wink.

'I do believe it, and I'm not going to.'

John picked up the coffee and left, smiling. This really was a small town.

He sat by the rock and drank the coffee, which was very good. He looked at the sheriff's office, but nothing was happening. There were two cruisers parked outside but no sign of anyone actually doing anything. He drank up and decided to head to Howarth. The sooner he got there, the sooner he would get back. With the FBI pass he probably wouldn't have to stick too closely to the usual visitor rules.

He threw the cardboard cup in the bin and then walked back to the motel and got in the car. On a whim, he decided to drive out to the east and check out the army base, Fort Blunt. He wanted to see what else was around and if it was as big as everyone said, after all he had plenty of time. He drove down the hill then turned left in front of the town hall. The road ran straight off to the east, with a slight southerly bearing. He passed the gun club, which was still there and looked identical to eleven years ago. He passed through a small town that consisted of next to nothing, which had a huge roadhouse just outside, no surprise there, it would be packed most nights with soldiers he guessed. A few miles further and there it was. The base was more of a distance from Gray Rock than he had thought, over thirty miles but he saw it from a long way away, the surrounding land all around was pretty flat. There were high fences, and then a long stone wall, which curved in elegantly at the centre point where there was a wide access road. A huge sign said US Army Fort Blunt, and there was a large sentry hut in the centre with barriers across lanes on either side. In and out. He could see soldiers inside, and beyond lots of buildings spreading out far into the distance. Neat and tidy, white painted kerb stones, lots of landscaping. An Abrams tank in the centre of a round grass lawn, visible behind the gatehouse. He had met many US military personnel over the years. Squared away, they would describe it. He drove past and then turned around at the next turning and headed back into Gray Rock, picking up the road north up the hill past the plant. He filled up at the petrol station and bought a bag of sweets for the journey then set off. An hour and a half later he reached Fort Stockton and his phone rang.

With the long straight roads and boredom he had bothered to connect his mobile to the car . He glanced at the number displayed which meant nothing. What the hell. He pressed the button on the steering wheel.

'Hello?'

'John?'

'Er yeah, who's that?' he asked, knowing full well and with a big smile.

'It's Rita! Asshole.'

'Yeah, I knew that. Sorry. So, how's it going?'

'Boring. It's a bunch of Japanese people, all oooh and aaah at everything. You know. Their English ain't too good so it's kind of hard to follow what they are saying but they seem real excited by what they are looking at. They're nice enough, these guys aren't gonna show up at the party, trust me. Anyways they are getting shown round the research building so I'm sitting down at last. Hey fancy phone sex? I never did that.'

'Me neither. But I'm driving, so probably not the best idea.'

'Guess not. Well, I thought I'd check you hadn't given me some bullshit phone number.'

'Why would I do that? I'm looking forward to tonight.'

'Yeah me too. Am I still pretty?'

'Oh yes. Very.'

'Good boy. Right answer. Now I know what I'm wearing tonight. Oh crap, what are these guys doing here?'

'What?' John was confused.

'Jeez, I can't stand these assholes. Sorry, I better go, see you later.'

'No problem, see you at seven.'

'Bye.'

John hung up and chuckled to himself. He would be leaving tomorrow, but with some fond memories. He would encourage Rita to get out too. After watching her in the diner that morning he could see some shiny poles on her journey, but she could make her own choices, live her own life. And she was sharp enough not to get taken.

He followed the road north and headed for Monahans, then Odessa. It was a long drive, the day was grey and dull. He picked up the signs and turned off halfway between the towns, the road he was on now narrow and straight as a ruler, nothing to see at all but wilderness on either side. After a long while a sturdy fence came into view to his left. Then there it was; the prison, massive, out in the middle of nowhere protected by a screen of three separate fences all topped off with miles of razor wire. The huge inner buildings were surrounded by tall white walls with watchtowers dotted all around. It was way more than a mile from the road to the inner wall. He couldn't see how anyone could escape from here. If it was possible to clear the wall and then the series of fences where would anyone go? There was nothing for miles. He passed through a vehicle checkpoint without incident and then there was a huge 'Texas Department of Corrections' sign, with the name Howarth underneath. He slowed to make the turning and pulled up in front of a barrier. A guard walked slowly out of a small glassed in building at one end. John buzzed his window down and produced the authorisation email and his passport. The guard said nothing; just took them both back to his hut. John sat and waited patiently, listening half-heartedly to some dreadful songs on the radio. Five minutes passed and the guard reappeared, returning the documents, and the barrier went up. So far so good. The guard told him to drive through to the building instead of using the pedestrian entrance and visitor's car park. He drove into a cage, with high thick mesh sides and a mesh roof. There were double gates closed in front of him. He stopped, and the set of gates closed behind him, and when they were completely shut the second set in front opened and he crawled through, to be stopped again by another pair. It was the same process; the gates closed behind and then the ones in front opened afterward. It was all controlled electronically. Once he was through the last set there was a car park to his right and he pulled up. He emptied his pockets; locked his wallet and mobile in the glove compartment and then made his way over to the visitor entrance. This was a narrow doorway, with a guard behind a thick glass window on one side and a heavy steel door in front. Once again John passed in the email and his passport. The guard looked closely at them and picked up the phone. It was impossible to hear his conversation but eventually he passed everything back and the door in front clicked open.

John walked in, and was immediately hit by the institutional smell of sweat, disinfectant and fear. He was now in a small lobby. In front was a closed in counter with two guards looking out, again sitting behind thick glass. There were cameras everywhere. One more time John pushed in the documents through a small slot in bottom of the glass. So far nobody had mentioned any lockdown, and he had got this far so he was optimistic. There were the same steel doors set on both sides and in front of him. The guards took their time reading carefully through everything and finally one moved to a microphone, pushing the email back through again.

'Ok, Mr Smith. We've been expecting you. We'll be hanging onto your passport. Go straight through the door to your left and wait. You will be met by an officer who will escort you through.

The door clicked open and John shoved the email into his pocket then pushed through into a small windowless waiting room with six plastic chairs bolted to the floor. More cameras. It was too warm in the prison, stifling with little air. There was a vending machine in the corner, so he got himself a coffee which was scalding hot and then sat down to wait. This time it took a while, but eventually a door opened on the other side and an elderly prison guard slowly walked in the room, wearing a smartly ironed uniform.

'Mr Smith,' he said.

'Hello,' John replied, standing up.

The guard gestured to him to raise his arms and then searched him carefully.

'Follow me please sir.'

John stood up and followed the guard into the prison main. They went up two flights of stairs and down several passages and through a couple of controlled doors which followed the same stop/start procedure as the gates on the way in and then into a corridor which had numbered doors on the left and windows on the right. John glanced out as they passed, he could see into the exercise yard. There was a bunch of beefy black guys around the weight machines at the back, while many more prisoners; a mixture of black and white were playing basketball. Some were just sitting there watching. It actually looked quite peaceful but John knew these places were a powder keg.

The guard stopped at a door with the number three painted on it.

'Ok Mr Smith. I have to tell you your conversation will be recorded. If you want to give anything to the prisoner you'll need to knock on the door and give it to me first so it will be checked before I can pass it over, Ok?'

'Fine, I don't have anything anyway. Well, you searched me.'

'I did, it's just procedure, I got to tell everyone the same script.'

'Got it. I'm just glad it's going ahead. I was worried this place might still be in lockdown.'

The guard looked at him.

'Lockdown? We haven't had a lockdown here in a couple of years.'

That's interesting thought John. He looked for somewhere to put his coffee cup but the guard grinned at him.

'Hey, take that in with you. That'll really piss him off.'

'Oh yeah?'

John smiled back.

'So can I ask how he's been, any problems? Because of all the original fuss I'm told that they didn't get any reports from here. To be honest, I'd forgotten all about him.'

'Hell, I'll tell you anything. It ain't like I'm breaking any laws or invading his privacy. There ain't none in here, believe me. Well personally, I think he's an asshole, but then I got a long memory. This place opened eighteen years ago, and I been here since day one, so I remember his first day. He was cocky, totally sure he was getting out. The guy behaved like we were all way beneath him. This was in the jail. Once he was in the prison, it was all different. We have a separate segregation system here. We got solitary, like usual. And we got restricted, same as everywhere. But we also got this wellbeing unit, which speaking for myself I think is all bullshit. They started it about six or seven years ago, maybe longer. Anyways, he's been in there ever since, he ain't a popular prisoner here, was always whining and demanding. But he ain't getting the shit kicked out of himself every day no more because of it. Last couple of years he's been real quiet. Must have finally dawned on him, right?'

'He had many visitors?'

The guard considered.

'Tell you the truth, before the last couple of months I don't recall any. Not one. But he's had an attorney in here recently, month or so ago I guess. Didn't stay very long.'

The guard opened the door and John walked in. He was in a small, square room with one plastic chair in it. In the centre of the room was a solid block wall over a metre high and the rest was thick glass up to the ceiling with a speaking grill set into the centre right in front of the chair. Through the glass John could see an identical setup on the other side. High on the wall on both sides was a camera. He sat down in the chair to wait, sipping the coffee which was still very hot.

Five minutes passed and then the door on the opposite side opened. A guard walked in and stood to one side, followed by

Anthony Collis, who slouched into the room looking at the floor, the guard walked back out again and shut the door.

Ten years in prison had not been kind. Collis looked at least ten years older than he actually was. Pale and pasty faced, what little hair he had left hung raggedly about his ears. He had put on weight; not easily done in prison so presumably through lack of exercise. He was wearing thick glasses and peered uncertainly at John as he walked across and sat down. He dropped heavily into the chair and licked his lips nervously, his face expressionless.

'Hello Anthony,' John started.

Collis nodded back.

'What the hell do you want? I never thought I'd see you again.'

'Well, your old friends in the FBI thought it might be an idea for us to have a chat. Especially with everything that's happening at the moment. So, they asked me to help out and I thought why not?'

Collis looked sullenly back.

'Yeah right. So what, you gonna say sorry now? I've been in here near enough eleven years asshole.'

Collis picked at the frayed edge of his white uniform shirt sleeve. John watched him and frowned.

'No, I'm not apologising for anything. You are guilty. I don't care what some ignorant prick of a judge thinks, he wasn't involved, he knows nothing more than what he's read in the papers. You did it. No question about it at all. And you're in here. But it sounds like you're getting out, and we wondered how you did that.'

John anticipated something triumphant, some bullshit about how much cleverer they were but Collis said nothing, didn't even smile. He looked up at the camera and then back at his sleeve, then rubbed his face and licked his lips again.

'I didn't do nothing about that,' he spoke quietly, almost a mumble.

'Well someone did.'

Collis said nothing. John looked hard at him. Something was wrong here. He hadn't expected this, from his memory of

Collis he had believed he would be in for a whole load of 'how smart we are' and 'how much are we going to sue' rhetoric, with a lot of injured pride and Texas is better than you thrown in. But that wasn't how it was. Collis was subdued, nervous, scared. For a man promised release by the highest judge in the state this didn't make a whole lot of sense.

And now John saw how prison had been, close to eleven years. Collis had several scars on his head, face and neck, and his left hand was at an unnatural angle to his wrist. There was fading yellow bruising on his right cheek and the eye above was swollen and blackened.

'Eleven years. Been tough on you right, Anthony?' John asked gently.

For the first time Collis looked at him.

'What do you think?'

John thought about why he was there, what Patrick had wanted. Maybe this could work after all.

'Well ok Anthony, talk to me. So tell me, how did all this start with Judge Raymer? It seems like a long wait for an appeal to me.'

Again, Collis glanced up at the camera. He shrugged, liquid eyes looking around.

'I didn't know. I was told about it. Just like that. I was in the computer class, a boss told me all about it. Showed me the newspaper. Till then I hadn't heard nothing. Nobody contacted me.'

'That doesn't make any sense. It read like they had been working on it for the last ten years.'

Again Collis looked at him. The weird eyes were still there, but had faded somehow, like all the life had been removed, something had been switched off.

'You know what? Just fucking ask me. Why do I care? I don't give a shit anymore. Ask me, and I'll tell you,' Collis whispered.

This guy is terrified, John realised. Of what or who, he didn't know. He decided to change tack. looked up at the camera and smiled at Collis.

'Listen Anthony, whatever you say today, I will pass onto the FBI. That's why I'm here. But look, they can get copies of the recording. Nobody can do anything with this. You got nothing to fear. It can't get edited, or changed. If necessary I will check every second of it. If there is anything you say that is helpful to the FBI then in turn it could be of use to you. But it sounds like you're getting out anyway.'

Collis rubbed his face with his hands, the left moving slowly. Then he sat back and nodded, saying nothing.

'Anthony. Your attorney has been in, right? So, you have been working on this, you must have,' John prompted.

'No, I could never do shit. I tried but got no help at all. Then years later that guy shows up here. He came to see me about a month ago maybe. Just to get me to sign some paperwork. But this was a while after I read about it, and nobody called or nothing.'

'So he just turned up? Out the blue?'

'Yeah. I never knew nothing about it. I never get visitors anyways, so I just went to meet him. It was in the governor's office. I was never in there before neither.'

'What paperwork did he ask you to sign?'

'Some documents, that I have been denied an appeal, and not allowed to speak to counsel, or any legal people.'

'That's bullshit.'

Collis half smiled, and nodded.

'Oh yeah, that is bullshit I was trying to get something done ten years ago.'

'Why do you say that?'

'When I was sent here, I was told don't worry, we're on your side, we'll get you out, you're not on your own. We'll look after you. And I believed them, why wouldn't I? But I never heard nothing. Nobody ever came here. Not once. I couldn't get hold of nobody. It turns out that yeah, I was completely on my own. And let me tell you, I wasn't prepared for this. I thought I would be straight out the door, that's what I was told, and I really believed that someone would be looking out for me in here. How wrong was I. First three years, I was in hospital more than in the block. I don't wanna talk about that.'

Collis's lip trembled. Although he didn't want to think about it too much, John could imagine what he had been through, best not to remind him, he decided.

'You played your part right? But then they just forgot about you.'

'That's it exactly. Man, how stupid I was. Like I knew I was low down on the ladder right? Of course I was, I was just the hired hand. But I really believed they would look out for me. They fucking promised, over and over and like a fool I listened to every word.'

'You probably don't believe me, but I'm sorry about that.'

'Sorry? Why the fuck would you care.'

'It ain't right you were left hanging, if you were made promises.'

'Yeah, I was made a lot of promises. But nothing. Nobody ever even answered the fucking phone.'

'So what did this attorney say?'

'He didn't know nothing. I think he didn't really even know why he was here, I could see it. Written all over him. Barely knew my name. Got me to sign the forms and then he got the fuck outta here. And yeah, I was excited, I want out. Of course I do. Like I asked him, how long, he just said real soon, it will be real soon, then he was gone. I tried calling since, but there ain't a proper answer, some bullshit message service. And I never got no call back.'

'Nothing since?'

'Nope.'

'So what's going on?'

Collis leaned forward and looked back up at the camera.

'You mean it? Feds get this recording?'

'Yeah I mean it. I will arrange it soon as I get to my phone.'

'Right well I'll tell you what I think. This is a distraction. I've been suckered, again. Look, I ain't totally fucking stupid. I can see what's going on. I ain't fucking getting outta here. But enough noise gets made, plenty people start talking, papers are full of it and the high and mighty in the state of Texas can sweep a lot of other shit under the carpet when there ain't anyone looking. Nobody will ever notice.'

John nodded.

'Ok, well, that makes sense.'

Collis sat back again and crossed his arms.

'And that's it. I got nothing else to tell you. Do whatever you want, it can't be any worse for me.'

'I'm not going to do anything. I told you the truth, I'm here because the FBI asked me to come and talk to you.'

'Yeah, well, we can talk. I've got fuck all to lose, nobody gives a shit about me anyhow.'

John nodded slowly. He had got a lot more than he expected, and it was going to help Patrick. He could ease off now.

'But it's better here for you now right? The guard said you were in some different unit or something.'

'Well I don't have to bed down with the animals anymore. Haven't done that for years thank Christ. I got my own cell, and I ain't stuck in with the rapists or the other monsters neither. So yeah, that's better. But I still got to watch out you know. I still got to eat. I don't go in the yard, I stay where the bosses are, but if anyone wants to, they can get to me.'

He rubbed his face where the bruises were.

'Yeah I can see that.'

'I got this because of all this shit in the press. Everybody immediately think I'm in the boss's pockets, I'm special. Suddenly everybody got to speak to me. Lot of wolves in here. This is a bad place. Don't get me started.'

'What's this about computer class? I thought all that would be a big no-no.'

'I teach computer stuff. You know, write a letter, send an email, real basic, and also some website stuff. But it passes the time, and gets me credits too. My councillor says I could be out in about seven years, I got a good record.'

'Well at least that's positive. I appreciate you talking to me, I just got a couple more questions. What's your connection to

Barlow? Abel? I can't figure out how all this started, with One Race I mean. I've met them, and I'm struggling to make it all fit. I know it was a long time ago.'

Collis looked hard at the camera, then picked at his sleeve again.

'I don't really know them. They were backing One Race, and they're from Texas. I think Barlow had the vision, you know the whole White America thing. Abel was always loud in supporting him. But I didn't really speak to them, I met them maybe twice, never for long. I just used to get emails. You know. Instructions.'

'Really? That's surprising, they live in Gray Rock.'

Collis stared at him.

'You sure?'

'Oh yeah. That town has changed, you wouldn't recognise it.'

'I didn't know that.'

'Nobody ever comes to see you?'

'Like who? My brother's dead. My parents ain't around a long time. Anyone I thought was my friend I soon found out wasn't.'

'I heard about your brother. I'm sorry.'

Collis shrugged.

'Yeah, well he was a kind of a mess, some people were not helping. But he made his own choices and didn't want to listen to anyone. I don't blame nobody else for that.'

John had never expected to feel any sympathy, but it was impossible not to; the man opposite was an empty shell.

'What about Paul Hunter? That was who you called all those years ago.'

Collis looked surprised.

'You know him?'

'Not personally. But he is around Gray Rock.'

'I wouldn't have expected that. He likes to be out the way. But I don't really know him that well, he just seemed to be a guy who would get things done.'

John nodded, it was what he had already assumed.

'How are you doing in here? Changed your mind about the white supremacy Ku Klux Klan thing?'

Collis sat slowly shaking his head, looking even more lost, eyes wet.

'It was all bullshit, all fucking lies. I found that out real quick. In here, it's all about colour. It's mob rule, like a hundred years ago. But I believed it. I thought I was right. They found me and I bought every word they told me. When I was in school I never took no notice of anybody's colour. I wanted friends, like all kids do. That all changed once I left, I got in with some guys and then I became who I was. I had problems, lot of difficulty fitting in and they made me welcome, like I was important I guess. It wasn't real, it took a long time for me to work that shit out. Yeah, they used me. And now, well, I ain't got any friends in here neither, white or black. They all treat me the same, good or bad. Because there ain't no difference in any of us. I learned the hard way. And to tell you the truth, the only men I ever seen in here with even a shred of decency have been black or Hispanic, and I mean that.'

'Regret is a part of life, unfortunately. We all regret things we did.'

'Yeah, I got regrets. Biggest is I regret believing all the shit I was told, and that we would make a difference, it was all bullshit. I know that now.'

'You killed three innocent people Anthony.'

Collis went to speak, glanced at him then looked up at the camera and then down at the floor, saying nothing.

'Well once you're out you can start again. You'll get help.' John told him gently.

'Maybe.'

John checked his watch.

'Anthony, I will be reporting our conversation to my contact in the FBI, and they will subpoena the tape straight away. You've been very helpful. We could do with more information on Abel and Barlow.'

Collis leaned forward.

'I think I've proved my position. You tell your guy I could be persuaded to talk more, but they got to move me from here. This place is fucking crazy. I don't care where it is, just somewhere I can get some peace. I'll answer any questions. Like I said, I don't know those guys really but there are a couple of others who work for them that I can talk about.'

'Ok, I'll pass that on. I think they'll be interested.'

'Good.'

Without another word Collis stood up and walked over to the door, banging on it hard. It was opened straight away and he was gone. John stood up too and walked out. The guard was waiting at the end of the corridor, and he was led out back through the prison, then collected his passport. As he drove out through the gates he was suddenly grateful for the journey in front of him.

He needed to think.

Chapter Thirteen

Once he got back on the road John called Patrick and relayed the conversation. After some initial confusion and then outright disbelief, Patrick agreed to get the recording immediately and also to arrange for an agent to call by the prison. John politely suggested not using anyone local, which Patrick agreed to. John hung up and checked his watch; just gone three. He should be back about six, perfect.

He settled in for the long drive, trying to find a decent radio station. He had nearly given up when suddenly the female DJ announced it was time for Madchester! A celebration of British music and then the opening riff from 'Driving South' came on.

That'll do well he decided.

He filled the car again halfway between Fort Stockton and Marathon, but got held up for a while further down the road as a tow-truck recovered a stricken panel van which had lost a wheel and slid across the road, so it was close to six-thirty when he finally rolled down the hill past the plant, and then stopped sharply.

Something major was happening in front of the motel. He could see two State Police cruisers plus both of Gray Rock's Sheriff's own, all scattered around on the road outside the motel with their roof lights flashing. There was also a dark sedan with lights lit in the grille and a couple of vans parked randomly around.

He wondered what was going on, must be an accident or something, and pulled up just behind the nearest cruiser. He climbed out and walked down the hill. There was a small crowd gathered just up the slope from the diner. He made it to the motel and started across the car park when there was a shout, and the next thing three state policemen were running toward him with their guns held high. He froze and raised his hands. The fat sheriff appeared from the corner by the stairs to his room and waddled forward wheezing.

'That's him! That's the murdering bastard right there!' he shouted.

Murdering?

John looked around confused, still holding up his hands.

'What's going on?' he asked.

'You shut the fuck up!' panted the sheriff and two state policemen, one a big young white guy with a red face and neck and the other a smaller, even younger Hispanic man got on either side of him and held his arms. They started walking him toward the corner without saying anything.

'You keep a tight hold of him y'hear!' shouted the sheriff moving closer.

The two policemen ignored him and carried on walking. John allowed himself to be led, wondering what the hell was happening. Then an older black man with short white hair, smartly dressed in a grey three piece suit with a dark red tie done up tight appeared from around the corner. The policemen stopped, still holding onto John and the black man walked across, looking intently at him. He halted and stood still a few feet away, and nodded slowly.

'You Mr John Smith?' he asked, in a deep, cultured voice.

'That's me. What's going on here?'

'He's asking the questions asshole!' shouted the sheriff, who had moved closer.

The black man held out his hand without looking.

'You mind sheriff?'

He nodded to the smaller policeman who searched through John's pockets, handing over his wallet, mobile phone and passport plus a handful of coins to the black man, who looked through them carefully without saying anything. The policeman took John's arm again.

The black man produced a clear plastic bag and dropped everything into it, then looked back at John.

'My name is Frank Slater. I'm a detective out of Odessa.'

John said nothing.

'Mr Smith, do you know a Miss Rita Gellar?' Slater asked slowly.

John stared at him. Something was very wrong here.

'I know a Rita. Right here in Gray Rock but I don't know her last name. What's going on?' he asked again.

'This way please.'

Slater turned and walked back around the corner, and the policemen guided John after him. They started up the stairs, the sheriff following. Slater reached the top and turned around.

'Would you be so good as to stay down there please sheriff?' he called out, and then walked into John's room, stopping just inside the door. The policemen carried on moving John up the stairs and suddenly he knew. He looked in through the door and froze.

Rita was lying on the floor on her back, facing the door with her eyes open. Her skirt was pulled up, and there was a lot of blood. Her hair was matted with it and her blouse was soaked. John felt weak, he dropped his head. Nausea welled up inside.

The bastards.

'What happened to her? I didn't do this,' he whispered, his face pushed into his shoulder.

'Well, we need to see about that,' Slater replied.

There were people everywhere in the room, everything getting picked up, and brushed and looked through.

The policemen took John outside and back down the stairs, Slater following. They led him over to a patrol car and pushed him hard up against the side of it, the Hispanic cop snapping handcuffs on to the front. Slater stood to one side, silently watching.

'John Smith, I believe you to be involved in the murder of Rita Gellar. You have the right to remain silent. Anything you say can and will be used against you in a court of law. You have the right to an attorney, and to have one present during any questioning,' he relayed. The big cop pulled the rear door open.

John looked at the cop and then at Slater, and the familiar anger welled up inside, replacing the grief and shock. He pulled away from the cop and stared over at the sheriff, who was standing on the other side of the car watching and smirking.

'Hey fat man!' he called out. 'You did this. You and you're fucked up bosses. And I am making you a promise, I will be back here. I will be free and clear, I did not do this and you know it. So you better start counting the minutes, because I'm coming after you. You, and all your fucking mates have fucked up. You are fucked. You will be fucking sorry, you all will be. You start looking over your shoulder you fat useless lump of shit. You are going to pay. You all will. You make sure you pass that on.'

The sheriff's eyes opened wide, and what little colour he had fell from his face. His mouth opened, then closed. He spun around looking wildly at everyone in the car park

'You hear that? He threatened me! He threatened an officer of the law! You all heard that right?' he shrieked, his voice becoming shriller. 'He threatened me! He …'

The squeaking voice was cut off after the big officer pushed John into the car and slammed the door shut. There was a pause while the two officers spoke with Slater and then the young Hispanic man climbed into the front passenger seat. The big one trudged slowly around the car looking at the sheriff who was now wandering around still speaking to nobody with his high pitched voice. John caught site of Gilbey walking across the road from the diner. John didn't want to think about what he would be feeling.

The big officer got into the driver's seat and started the car. He carefully negotiated a turn through all the other vehicles and then set off up the hill past the plant on the same road that John had just driven down fifteen minutes earlier.

John sat in the back saying nothing, staring out through the black steel mesh that separated him from the front. His mind was numb, nothing seemed to connect together. The two officers didn't speak either, the Hispanic man would turn and look back at him occasionally, then about an hour into the journey after they had cleared Marathon and the road had improved he turned again and tapped on the mesh.

'Hey!' he called out.

John looked at him, but said nothing in reply.

'What did you mean?' the cop asked.

'What did I mean about what?' John replied.

'What you said, about the sheriff back there. Carter.'

'What, did I mean I'll make him pay? Yeah, I meant that.'

'I know you did. You said "You did this" to him. Why did you say that?'

'Because he did. There's something wrong with that town, and he is up to his neck in it.'

The big officer grunted something and the Hispanic cop shrugged and turned back to the front. John sat back and waited.

Abel parked his car haphazardly on the drive at Barlow's house and hurried up to the front door. He went to knock but it was opened immediately by a man he recognised but didn't know the name. A man wearing a pale grey polo shirt. He walked in and the man closed the door behind him, waiting there. Abel practically ran into the large living room, expecting pandemonium.

But everyone was relaxed, calm. Barlow was even smiling. He was sitting on the end of the long sofa, Hunter in an armchair opposite on the other side of a coffee table. Cane was standing by the glass doors that led onto the garden which was now in darkness.

'Abel! Dennis, please sit down,' Barlow sang out.

Abel sat down in the chair further along from Hunter. He looked around carefully. He had been at the Country Club when Cane had called him saying he needed to get to Barlow's house urgently, and he had jumped in the car fearing the worst. Now he wondered why he had got the call. But he knew better than to ask, so he sat there quietly.

'Mr Hunter has done us yet another great service,' Barlow told him reaching down, picking up a brandy glass from the table and raising it in the air.

Hunter picked up his own glass and reached over, clinking it with Barlow's. There was a bottle but no other glasses on the table. Abel looked at both men and glanced at Cane, who stood very still looking uncomfortably into the room.

'It just needed some lateral thinking. It's my military brain,' Hunter said and sat deep into his chair.

Barlow smiled and drank from the glass, also settling back.

'So, what are we celebrating?' Abel had to ask, it was clear that nobody was going to actually say it. Cane obviously knew, but he was never going to speak out.

'Celebrating?' asked Barlow. 'Yes, I suppose we are. Mr Smith is no longer an issue. It's back to business as normal. Tomorrow is Friday. We can make sure everything goes well, and we are the hosts with the most over the weekend. Everything will be signed Monday morning and the ink dry. Then we are set for life. Nobody will ever interfere again.'

'That's good news,' Abel replied carefully, still wondering what was going on.

'No. It isn't!'

The voice came from behind, confusing everyone. Heads turned. It was remarkable; Cane, had actually said something? He was standing in the same place, trembling slightly, eyes wide.

'He killed the girl!' he blurted out.

'Ssshhhh,' Barlow said shaking his head, but still smiling.

'What girl?' Abel asked.

Hunter stood up.

'It's not important. It's ways and means. I saw the opportunity. She is of no consequence, it was for the greater good,' he announced grandly.

Barlow nodded happily.

'Rita. You know her,' Cane told Abel, ignoring Hunter who scowled back at him and sat down heavily.

'Rita? She worked for us,' Abel remarked, now looking at Barlow.

'So what? Lots of people work for us. We aren't going to miss her. Forget about it,' Barlow's smile was slipping fast.

Abel looked at Hunter, who sighed.

'Like I said, it was a means to an end. Smith is now in the care of the Odessa PD. He ain't getting out of there quickly I promise you that. A loner, an oddball tourist who just hangs around the town all day and then gets lucky with the local slut and it all goes wrong. Who cares.'

'This is not right at all. Rita was no slut,' Cane said.

Hunter flapped a hand at him.

'Whatever. We'll need a replacement for Friday,' Abel said, unable to think of anything else to say.

'Then find one. Plenty of young girls in this town. In fact, just ask Tiffany to sort it out,' Barlow replied dismissively.

'Sure,' Abel replied, but looking at Cane when he did it.

Barlow poured some more brandy for himself and Hunter. Cane walked stiffly across the room and then out of the house. Hunter grinned at Barlow, who glanced at Abel.

'Make sure everything gets sorted. And tell Cane from me, that I expect more of him.'

The big guy turned onto the 10 at Fort Stockton and headed west, after a couple of minutes he hit a switch and the roof lights came on, a haze of red and blue lights flashing across the buildings on either side of the road in the dark. Then it was emptiness and he bumped off the road onto concrete, finally pulling up in front of a long low office. The Hispanic cop got out the car and then walked around and opened the door on John's side. He had his handgun drawn and aimed in at him. John raised his cuffed hands and shrugged. The big cop appeared and pulled him out of the car, and then the pair of them marched him into the building.

Inside it was a grey painted rectangular room, with a small drunk tank cage on the right and a counter along the wall straight in front. There was a heavy iron gate set in the wall to the left. The drunk tank was empty, and there was a bored looking woman cop sitting behind the counter. She looked up as John was led over and went through the procedure as she had no doubt done before many times over. He answered all her questions, and she entered the details into a computer which was out of sight below the high counter.

'He been searched?' she asked.

Both cops nodded.

She stood up and walked over and unlocked the gate.

'Need to take them boots off,' she said.

With difficulty in the handcuffs John undid his desert boots and slid them off, and then stood up again. The big cop checked he wasn't wearing a belt. She walked through the gate and John followed with the Hispanic cop behind. John followed her down past a couple of simple cells and then she stopped and unlocked the next one. He walked through. There was nothing inside, just a stainless-steel toilet with a sink set in the top and a low metal bunk which jutted out from the wall. The front was thick vertical iron bars from top to bottom, the sides and back all painted concrete block walls. All the other cells he could see were empty. She slammed the gate shut and then gestured to him so he walked across.

'Stick your hands through,' she told him.

John did so and she uncuffed him.

'Where are we? Detective Slater said he was from Odessa.' John said.

'State Police Office Fort Stockton. You're here in case they find anything else in Gray Rock. Chances are you'll stay the night then be taken to Odessa in the morning.'

'So what now?' John asked.

'You sit right there real nice and quiet and wait. Detectives will be here soon enough, and they will want to talk to you.'

'I need to make my phone call.'

'You'll get your chance.'

She walked off, the Hispanic cop gave him a long look and then followed her out. He heard the gate at the end of the corridor slam shut.

He sank down slowly on the bunk and looked around. There wasn't much to see. The short row of cells went down one side, there was just a another painted block wall in front. No windows anywhere. Fluorescent strip lighting in the corridor and a single bulb behind a wire grille above his head. A clock away to his left high on the wall opposite read 7.55. Next to it he could see a CCTV camera.

He put his elbows on his knees and buried his head in his hands. How could he be so stupid? This was all his fault, he had guessed he was being followed, but he had only considered himself. Now he had Rita's death on his conscience. She was an innocent, just a young woman who wanted a better, more fulfilling life. She didn't deserve this, she had done nothing wrong other than mix with him and end up in the wrong place at the wrong time. He took his head out of his hands and stared at them. These hands. Hands that had done so much good, and so much wrong. He wasn't a good man. He had done his share of dirty work.

But he had never killed an innocent. Never.

The anger grew in him again. They would pay. He would go back. And he would make every single one of them sorry.

Chapter Fourteen

They came for him just over an hour later, the clock said 9.05. It was the woman and another cop he had never seen before, a nervous looking guy dangling a pair of handcuffs.

'Am I going to have trouble with you?' she asked as she unlocked the cell.

'Not at all,' John answered, standing up.

'Good enough. After you,' she gestured back down the corridor and stood there with the gate open behind her. The nervous guy snapped the cuffs on in front, not too tight. John walked down after the woman and got to the gate at the end. The nervous guy squeezed past and opened it, and John was standing back in the booking area. He could now see there was a door directly opposite behind the drunk tank, which was still empty. But it was early he supposed.

The woman walked past and punched in a code on a pad alongside and the door opened, they walked through into a short corridor. There was an open office at the end, and a door on either side. She rapped hard on the left hand one and opened it, motioning inside. John walked in. Detective Slater was standing there with a younger man, also wearing a suit. In the room there was just a square table pushed against a side wall with four simple plastic chairs, two on either side, and some recording equipment on a shelf above.

'Please Mr Smith, sit down,' Slater said, his deep voice seeming loud in the small room.

John did as he was told, and Slater and the other man took their seats opposite. The nervous guy removed the cuffs and with a loud cough, left the room.

'So would you like us to provide you with an attorney Mr Smith? We are happy to wait if necessary,' Slater asked as they made themselves comfortable.

'No, I don't need one. But I would like my phone call,' John replied.

'Yes of course, in time. Mr Smith, I am chief of detectives, Slater, and this is detective Myers,' Slater announced while Myers fiddled with the recording machine. There was a beep and a red light came on, and John saw there was a camera high on the wall opposite, also now with a glowing light showing. He nodded but said nothing.

Slater went through the introductions for the benefit of the tape, who was in the room, the time and date, and took John's full details down, including his address in St John's Wood. Then he placed a brown cardboard folder on the table and opened it. John hung his head and didn't look at it.

'Well, this is serious shit alright,' Myers said brightly.

John's head snapped up.

'Of course this is serious. A young woman, a total innocent has been murdered. Yeah, this is very fucking serious you idiot,' John told him, eyes flashing.

Myers stared back at him, speechless.

'Ok, ok, ok, let's just concentrate on what we know and what we need to find out,' Slater interjected smoothly.

He picked up a sheet of paper from the folder. Myers slowly and deliberately slid out some photos and spread them on the table. Crime scene photographs. He had done it to shock. John looked at them carefully and spotted something immediately.

'So her body was dumped in my room then,' he said.

Myers went to speak but Slater got in first.

'What makes you think that?'

John sighed averting his eyes. He did not want to look at the pictures laid out in front of him. He knew exactly why it had been done. Myers needed a kicking.

'The blood. She's covered in it, but there's hardly any on the floor.'

Slater said nothing, just read the sheet in front of him.

'So this is the preliminary report,' he said eventually. 'Not a great deal here but it's a start. The body has been taken to Carline hospital, they got a mortuary there. PM will be done tonight.'

'Well?' John asked.

'Ok. Rita Geller was raped and murdered. Cause of death severe head trauma but she also had deep wounds to the chest and abdomen. She had been beaten. We have witnesses state that she was with you last night, and you were seen together earlier today. Her body was found in your room. Now, as you say, she was not murdered there, in fact the report states that she was placed there post mortem.'

John shook his head slowly, tears pricked his eyes. He couldn't do this. He swallowed.

'She was raped?' he whispered.

'Yes.'

'And what time of death do you have?'

'Again, this is unconfirmed, but the initial findings are between two and four-thirty this afternoon.'

They were talking about Rita, who had been so full of life when he had said goodbye to her at the plant. He recovered himself with an effort.

'Right. So ask me,' John sat upright looking hard at Slater.

'Ask you what, asshole?' Myers asked.

John ignored him, focussing only on Slater.

'Mr Smith, please can you verify your whereabouts today, listing all your movements that would be relevant to my investigation,' Slater asked very properly and politely.

And John told them. Everything, from waking up next to Rita, breakfast, taking her home to get changed, then to the plant, getting coffee, driving out to look at the base. And then he dropped his bombshell.

His visit to the prison.

Slater had been scribbling furiously while John had spoken but now he froze. John paused, waiting. It would be funny if it wasn't so terrible.

Slater looked up slowly.

'Mr Smith, are you saying you were visiting at Howarth prison this afternoon?'

'Yes. That is exactly what I'm saying.'

Slater puffed out his cheeks and glanced at Myers.

'Thank you. Please, just go over the timeline for me again, your travel and so on. Try and be as accurate as you can.'

So John repeated it, then remembered something.

'Actually, Rita called me. About one thirty or so. That will be on my phone, you can check.'

Slater made more notes.

'Why did she call?' he asked.

'We had plans for this evening. I gave her my number, she said she wanted to check it was real.'

John smiled at the memory. Poor Rita.

'Where was she when she called?'

'Still up at the plant. She was doing this hostess thing there, she's done it before.'

John stopped, thinking back.

'Yeah, we were chatting, then she said she had to go. I can't remember exactly, she told me some assholes had showed up or something like that.'

'Ok. And how did you meet Miss Geller?'

'At Big Lil's, it's a bar near Gray Rock.'

'Yeah, I know it.'

'We met there last night, I was introduced to her by Gilbey. Sorry, I can't recall his first name but everyone knows him. And the barman, he can tell you.'

Slater made more notes and put his pen down.

'Anything else?'

'Yeah, there is. On the way back I had to stop, there was some kind of accident with a van on the road past Marathon. You had a couple of highway patrol guys there, probably about five, five-thirty. You can check that too. And, you got my wallet, I've got a receipt from the petrol station in Gray Rock, and another near Fort Stockton so that will confirm the times I'm giving you.'

'Well, we do know our job Mr Smith. Be advised we will be doing what needs to be done.'

'And the prison of course. They know exactly the time I arrived and left. They took my passport while I was inside.'

Myers sat uncomfortably, Slater stood up.

'Right Mr Smith, we got some work to do I guess. We need to check all this out for ourselves, you understand. So, I'll get you taken back to your cell for now, we shouldn't be too long. You can make your phone call first.'

'Thanks. And can I get something to drink? I had a coffee about six hours ago.'

'Sure, I'll sort that out. You hungry?'

John realised he was. He hated himself for it but admitted it.

Myers stood up and walked around, pressing a buzzer by the door. It was opened after a short time by the nervous guy and they all filed out into the corridor. Myers immediately disappeared off to the office at the end while Slater led John back into the custody area. He arranged the phone call and then stood to one side with the woman cop talking quietly in her ear.

John called Patrick and explained everything that had happened.

'Shit,' Patrick said.

'Yep,' John told him.

'Jesus Christ. What the fuck is going on down there? OK, look try and stay cool. I'm all over it,' Patrick replied and hung up the phone.

The woman cop came over and took John back to the cell. There were no handcuffs. This time, she was almost friendly; the dynamic had changed. Slater must have divulged something.

John sat back down on the bunk wondering how long it would be this time. The prison would be first, and that would be quick and simple. They would also confirm John's vehicle was there. They would have the absolute facts; John had driven from Gray Rock to Howarth, and then after the visit all the way back again. Total close to seven hours that he could account for being nowhere near the motel, in fact even the town. He knew there would be other details to check, which maybe could take some time. He wasn't sure how easy it would be.

He was getting angry, he needed to be out of here, back in Gray Rock.

He had work to do. Work that he really wanted to get done now.

Forty minutes later the woman cop came back with a McDonalds meal in a paper bag along with a Coke. He took it gratefully and sat there eating and drinking slowly, clearing his head, concentrating on nothing at all while he ate. He balled up all the rubbish and placed it by the gate and washed his hands.

Then he sat back down again to wait.

Myers was back a couple of hours later, with a hangdog look on his face. The woman cop was with him, and with a beaming smile unlocked the gate. No handcuffs. They walked back to the interview room; Slater was already sitting there, with a small stack of paperwork in front of him. No folder.

John sat down again in the same seat as before, and Myers did the same, starting the recording. Slater repeated the introductions and the new time.

'So,' Slater said.

John looked at him.

'Well, we have checked your story. And I have to tell you, it is watertight. You were telling the truth. You were at Howarth between 2.30 and 3.20 today. You filled your car at 11.10 in Gray Rock, and then again at a filling station about fifteen miles from here at 4.55. There was a road traffic incident just outside Marathon, the Highway Patrol did attend and they confirm the road reopened just before 5.30. So Mr Smith, we do not believe you murdered Rita Geller.'

'But,' John said.

'But. There is evidence that there were at least two people responsible, at this time believed to be the men who perpetrated the crime. We cannot rule out that you are involved in some way.'

'Why would I want to kill her? I only met her last night.'

'For what it's worth Mr Smith, I do believe you. I don't think you had nothing to do with it. And I have more information if you wish to hear it.'

John sat back, heart speeding up.

'Please.'

'Well as you rightly say, Rita was not murdered in your motel room. We have checked your car, there is no blood or trace evidence at all other that some fibres from her skirt on the front passenger seat, which fits your story.'

'Right.'

'Rita Geller was asked to be at the plant today by a Mr Victor Francis, who is a PR manager there. We have interviewed him. He tells us that Rita has worked for him several times and is popular, he likes her. Today, she disappeared. He was annoyed about it. Mr Francis was showing the guests some more secure areas and when he returned he expected Rita to be waiting with coffee. However, there was no sign of her. Security have no record of her leaving.'

John thought hard.

'She said something about some assholes, she asked what were they doing here? Something like that.'

'I heard you say that, so I checked with security for that time you said she called, around one-thirty. At one-twenty, a van came into the plant, with a driver and one other man. The guard didn't get a real good look at either of them. We have checked the security tape; the guys clearly know about the camera and keep their faces obscured all the time. They were there to collect some office furniture, they had paperwork which we are checking now. The guard let them in. They left about twenty minutes or so later.'

John nodded.

'Ok, so have you got the van details?'

'Yes, and the state police already found it, up at the airport in the goods yard. They have checked it, and it's been impounded. It has been cleaned, but there is a lot of trace evidence. Gary Webber, who is the manager at Big Lil's confirms you met Rita last night. She sent him a text message actually, asking if you had left at nine PM yesterday evening. You just had so he sent her one back. He guessed the rest.'

Slater picked up the next sheet.

'Time of death confirmed at between two-thirty and four-thirty. So no, you didn't do this.'

'No, I didn't.'

'But you understand we have to act on the information and evidence we have?'

John tutted.

'Yes of course. What else is there?'

'Well, we have a witness who believes the van was in the motel car park about four-thirty. A waitress at the diner saw it. The body was discovered and called in at four-forty-five by a Mrs Walton, who is the motel manager. I was there at five-thirty, it just happened that I was on my way back from Carline.'

'How did Mrs Walton find it?'

'She says she was doing a routine housekeeping inspection.'

'No, she was told to do it.'

'Told to by who? I have no evidence of that.'

'I need to get back to Gray Rock.'

'Mr Smith, I advise very strongly that you do not attempt any independent action. Leave this to us, this is what we do. It's a police matter.'

'Ok then, so Mr Police talk to me. Tell me about Gray Rock.'

Myers looked at him briefly, then up at the clock on the wall, disinterested. Slater pursed his lips.

'What's to tell? Small town, like so many others round here. Nothing special.'

'So, a whole brand new town springs up in like, ten years, completely cutting off the original residents, and seriously rich guys are running around making their own laws as a result and the police aren't interested?'

'Today was the first time I've been to Gray Rock, in what, six years I guess. I don't know it, we're not local PD for the area. I couldn't even remember where it is, had to check the place out on a map before I went there.'

'But there's never any complaints, never been any problems, nothing on record?'

'Again, I don't know the town Mr Smith. Last time I was there was a missing person's case. I only got called in because there was already a similar one on file.'

'Missing person? Let me guess, Mexican family, from the south side.'

Slater looked uncomfortable.

'Yeah ok Mr Smith, I can see where this is going. As it happens yes, you are right. The missing person was a gentleman in his fifties, a car mechanic whose business recently closed down. He'd been depressed according to statements we read that the local sheriff took. Reported missing by his family, daughter from memory. The man was Mexican born but a US resident for over twenty years.'

'And?'

'And nothing. It was handed back to the sheriff. There's only so much we can do in these cases; depressed man disappears surrounded by thousands of square miles of nothing.'

'And the previous case was the same.'

Slater sighed.

'Look, I know how this sounds now. I get it. We couldn't be bothered. But we did all we could. The previous case was about six months before, man of similar age, I don't recall all the details, I wasn't directly involved with it. But again, the sheriff dealt with it. They're right there, on the ground, they know the people and the area. I can see how this looks, elitist whites living in luxury, with a ghetto to the south. I am a black man Mr Smith. But there is no record of any serious crime in Gray Rock within the past ten years.'

'The sheriff is an arsehole, who is up to his neck in the shit floating around down there.'

'If there is any corruption, and if there is any collusion with law enforcement, then we will find out and get to the bottom of it. And this is a murder enquiry, it needs police involvement. We won't go away, we will find out who did this.'

'I know who did it.'

Slater folded his arms.

'I had a call from the FBI. They aren't very happy with me. You got quite the fan club there. I have already called them back and appraised them of the revised situation. I would ask that you inform them that I have freely advised you and supplied you with full information. But we need to ask the questions, you understand?'

'I do, but you need to listen. I can tell you right now who to talk to. Start off with the woman from the motel; Mrs Walton, she is in deep there is no doubt. And that fat fucker of a sheriff. Keep moving up the chain. You'll get to three men; Barlow, Abel, Cane. They are at the heart of this.'

Slater looked hard at him for a while, and then wrote down the three names. John wondered if he was already aware of them.

'Now, can I get out of here?'

'Mr Smith, I advise you not to return to Gray Rock. We can find alternate accommodation for you if you wish to remain in the area.'

'Unlucky. I'm going back.'

'Mr Smith …'

John got out his chair and pressed the buzzer by the door.

'I do not believe you can stop me,' he said quietly.

Slater shrugged and stood up.

The door was opened by the nervous guy, and Slater took John back to the booking area. Myers, who had said nothing at all the entire time, vanished again.

The woman cop stood back while Slater spoke to her. She unlocked a cabinet and produced the plastic bag with John's wallet, passport and mobile in it, and also his bag from the motel, now covered in fingerprint powder.

'Where's my hire car?' John asked.

'It was taken to Marathon, but it will be returned to the sheriff station at Gray Rock,' the woman told him.

'I don't want it there. I'll collect it from Marathon myself, you just need to get me there.'

Slater shrugged again.

'Mr Smith, you are not making this easy on yourself, or me.'

'I don't care.'

The outside door opened, and the big young cop from earlier walked in. He looked pissed off. He glanced at John and waited. The woman cop walked out from behind the counter. She told the cop where to take John, and he looked even more unhappy, but walked back outside without saying anything. Slater and John followed. There was a cruiser in front of the door with the engine running. John threw his bag on the back seat and transferred his belongings back into his pockets.

'I'll be seeing you Mr Smith,' Slater said.

'Maybe.'

Much to the young cop's annoyance John got in the front passenger seat.

Slater watched the car drive away and looked at the woman.

'We have not heard the last of that man. Better warn that fat turd of a sheriff down in Gray Rock.'

'I'll get round to it.'

She looked at Slater.

'He got something don't he?'

Slater nodded.

'Yeah, he does. It didn't fit as soon as we started to talk.'

She smiled.

'Myers is super pissed.'

Slater smiled back.

'Oh yeah. Myers is all about the statistics, he wants the quick arrest, the numbers on his record. To him this was all gift wrapped soon as we got him here. He'll get over it.

The woman turned to go back inside.

'Gonna rain,' she commented as she pulled open the door.

The young cop did not say a word for the entire journey. But John was ok with that, lost in his own thoughts. He watched the dark landscape drift past, occasional traffic, nothing really to see. The rain started about halfway, falling hard. He was dropped off at the sheriff station in Marathon, and retrieved his bag from the back seat. He had barely closed the back door before the car was powering away, accelerating hard.

John walked in and spoke to the desk guy, a civilian. Slater had called ahead. The desk guy got on the radio and a few minutes later another cop walked in, eating a sandwich.

'You John Smith?' he asked.

'Yeah.'

'Got ID?'

John showed him his passport. The cop walked out the front door, and turned into a yard at the side. John's hire car was parked against the wall. The cop dropped the key in his hand and walked away. Both inside and outside the car was covered in powder, it was everywhere. But the rain had cleaned the roof, bonnet and boot and there were streaks down the sides.

John climbed in and closed the door, then adjusted the seat and got out his mobile. He sent a text message, and then waited. A couple of minutes passed then the phone rang.

'Hello John.'

'Hi.'

'What can we do for you?'

'Right. There's a town in West Texas called Gray Rock. They have a Radisson. I need a room, but I need it for a week from say three days ago.'

'Yes, ok.'

'And can you show me staying there with a wife, and that I am already checked in?'

He could hear some faint keyboard activity on the other end of the line.

'Yes of course, in your name?'

'No, use …'John thought hard, he hadn't considered this. 'John Lampard. That'll do."

'I will confirm once completed.'

'Thank you.'

He hung up and then called Patrick, who already knew everything anyway.

'John don't go fucking crazy down there,' Patrick warned.

'I won't,' John lied. 'Patrick, you need to get Collis out of

Howarth, and I mean quickly. This shit is about to explode, I don't want anyone else killed.'

'I'm already on that, but I will push it through. Safe house if necessary.'

John hung up and started the car, and set off back to Gray Rock.

The drive took longer than previously, he was careful to keep the speed down and to concentrate. The rain was still falling heavily, and the roads were slippery. His brain was spinning with a lot of bad thoughts, but eventually he was driving down the hill past the plant, which was all lit up, even at two-thirty in the morning. He passed the motel, and the diner, and then turned west and cruised past the rock, turning right at the far end. He didn't want to use the hotel car park so he drove on up the hill and parked up near a couple of other cars in the turning which led to Collis's house, got his bag and jogged across and down the road to the hotel. He had calculated that the Radisson would probably not be full, but it would still operate twenty-four hours a day and that the staff would rotate. So it was entirely possible that they could have guests staying that some staff would never actually see.

He checked his mobile, there was a text to say it was all done. Room 602. And it included breakfast.

He was all set.

He walked up to the hotel entrance and the doors opened automatically. There was a man behind the counter, dozing, his eyes snapping open when he heard the doors. John hurried over and affected an American accent.

'Hi, I'm John Lampard, room 602? I am real sorry, I had a meeting which dragged on and my wife has my room key. I am sorry.'

The man gave a rueful half smile, and tapped some keys on the keyboard in front of him.

'It's no problem,' he said, and slid a key card across the counter.

'Thank you.'

John walked quickly across to the lift. He saw a small bar and restaurant in front of him that was empty. He went up to the room and let himself in, then closed and locked the door. He dropped the bag on the floor and walked over to the window. He was overlooking the rock. To his far left he could see the town hall and sheriff station and to his right he guessed he would be able to see the neon lights of Lil's if it was open.

He would be reasonably safe here. They would never think to look for him in this hotel, and even if they did the reservation wouldn't fit. And he knew he was better than them. Hide in plain sight, it had always been successful in the past.

He stripped and had a long shower, and scrubbed his teeth. Then he climbed into bed.

He didn't think he would be able to sleep, but after a while he drifted off, his body shutting down completely.

Chapter Fifteen

Barlow had barely eaten any breakfast. Fury boiled in his face. Abel, normally excluded from any of the usual ranting, tirades and threats had been worn down already, and they had only been together half an hour. Cane however, was unusually sanguine. He felt good. For once. Because last night, as usual, he had been ignored, which was no surprise and today, almost welcome. It had become his habit to remain silent because nobody ever listened to him anyway. He had been very shocked by what they had done to the girl, he couldn't imagine anything more appalling. He had tried to reason, tried to warn Barlow, but the man would not listen. So, he ate his breakfast, and drank his coffee, and looked out the window as usual, saying absolutely nothing while Barlow cursed and raged next to him.

Just as it was becoming painful to the point that Abel was about to walk out Hunter appeared, walking slowly across the room, his usual cockiness gone.

'Finally,' Barlow growled

Hunter stood awkwardly, and then moved a chair and sat down on it.

'Look,' he started but Barlow cut him off.

'No, you look. I asked and asked for this to be resolved. And it just gets fucked up over and over, and you have just fucked up the most. He was at the fucking jail! How the fuck did you not know that! Watertight alibi Carter tells it, and I bet my house that useless fat ass is shitting himself right now.'

Hunter coughed, and grabbed a cup, pouring coffee in and spilling most of it all over the pristine white tablecloth. He was buying time, and everyone knew it. Barlow just sat staring at him, and in the end he had no choice but to speak.

'Ok, look. We knew the girl was with him. We saw them go to breakfast. He dropped her at the plant, and then he was just fucking around. He went off in his car towards Carline for Christ's sakes. How were we to know? Once again, I am telling you, I didn't have the right fucking information. I was told that the jail was still locked down as far as anyone was concerned.'

He peered hard at Abel, and Barlow did too. Cane turned to look. Normally it was him under the microscope.

Abel coloured. Barlow stood up and looked around. The young girl hurried over with a fresh pot of coffee.

'This is not my doing. I was given information, you all heard me. The FBI had not been notified the lockdown situation was changed. Hunter is right, we could never have known he would go up to the prison,' Abel stammered.

'Never have known?' Barlow mimicked in a high voice. 'You are supposed to know, that's how this works goddammit. We're always in front. Jesus how is this so difficult? It's one fucking man! And how come we still don't know anything about this fucking guy?'

'Ah,' said Abel, on safer ground. He pulled a sheet of paper out of his notebook.

'John Smith. Joined the British army aged eighteen, just as a basic soldier. At nineteen, he goes in front of a selection committee for First Paratroopers, which I understand is like their Green Beret's. He gets in, and then three years later he is Special Forces. The SAS. He does seven years with them, I can't get their operational details but he makes captain. Then, he becomes some government super-agent. Again, I can't get any real information. They call it the department, but it's real name is F7, External Operations. He is with them ten years, one of his jobs as we know was Anthony Collis. He left, and there is no record of employment since, no trace of him.'

'We know where the hell he is.' Barlow grumbled.

'Not right now we don't,' countered Cane.

Hunter glared at him but said nothing.

Barlow sat down again.

'We agreed. He wasn't to speak to Collis, at least until after we had everything signed. That's what we all said, and that left only today, as Collis can't get any visits on the weekend at Howarth anyway.'

'And I said remove Collis from the equation,' Hunter said, pouring himself more coffee.

'Yes. You did,' confirmed Barlow, both men now staring at Abel again.

'It was felt that any action would bring attention, bearing in mind what the papers are full of currently, if you recall,' Abel spoke quietly. He wasn't accepting all the blame here.

Hunter changed tack.

'The SAS, those guys are real badass. I should have known about this, I could have been prepared. I've been left wide open here, no chance of getting the setup in place that would have avoided all this horseshit.'

'I didn't have the information at the time,' Abel replied deliberately.

'Well, you should have,' Barlow said forcefully. 'Thomas could have got hold of all that.'

'Thomas? He's disappeared. Some bullshit about the FBI needing him in Washington. That's crap. He can't handle the heat. But yeah, you should have been able to give me more than you did. I can only work with what I have,' Hunter said, staring fixedly at Abel.

'Like I keep saying. I didn't have the information. And you told us you would deal with it.' Abel could feel himself getting all the blame if he wasn't careful about what was said.

'I would have. I've done the best I can.'

'Interesting you should say that. Carter also said that there were no guns found in the room, no weapons at all. So where are the Berettas he took? I was told just last night that would be the icing on the cake, it would sign and seal everything. But once again, it was crap.' Barlow hissed, now completely fixed on Hunter.

'I don't know. I mean we can't get involved. He must have stashed them somewhere, probably in his car.'

'No, they searched that too. On Carter's insistence. So, wrong. Again.'

'If I had been told everything from the start this would have been different,' Hunter insisted.

Abel said nothing, just sighed.

'So what do we do now?' asked Cane, which was a very good question.

'What did Carter actually say about his release?' asked Hunter.

'Not much, just that the PD threw it out. John Smith is innocent. Unbreakable alibi, and they have been speaking to the plant. They got security tapes, and they tracked the van down quickly as we know. So they will be coming back here, that's for sure,' Cane replied.

'And how in hell did they find that van so quickly? It was at the airport, along with Christ knows how many others up there,' Barlow rasped.

'People are starting to talk,' replied Cane.

'What the hell does that mean?'

'It means what I said. People are starting to wonder. It's not as if we've been very low-key. And once the police show up, the real police that is and they start asking questions it's no surprise if there are some of them who will want to say something,' Cane told Barlow, sticking to the point.

'These people, whoever they are, have no loyalty. We should find out who they are,' Barlow replied.

'Now that would be a bad idea,' Abel said drily.

'The police knew they were looking for a van because one was seen at the motel. Somebody must have tipped them off to look at the airport,' Hunter explained.

'This is becoming a mess,' for once Abel was unhappy.

'It may be necessary for one of your guys to take a fall,' Barlow told Hunter.

'No way, I can't spare anyone,' Hunter replied.

'I don't want any names but they should have considered that before they decided to fucking rape her.'

'I have spoken to them about that. It seems like there is some history there. Rita Geller had not been very respectful.'

Barlow grunted. He didn't care. He shifted his attention back to Cane.

'Where did Carter say Smith went to?'

'He doesn't know. He doesn't know much actually. Apparently Smith got driven away, but Carter's contact at Fort Stockton wouldn't give anything more than the bare details.'

'Well that's bullshit. He ain't got any contacts. They must know what a fat fool he is,' Hunter said.

'So what I am hearing is, we don't have any idea where he is,' Barlow stated.

'Anywhere but here would be my guess,' Abel said confidently.

'Why not here?' asked Cane.

'Yes, why not here?' repeated Barlow.

'Because, well, because, why would he? The girl is dead. It could well be him. And where the hell would he go, he can't stay in the motel. He knows we are watching for him. He won't come here.' Abel spoke deliberately.

'What about the Radisson?' asked Cane.

'What about it? We're right next door to it, he knows that.'

'Not that we're there very much,' Cane pointed out.

'Alright, alright.' Barlow raised his hand, long bony fingers straight up in the air. 'Hunter, make sure your people have their eyes open, in fact that goes for all of us. And check the Radisson, just in case. I must admit it seems unlikely he would come back here, but we can't rule it out. Tonight is the night, we cannot make any more mistakes. Dinner here, we have other guests to make the numbers look good, all the tables will be full. And of course, entertainment later. Plant and site visits tomorrow plus dinner later. Sunday will be plans review and general inspection and dinner again, then on Monday back here for breakfast 8am sharp for signature. Nothing can stop us.'

He paused and looked down at the cold food on his plate. He picked up a fork and savagely speared a sausage, took a bite then continued.

'Mr Abel, I need you make sure all the arrangements are complete for this evening. And you better speak to Tiffany, she needs to be certain she has everybody she needs. Mr Hunter, take care of everything from your side. Mr Cane, as you know we will be visiting the plant tomorrow. I want you to go and make sure that they are aware of the importance of the visit. And one more thing Mr Abel, Plan A is back in play. Mr Hunter was right all along. Speak to your man at Howarth. Anthony Collis is to be removed from this equation.'

All three men nodded. Barlow ate the remains of the sausage and surveyed the uneaten breakfast on his plate. His appetite had returned.

John woke up with a start. He hadn't drawn the curtains last night. He rubbed his eyes and checked the time, just after eight. He needed to find Gilbey, he had to talk to him.

He got out of bed and walked into the bathroom. He caught sight of his naked body in the mirror and immediately thought of Rita. Sadness washed through him, quickly replaced by anger. They were going to pay.

He showered and cleaned his teeth, then dressed. He was running out of clean clothes, he hadn't anticipated being in Gray Rock more than a couple of days. He had only bought some extra as he had planned on going to New York straight after to see his daughter.

He picked up his room key, walked out and into the lift. It wasn't a big hotel; the sixth floor was the top and there weren't that many rooms to each one. The lift doors slid open at the bottom and he stepped out, scanning everywhere. There were three Oriental men and another couple eating breakfast in the restaurant, a single waiter present, carrying a coffee pot. A man sitting on a sofa in the lobby reading a newspaper. A woman behind the counter talking to a man.

A man he recognised.

He slipped back into the entrance to the restaurant and pretended to look at the menu. From where he was standing he could see right through the lobby to the front door. If the man turned his way, it was likely he would be spotted but there was nowhere else to hide if he wanted to look out.

The man had a closely shaved head and was wearing a green bomber jacket. John had definitely seen him before somewhere. The woman was tapping on her keyboard and talking. The man straightened and drummed his fingers on the counter, then nodded his thanks and walked out without looking around. John continued to look at the menu, then a woman come out the lift and walked over to the counter and started talking, so he used this distraction to move past quickly and out into the street.

There was no sign of the man in the green jacket. The door to the three wise men's office was just down the street, closed.

It was a grey, cool day. The street was wet with puddles everywhere, it wasn't raining now but it must have been for most of the night.

Hide in plain sight. John turned and walked casually along, one thing he was good at was being anonymous.

Chapter Sixteen

He safely travelled the entire length of the street and walked across the road into the diner. There was no reaction from anyone inside. Gilbey would normally be in around now. He sat in a booth by the window and ordered bacon and eggs and a milky coffee. Carrie was over on the other side, she hadn't noticed him. He rubbed his head and stared out the window. His coffee arrived and he took a grateful sip, remembering being here with Rita, and her entertaining the entire restaurant. He smiled sadly, and then there was the familiar rumble and Gilbey swung into the car park avoiding the puddles, killing the engine, kicking down the side stand and taking off his helmet in one smooth action. He walked up to the door and spotted John. He paused, then went inside.

He walked over and sat down opposite.

'I'm really sorry Gilbey,' John told him simply, there was nothing else to say.

Gilbey eased himself out of his jacket.

'What do you know?' he asked.

John told him everything that Slater had said. Gilbey nodded.

'They fucked up. They can't have known you was at the prison.'

'I know. The lockdown was all bullshit, the guard up there had no idea what I was talking about. So they set it up, must have someone inside up there, someone who could legitimately pass it onto the FBI. My guess is they were following me, but I did suspect that anyway. I drove down to look at the base, they would have seen me drive off in the other direction. Must have lost interest.'

'Tell me straight John. What happened to Rita?'

'Head trauma, died sometime between two and five yesterday.'

John didn't mention the rape, it would get out anyway and he didn't want to make it any worse than it was right now.

'Who did it?'

'Well, I don't the person, but we both know who's behind it. Detective Slater told me he saw some security footage at the plant, a van pulled in, two men in it. I wondered if you knew anyone up there. I would like to look at the tapes myself.'

Gilbey thought for a while. Carrie walked over and gave him a kiss, and patted John on the arm, which he was grateful for.

'You know, I think I can do something with that,' Gilbey said.

'Really?'

'Yeah, the security manager is ex-military. Army. He helps out with the National Guard, he's a good man. I don't know him real well, but I've met him on occasion. Seems like a smart enough guy. I reckon he would help.'

'Right, so let's start there. You may even recognise someone.'

Gilbey shrugged.

'Well, maybe. But like I said, these Regulators are like a myth. But yeah, it's worth a try.'

Carrie brought their food over, and a coffee for Gilbey. He thanked her and they started to eat.

'They didn't need to kill Rita,' John said quietly.

'No, they sure didn't. And I'm gonna fucking well make sure they regret it.'

'I am sorry Gilbey. This is my fault. I knew they were following me. I got back to the motel and she was waiting for me. I should have been smarter. She was a good kid, well, young woman. I really liked her.'

Gilbey shook his vehemently.

'Bullshit. This ain't your doing. Hell, look, we're all adults here. She rang me you know? She called, told me she was a big girl, and she liked you, and if I was going to whup anybody's ass it better not be yours. But we know who did this. No point blaming yourself. She'd be real upset about that.'

John's throat thickened, he didn't trust himself to speak.

Gilbey chuckled mournfully.

'Jeez I told her I wasn't about to start any shit with you. I wouldn't dare.'

John smiled, and finished eating. He drank his coffee and looked around. As usual for the time of day, the diner was pretty busy. But mostly white folks. There was young black couple close to the door, and that was it. He had used this same diner eleven years before, and it had been a mix of everyone. A happy place. It was most likely nothing to do with the actual restaurant, the division had been set in place a long time ago. It was all so pointless. He looked up at Gilbey and cleared his throat.

'Listen Gilbey. I know you have been watching and you've been waiting, and now I come along out the blue stirring up the hornet's nest and you are happy about that. At last somebody feels the same way that you do and now it's causing problems. But we don't need to be making a stand. It's gonna unravel from the inside. I spoke to Collis, he is broken. He is ready to talk and although he never had any face to face dealings with Barlow I reckon he knows a lot. He turned up at Howarth all those years ago, all righteous, believing he was going in one door and straight out another. They told him he was special, he would be protected, he would be out in no time. All he had to do was keep his mouth shut. And look at him, eleven years later and nobody has even been to see him. I spoke to Patrick at the FBI straight after, they are getting him out and on the record. It was a long drive back from the prison and I had a lot of time to think. I figured a lot of it out. Barlow, and Abel, they have been rich a long time. And they got buddies all over the country who are also rich right? So they get their heads together and come up with One Race, a supreme society, the white man is king, and they believe in it and bang their drums but nobody takes any notice. Which pisses them off. But then, look what happened.

The financial crisis. Everything went bust, all over the world. Massive unemployment, everyone broke. So suddenly out of the blue, people start listening. They want someone to blame. And it takes off. That's how I got into this in the first place all those years ago, hanging out in a crappy pub on a Tuesday night listening to a bunch of losers complain how terrible their lives are and how it's all the immigrants fault. On and on and on. I hated that job, but I was told to do it, so I got on with it. Thing is, those people weren't rich. These were just pissed off, broke people at the end of their tethers and looking to lash out. And this happened everywhere, all over the world, it even got to the point where One Race were trying to get elected for parliament in Britain, and also elsewhere. But the reality is, the world recovered reasonably quickly, and as suddenly as it became popular One Race is disappearing again. Fast. So Barlow and his friends come up with the idea of raising the profile, and lucky old Anthony Collis is picked. I suspect it was because Gray Rock was already in the works and where they wanted to be or I suppose it could be a coincidence. But he gets given a shiny new gun and some plane tickets and gets told to bump a few people off, anyone that has a negative on One Race and at the same time raise the profile. Meanwhile, Barlow and Abel are already well on their way with their masterplan, to create Utopia, right here in Texas, a town for the white man. Yeah, there's space for others, but on the other side, away from the nice folks, and they can do all the shit jobs that nobody else wants for half the pay. But the wheels come off, like they invariably do, and Collis is stuck there in Howarth, forgotten, but never speaks a word. He heard about this grand announcement all about his impending release after one of the warders read it in the paper. Nobody ever contacted him before or after. An attorney went to see him once, got him to sign some nonsense papers about him being refused legal access, and nothing since. He knows he is not getting out. He says this is just a distraction, a smokescreen. Something else is happening and they are using this to distract away from it. And Collis is prepared to tell everything, in fact he wants to, and he will be naming names. He believed in One Race but knows it is all but forgotten and not just by him.'

Gilbey whistled softly.

'Wow, that was a long speech! But a good one. And it makes a lot of sense.'

'Well ok. And I want to get some payback for Rita. So, how do we do this, do we get up to the plant?'

'Let me go first, I'll call you ok? Right now we don't have any idea who we can trust, so let me keep this casual. Where are you staying, not the motel?'

'No, not the motel.'

Gilbey held up a hand.

'You know what? Don't tell me, just in case. But I'll call you, ok?'

'Do it.'

They checked each other's mobile numbers, and Gilbey looked at his watch, then slid out the booth. He reached forward and the two men shook hands.

'Let's go to work,' he said, and left the diner.

Cane became properly aware of his newly elevated status when his mobile rang. It was Hunter, he had some news.

'Say, you at the plant Mr Cane?'

'Yes I am,' Cane replied cautiously. He was at the plant as requested, busy doing nothing; sitting drinking coffee in the enormous canteen while everyone else was hard at work.

'Right, well I just got a call. Gilbey is there. Right now. I'm sending a couple of guys ok? So if you see him, act all friendly. I'm dealing with it.'

'Er ... ok, right, yes I will. And what about Smith?'

'Nothing so far. No sign. He ain't at the Radisson, no surprise there. But Gilbey is nosing around, he was close to the girl. I got to take care of it.'

'Right.'

Cane hung up. Normally Hunter barely spoke to him, and when he did it was always with disdain. Yesterday that call would have gone to Abel. Suddenly he didn't feel so useless anymore. He was important. He puffed his chest out and looked all around. This would be good for him, he could feel valued again. Maybe he could get one of the big houses. He'd been made a thousand promises, none of them ever fulfilled. Well, it looked like that was all about to change, at long last. He smiled to himself. What he should do is prove himself further, make himself look even better, he just needed the opportunity.

John got the call close to two hours later. He had been trying hard to stay off the radar, basically hiding out at the Radisson keeping out the way, stewing. He didn't want to be spotted before they had something to work on. Hiding out in plain sight was all very well but in this town he had no idea who or what was good or what was bad. He called Patrick, who was working on getting Collis out, there were some politics involved as usual, red tape to get through but it would be achieved. Soon after that his phone rang. Gilbey had something. John needed to get his ass up to the plant. Tell the gate man he had a meeting with Rob, security manager.

John went quickly over to the car and fired it up, then drove down past the rock and turned left up the hill. As usual there was hardly anyone around and those that were took no notice. He checked frequently but he wasn't being followed.

At the gate he passed on the instructions that he was there to see Rob. The guard took his time making the call, but eventually raised the barrier and waved John through, told him where to park for the security office. He saw Gilbey's tired Harley standing forlornly and parked up next to a shiny white SUV with BRP SECURITY written across the bottom of the doors and then walked in through a glass entrance. It was a short corridor with doors on either side. He could see Gilbey in the left hand room so he knocked and opened the door. He was in a small office, Gilbey sitting in a chair in front of a desk, behind sat a man with bright red hair, who stood up when John came in. They introduced themselves and shook hands.

'Let's go next door,' Rob said, and they filed back out across the corridor into the room opposite.

Inside there were racks with DVD recorders on, and a long bench with several lines of monitors above. They were all active showing different areas of the huge plant, the pictures changing all the time. It was a good quality system in full colour. Everything was fully automated, there were several chairs in front of the bench but nobody in the room, there was no need. Rob walked over and sat down and inserted a DVD into a machine then pressed a button. He produced a tablet and started scrolling through menus and then one of the screens above blurred into life.

The guard hut came into view, looking along the barrier. A big dirty white panel van arrived, slowed then stopped at the line. Both the driver and passenger were clearly visible but they kept their faces hidden, the camera was perfectly set and obviously the men had been told. Rob pressed a button and the picture changed, now a shot of the entire front of the van. But clearly both men inside knew all about the cameras. They wore baseball caps and kept their heads lowered and turned the whole time. At no point did either camera show their faces.

'You need to have a word with the fucking gate guy,' growled Gilbey.

Rob nodded.

'Not sure this helps Gilbey,' John said.

Gilbey smiled grimly.

'Rob wasn't here when the detectives who pulled you in came calling. They spoke to the gate, and they got this disk. The guy they dealt with wasn't the most helpful. But Rob was one of the smart asses who designed all this shit and knows every inch of this place, check it out.

Rob changed the DVD and worked the tablet again. Now the view was of a long loading bay; with two big trucks reversed up, fork lifts and people moving around. Rob fiddled with the complicated controls and the picture ran forward. A van appeared under the camera, moving away, the same dirty white one from earlier. It drove the length of the bay and pulled in, turning all the way around then reversing toward a single door visible at the far end. It was possible to make out the shape of two men inside. The van stopped. The passenger door opened and a man got out. Tall and thin, mobile phone glued to his ear. Nodding and talking. Then gesturing to the driver who also got out. No baseball cap now. Face not clear but a mop of blonde curly hair, shorter and wider than the other man. They disappeared around the back of the van. The door was obscured. Rob used the remote again and the time ticked past faster. Four minutes, and then the van could be seen to move around, rocking slightly on its springs, then the man with the curly hair appeared, moving fast. He jumped into the driver's seat and pulled away.

Rob stopped the player.

'I've spoken to the Odessa PD. A Detective Slater is on his way.'

John nodded.

'That's good, he's pretty smart. Do either of you recognise them?' he asked.

Both men shook their heads.

'She was bundled inside. The tall guy must have been in the back of the van with her,' Gilbey said.

'I'd like to help more, I'm going to check the internal footage. That door leads into the VIP suite and there aren't any cameras in there for obvious reasons,' Rob told them.

'Thanks Rob,' Gilbey replied.

'Yeah, thanks a lot. Slater will be interested for sure,' John told him.

They walked out and said goodbye to Rob in the corridor. Gilbey went outside first, while John shook Rob's hand again. He let go and turned, and saw a red pick-up immediately outside the now open door. Gilbey was already through. Automatically he pushed Rob backwards and ducked down and hurled himself out the door. Two men. Both wearing pale grey polo shirts. Both holding Beretta handguns. One was furthest from John, but closest to Gilbey. He had his gun raised high, pointing at Gilbey's head. The other man was grinning and walking around. Both jumped when John came barrelling out the door.

He aimed straight for the nearest man. They had parked very close to the door, and now that decision was working against them. John made the couple of metres gap in less than a single second, rising up fast. He knocked the gun away and planted a solid right hand punch straight into the other man's throat, with his left pulling down hard on the polo shirt. John heard a faint thump to his left, but concentrated on the man in front of him who was falling backwards and hit the ground, choking. John picked the gun up and whirled around to help Gilbey.

It wasn't needed. The surprise of John's arrival had been enough. Gilbey had delivered a devastating blow to the man's face, broken jaw, teeth everywhere, then had followed it with another which shattered his nose, the man was crumpled on the ground in front of the pick-up, there was an impressive amount of blood.

Two down, in less than a couple of seconds.

John straightened up. Gilbey looked at him.

'Mine's alive, how's yours doing. I saw the throat punch. Animal.'

'He's still with us.'

Gilbey picked up the other Beretta. Rob appeared at the doorway.

'Jesus Gilbey,' he started, but was interrupted.

'We didn't start this ok? But it's over now. You might want to edit whatever cameras you got here before that detective shows up,' Gilbey told him, then stopped suddenly, staring. He marched over to Rob then grabbed him by the shirt front and lifted him clear off the ground.

'Who did you tell you fucking snake?'

Rob was twisting from side to side.

'What?'

'Who did you call? You must have got on the horn straight away you fucker.'

'I didn't! I didn't call anyone Gilbey? Jesus! I have been with you, and why would I?'

'Well someone did!'

'Gilbey, it wasn't me. Christ, this plant employs over a thousand people! I didn't call anyone. Look, I helped didn't I? I found the other camera! I could have just shown you the gate. Shit that's all the cops have, I didn't need to do anything!'

'He's right Gilbey,' John told him. 'Put him down.'

Gilbey dropped Rob, then attempted to straighten out the other man's shirt.

'Jesus Gilbey …' Rob croaked.

Gilbey wasn't about to apologise. Rob looked at the men lying on the ground, aware he had been very close to joining them.

'It's ok, we'll tidy up,' said John. 'Maybe ask the gate to just let us through.'

'Yeah, ok, ok. Jesus.' Rob disappeared fast back into the building.

John knelt down. His guy was breathing, but uncomfortably. He was holding his throat and wheezing.

'Just relax,' John told him. 'You'll be ok.'

Then he took the man's right hand and laid in flat on the ground, and stamped repeatedly on it, grinding his heel, making all the bones splinter. The man shrieked. John then casually broke his other arm. Gilbey watched, eyebrows raised, and repeated the actions exactly on his man, with similar results.

'Let's get them in the back of the truck, dump them somewhere,' Gilbey said. 'We can't leave them hanging around here.'

John nodded, and together they lifted the two sobbing men into the back of the pick-up.

'Ok, I'll get rid of them. You go lie low, let's meet up later ok,' Gilbey told him, the old soldier's natural authority coming through. John was happy to hear it.

'When you say get rid …' he asked.

'It's a figure of speech. Don't worry, they'll be fine. Just nowhere near us. And they'll get medical help.'

John searched the two men quickly. They didn't make any attempt to try to stop him, just lay there whimpering. No ID, a couple of hundred dollars and a mobile each. He handed everything to Gilbey.

'Right, keep your phone on. I'll talk to you later,' Gilbey said and climbed into the cab. He started up and drove slowly away. John watched him go, then looked around. He was at the bottom corner of the plant, a straight line to the gate. He couldn't see any windows overlooking but that didn't mean they hadn't attracted some attention. He wondered whether he should go and apologise to Rob again, but decided against it. Better to not bring attention to himself or anything that had happened. Gilbey had been wrong but John understood it completely.

They needed to be sure of everything. Today could go either way.

Chapter Seventeen

William Franklin Cane; nee Cage was not having a bad day, certainly the best in a long, long time. He was striding around the plant being the man and enjoying it. Hunter, of all people had gone to him, asked him for help. He would surely now have the credibility he had been lacking.

But he wasn't used to feeling like this, and his judgement was not what it normally was, now he was about to make a decision that would change everything for him forever. It had been straightforward for him to find out Gilbey was in the security office, just a simple matter of deduction. He had found a discrete place to watch near the helicopter, and had seen the Regulators arrive. Cane didn't enjoy violence, but it seemed to have become part of his everyday life. It had looked like business as usual and then what happens? John Smith. Flying out of the door and the next thing both Regulators are on the ground. Open-mouthed at the speed and audacity Cane watched Gilbey drive off and Smith stand looking around. He took out his phone and found Hunter's number.

And that's when he had a thought. Maybe Hunter wasn't needed. Maybe there was another way, a way that would mean he was never underestimated again.

Perhaps it was the proximity of the helicopter. Or maybe the fact that he was now being regarded differently, at last. Or possibly bravado brought on by the fact he had a Colt 45 in his jacket pocket. The gun had belonged to his father, and was the only thing he owned of his. He kept good care of it, and had fired it a couple of times at the gun club. He had decided to carry it only recently, as the situation seemed to be on such a downward spiral, and was glad he had it now. Today was the day Barlow had said. Any issues with today was what he was most upset about. Well, Cane could completely resolve that problem, and he would be properly regarded for ever after. The plan grew in his mind, it was simple, fool proof. Actually, he admitted to himself, it wasn't really his idea, Barlow had done something similar some years ago dealing with the former mayor, and it had been extremely effective. It would be perfect now. He wondered what Barlow would say to him, and what Abel would say, or especially Hunter. They would be lost for words, and Barlow's gratitude would be endless.

The decision was made, and scrolling through the list of numbers he made an urgent call on the mobile, and then hurried around the building, keeping out of sight, guessing he had only minutes to get to where he needed to be.

He could do this. He would show the others what he was made of. He took the Colt out his jacket and felt the weight. The security office was in the front corner of the plant, with a square single story building alongside which butted out at right angles that housed the power and comms rooms. Cane approached the building from behind knowing he couldn't be seen and then carefully made his way around it until he was peering round the corner toward the security entrance. The door to the office was right in front of him at the far end of the low building, there were vehicles parked along the wall. John Smith was just getting into his car.

Behind him Cane heard the helicopter whining as it was started.

Everything was in place. Everything that he had instructed was happening. Now, he was in charge and it was time to show everyone what he could do. He moved forward just as Smith was closing the door. He held out the Colt, and tapped hard on the glass. Smith's head spun round and stared at him.

Smith smiled. What the hell? What was he smiling at?

Cane cocked the pistol and gestured to him to get out the car, which Smith did, and stood perfectly still next to the open door.

This is too easy thought Cane, although the smiling was niggling at him.

'Have you got a gun?' he asked.

Smith nodded and withdrew the Beretta he had taken just a few minutes before from the back of his trousers. He held it out straight in front of him, then dropped it into the footwell inside the car.

'Let's go, this way,' Cane ordered, pointing quickly, keeping the gun fixed on Smith, who closed the car door. They moved back around the building and headed straight over toward the helicopter, which was standing with the rotor blades spinning in idle mode. The pilot, a heavy man in his fifties with dyed black hair in a quiff, who could make good cash appearing as Elvis in Vegas, was standing by the open rear door, watching as Cane hurried Smith across the grass. Smith looked at him and then climbed inside and sat down on the back seat; Cane followed him in and sat in the corner by the door, still with the gun aimed at Smith. The pilot slammed the door closed and walked around to climb in the front. He strapped in and pulled on a headset, speaking rapidly into the microphone under his chin. Then he twisted on the throttle and raised the collective. The rotors spun faster and they began to lift straight up in the air, then the pilot moved the cyclic and the nose dipped and they turned hard and headed east, still climbing.

John hadn't spoken. He sat there, perfectly calm, watching Cane.

This was getting interesting he thought.

He wasn't worried, he just couldn't work out what was going on. It was just him, Cane and the pilot. They were heading away from Gray Rock quickly, so nobody else was joining them. And Cane offered no threat at all, despite the gun.

He smiled at Cane and sat back, looking out of the window. Soon the army base came into view far below them. They were still climbing and moving fast, so wherever they were going, they were in a hurry.

Cane sat very still watching Smith, and now they were underway he started to doubt what he was doing. Smith wasn't concerned at all, he didn't show the least discomfort, hadn't said a single word, and hadn't tried to appeal, or run even when they were still on the ground. Nothing at all, he had just done as he was told and now it looked as if he was enjoying the ride. The realisation that he may have made a big mistake began to solidify in Cane's mind.

John could see Cane was way out of his comfort zone. The Colt was an original, which is a big gun with a long barrel. Probably late 1930s. It fires a big bullet, with a hefty kick. It looked in reasonable condition, and John could see the shells visible in the revolving chamber. So it was loaded, and more than likely to fire. If it came down to it, he would have no chance. But what was Cane thinking?

They carried on, still climbing.

John looked around him. He had spent a lot of time in helicopters over the years, many, many hours. But nothing like this. Here, it was all leather, walnut finish, plenty of comfort and soundproofing. Helicopters are noisy and move around a lot, but this thing was reasonably quiet and steady. Two rows of plush seats facing each other in the back and the usual two for the crew in the front. The pilot was staring out the windscreen, no need for him to look around. The boss was here and he had a gun, so he didn't have to get involved. John looked back at Cane. It was quiet enough they could probably have a conversation, it would need to be loud, but probably not shouted, which was another first for him in a helicopter.

May as well try, he thought.

'So, where are we going? I only ask because I'm due to meet someone later,' he called out.

Cane's eyes flicked around. He didn't know what to say. How was it possible that Smith was so calm?

'You'll see,' was all he could think of.

John nodded, and smiled again. Cane was sweating hard. The other factor is that the Colt is a heavy weapon, particularly fully loaded, and Cane was sitting awkwardly with the gun held out in front of him, no arm support. The hand and wrist were shaking. John was suddenly concerned he might drop the gun, which could be disastrous.

'So tell me Mr Cane. Or should I say Mr Cage? No matter. Anyway, what's the plan? Throw me out somewhere? We're what, three thousand feet up, maybe a bit more. And not much for me to hit down there right? Miles and miles of nothing. I wouldn't be found for months probably. So, not a bad idea. But there is a problem. I'm not doing it.'

'You'll do what I say,' Cane replied licking dry lips, voice straining.

John shook his head.

'Nope. Doesn't work. I'm not doing it.'

'I've got the gun.'

'Yeah you have. So you'll have to shoot me because you ain't never gonna be able to throw me out unless you do.'

'No, that's not the plan,' Cane said, having to shout.

'Great. That's good for all of us. So what is?'

Cane glanced at the pilot.

'Won't work,' John told him. 'Not with those headsets. Listen, I am very impressed, it's like being in a Rolls Royce in this thing compared with the helicopters I've had to put up with. But he can't hear a fucking word, trust me. It's just you and me.'

Cane wiped his brow. The gun hand was shaking badly now. He said nothing.

'And here's the thing. You haven't thought this through Mr Cane. You see, you got the gun. We both know that. You're in charge. And what a gun! You pull that trigger and its game over for me, that is for sure. But there is a problem, and really, you should have considered it. That thing is a fucking cannon. Gut shot, chest, head, wherever that bullet ain't stopping. Through and through we call it. Hole in the front and a big old gaping chunk out the back. Which is a serious problem. Not for me, I'm dead. But helicopters are complicated things. I'm sitting right in front of the tail section. There are hundreds, probably thousands of God knows what back there. Right behind me, every single bit really important. Cables, hydraulics, electronics, you name it. All about to be destroyed. And what's Elvis gonna do?'

John nodded at the pilot, speaking loudly and slowly.

'Well, he will try to autorotate, we're taught how to do that in the army and it does work. A lot of the time anyway. But not from this height, and not in this thing. Way too heavy. It will drop like a stone. So we're all goners, not that I'm going to be around to enjoy watching it happen. I'll be honest with you, it all seems a bit pointless to me.'

Cane was sweating worse than ever, and the gun was wavering around all over the place.

Time to end it.

Calmly John reached out. Cane didn't move. John leaned forward, eyes fixed on the other man and gently plucked the gun out of his hand. Relief washed over Cane's face, and he just crumpled, tears streaming down his cheeks. John watched concerned, released the hammer back gently to rest on the Colt and then moved across to the front, tapping the pilot on the shoulder. He jumped and turned his head. John pulled the headset clear.

'Turn around my friend. Drop us down to a thousand feet and start heading for San Antonio, wherever that is.'

The pilot stared back wide eyed.

John leaned over, and patted the man down. No weapon, but why would he? There was nothing else, no bag, no jacket. Obviously going to be a simple job.

'Just do it, and slow down too. And before you think you can be a hero, I can throw you out the door just like that. I am one guy that you don't want to be any more upset. And I can fly this thing, so it makes no difference to me at all. Up to you.'

Which was a half-truth. John had a commanding officer once who had decided that special forces soldiers should have helicopter flying instructions in case the pilots were ever disabled. Made it sound like it was for the good of the men but it became clear later it was because choppers were so expensive. John didn't care, he had been selected along with half a dozen others and spent fourteen weeks at an RAF base in Shropshire, and had enjoyed it. He wasn't a natural, but had acquired the basics and passed the course. His instructor had been surprised, it just happened that on the day John managed to get it right. This had been a long time ago, and he had never had to fly one for real, never. But he thought he could muddle through, land it somewhere. Probably.

The pilot gaped, and looked at Cane, who was still sobbing. Then he nodded and eased back on the throttle and lowered the collective. The helicopter drone reduced and started to gently move down. The pilot pressed some buttons on a GPS screen and changed direction. John would have to keep an eye on him but he was in no immediate danger, the guy was no hero, he would do as he was told.

He sat back down, right next to Cane.

'Talk to me.'

Cane shook his head.

'Mr Cane, we know all about you. You did ten years for Barlow. Ten years without a peep. We've been through the Dallas PD records. You didn't do a damn thing that night, nothing. My guess is that you went there just because Barlow suggested it, without really knowing what it was. Wrong place, wrong time. You probably don't know this, but Barlow's prints and DNA were all over that house. But he had people looking out for him right? You probably thought you did too. You and Anthony Collis are virtually the same. And he talked by the way, still is. And he's got a lot to say.'

Cane looked at him, eyes shining, cheeks wet.

'You don't know. You don't understand.'

'No, I don't, and I never will. But you aren't Barlow, or Abel. So why the hell are you doing this shit? Why kill the girl? She had done nothing to anyone. You were already on my shit list but you crossed the line then, now I have to get payback.'

Cane covered his face and wept harder. John waited patiently. Eventually Cane looked up.

'I know. I found out they had killed Rita last night, I told them they shouldn't have done. But Barlow …'

'Who killed her?' John asked forcefully.

'I don't know. A couple of Hunter's men, the Regulators. I don't know who, really, I don't. They never tell me anything.'

'You need to help yourself Mr Cane. Now is the time to stand up.'

A large town was now visible, the pilot turned and shouted something. John moved over.

'San Antonio,' the pilot told him.

'ok, drop down to under a thousand feet and circle, make sure the locals know we are here. We ok for fuel?'

The pilot nodded.

John sat down again and dug out his mobile, he had a signal. He called Patrick.

He explained he was in a helicopter over San Antonio, and he had Mr Cane. He needed to meet. Things had escalated.

'Jesus Christ John, it's never a dull moment! I can't keep up.'

John listened to a muffled background conversation, he sat patiently, listening to raised voices, then Patrick was back.

'Shit. Ok, head for Freeman Airfield, it's a commercial place to the north of the city. Get up there and we'll meet you ok? We should be about twenty minutes.'

John agreed and hung up, then went back to the pilot and repeated the instructions, who once again went to the GPS. He pressed buttons and turned knobs, then stuck a thumb up.

John sat back down again.

'Ok, this is what is going to happen. As of right now, as far as I can tell, you have committed no crimes, other than any number as an accessory. The FBI will take you in. You aren't going back to Gray Rock. My suggestion to you is that you answer all their questions. I don't understand what hold Barlow has on you, but this is coming to an end.'

Cane nodded.

'He promised me a new life. He told me I would live like a king.'

'Yeah, I can imagine. Instead you have to sit and watch all sorts of shit right?'

The helicopter slowed, and started to circle tightly, dropping all the time.

John moved forward again and spoke to the pilot.

'Let them know who we are. And just to clear up any potential bullshit from your side, we are meeting the FBI here. That is the F.B.I. , by the way. I'm fairly sure you have heard of them.'

The pilot's eyes widened and he nodded, then started talking into the microphone again.

Cane suddenly reached forward and grabbed John's arm, wild eyed, feverish.

'It's worse. Worse than you know. It's been going on for too long. I hate it. I hate it. Tonight, it's happening tonight. Again. They're doing it again. At Brown's. Tonight. It's happening again. About eleven.'

John looked at him confused.

'What's happening? What's Brown's? Where's Browns?

But Cane clammed up, refusing to say another word. Just sat there weeping, shaking his head and shivering.

They were about a hundred feet up, the pilot was now moving around peering out the side and talking into the microphone. Below them was a large space, with hangars, warehouses, trucks and small airplanes dotted around. Eventually the message was received and they headed toward a clear square with a large white cross painted on it. The pilot lined up quickly dropping to the ground, landing right in the centre, and then shut down.

The silence was deafening.

Chapter Eighteen

John looked out the window. He could see a man carrying a clipboard wandering across approaching the helicopter, in no particular hurry. No sign of the FBI, but Patrick had reckoned on twenty minutes. John looked at Cane, who was now half lying across the seat, head down and weeping. John climbed up over the rear seats and dropped down next to the pilot. He was still holding the Colt, which now seemed a bit ridiculous so he dropped it on the floor in front of the seat.

'FBI are on their way, so stay cool. I don't know what your involvement is but you are gonna have some questions to answer,' John told him.

The pilot wiped his brow.

'I'm not involved in anything! I swear to God. I just fly this thing,' he replied.

John glanced back at Cane, who hadn't moved.

'So tell me, what were your instructions? Mr Cane says he wasn't planning on throwing me out the door, which I thought was the idea. Not that I'd have gone along with it.'

The pilot gulped.

'Look man, I don't know who the hell you are ok? Or what you've done. And I don't wanna know, believe me. Cane called me. He needed the helicopter and he's the boss. One of them. I just do what I'm told.'

The man reached the pilot's side and was looking up expectantly. The pilot opened the door and leaned out.

'We were told to put down here. The FBI are meeting us, they're on their way,' he said quickly.

The man looked across at John. From where he was standing he couldn't see into the back well and Cane was slumped down anyway.

'FBI? Well, I guess that's gonna be ok. You carrying any cargo?' he asked.

The pilot looked across at John.

'Nope. It's just routine I think,' he replied. The pilot nodded.

'Well, if you aren't staying long then I don't see a problem. You need fuel?' the man asked hopefully.

The pilot leaned forward and pressed a switch, then shook his head.

'No, we're good thanks, more than half a tank.'

The man nodded.

'Well ok, I guess.' He made a note on the clipboard. 'So just let the tower know when you're ready to leave.'

He wandered away, his work done.

The pilot looked around him and then reluctantly closed the door and sat fidgeting, anxious.

'So,' John resumed. 'You just do what you're told. So my guess is you have already done whatever this is before, am I right?'

The pilot froze, and then nodded.

'Which is?'

'Look I don't like it ok? But I get paid to fly this thing. Normally just in and out of Dallas or Houston, wherever. I pick up the VIPs and ferry them around. I'm a taxi driver, I guess. But yeah, I done this before. But we never threw anyone out, I swear. I never did that.'

'Tell me.'

The pilot sighed deeply.

'I don't like it,' he repeated. 'I never signed up for all this shit. But look I don't got no choice if I wanna get paid. Look, BRP got a dangerous chemical storage depot, about thirty-odd miles from Galveston. Middle of nowhere. Secure, unmanned.

I was going to drop you there, within the compound. No way out. That was it. Yeah, I done this before, couple of times. But not for a long while and nobody got killed.'

John raised his eyebrows.

'So I'm there and I can't get out? How is that not gonna kill me?'

'They have security patrols. You would work it out and flag them down through the gates eventually. Cane just said he needs you out the way. Like I said, I just do what I'm told.'

'Well your best bet is you should start thinking, because constantly wheeling out that same old bullshit excuse sure as hell is gonna get you nowhere. The FBI are gonna love you. You are in this shit up to your neck, believe me. You got a mobile phone?'

The pilot nodded and dug a smartphone out of the pocket in his cargo pants. He handed it over without looking at it.

There was activity outside, and John looked out to see two dark coloured sedans weaving quickly through the cars and trucks.

'This is us,' he said and opened the door.

The first car pulled up sharply and Patrick jumped out. He was grinning but looked strained. Three more agents got out the cars and stood around the helicopter in a rough perimeter. Typical in dark suits and uptight expressions.

Patrick was as always impeccably turned out, with neat grey hair ruffling slightly in the breeze. He looked older, and John suddenly felt guilty. The man was way high up in the FBI but somewhere he had a boss, and explaining, or at least trying to what was going on down here in light of all the grief the bureau had received, would not have been an easy task.

John jumped down out of the helicopter then stepped forward and shook Patrick's hand and the two men embraced.

'John, it is good to see you, but Jesus can't you do anything without a couple of tons of shit flying everywhere?'

'It seems not, and I apologise but this isn't over yet.'

'I guess not. So what we got?'

John walked around and opened the rear door. Cane hadn't moved.

'This is William Franklin Cane. And trust me, he has got plenty to say.'

John handed over the Colt and the pilot's mobile and stepped back. Patrick indicated to two of agents who climbed in. With difficulty they managed to eventually manoeuvre Cane out of the helicopter and into the rear seat of one of the cars.

'He is ready to talk, believe me. What's happening with Collis?' John asked.

Patrick turned away, and then rubbed his eyes.

'Ah shit. We were too late. We fucked up. I fucked up. The local agent, a man called Harlan Thomas was given the instruction, despite the fact that I specifically said not to.'

'Ah Jesus,' John said. He had really wanted to help Collis.

'Look, he isn't dead. He got a real bad beating, but one of the guards stepped in. Just in time. It was a setup, for sure. I'm sorry John.'

'So how is he? Where is he?

'In the hospital in Midland. He's in a bad way. Some crazy giant got him, who shouldn't have been anywhere nearby. But I pulled in Thomas, basically he's claiming not to know nothing about anything. I suspect he tipped them off. But I got him, and he'll talk. Look, I hope to Christ Collis makes it, and if he does and he can tell us something, I will make sure he gets something for it. I mean that.'

'Can we deal with him?' John nodded at the pilot who was staring out.

'Have to I guess, what's his story?'

'He's done this before. He was supposed to drop me at some BRP depot near a place called Galveston, I never heard of it, but it's unmanned. The idea is that in the end I manage to get a security patrol to let me out. But I would be hundreds of miles away from Gray Rock, a long way out the picture, for however long it takes.

'Galveston? It's down near Houston.'

Patrick had a long look at the pilot, eyes narrowed, evaluating.

'I don't think he's involved really Patrick. I think he's a lackey who gets a little extra for the odd trip here and there, his main job is flying VIPs to the plant,' John told him.

Patrick nodded, thinking fast. He looked lost.

'Jesus, where does all this come from,' he asked shaking his head.

'No idea. I never asked, you sound a bit local. You Texan Patrick?'

'Nope. Tennessee. Still southern, but a whole lot smaller.' He half smiled. 'Less everything. Less assholes, that's for sure. Especially with the friends you seem to be making.'

John looked at Patrick affectionately. He had known the man a few years now, there was a lot of mutual respect. He had to be in his mid-fifties at least, and while he was the most ordered and disciplined man John had ever met he had a tough streak, a desire to do the right thing.

'So what do you want to do now John?'

'Well, I need to get back to Gray Rock. Cane said something about it going down tonight, some place called Brown's.'

'Brown's? What's that; a bar?'

'Could be, there's a restaurant called that in London. I don't know, but I would say for sure it's in Gray Rock, or at least very close by. I need to speak to Gilbey, hopefully he'll have an idea. I can't get anything more out of Cane, with luck he'll open up to you.'

Patrick waved over an agent and spoke to him, and the man moved quickly around and led the pilot out of the chopper.

John looked at his watch.

'Tonight?' Patrick asked.

'Yeah. According to Cane, and he was in no state to start lying.'

Patrick thought again, weighing everything up. He made a decision.

'Ok. Right, well we need to contain this guy,' he nodded at the pilot. 'So here's what we do. We'll get the pilot to fly me, you and an agent back to Gray Rock right now. I'll get a team up close by, to be in place and ready for this evening. The agent can babysit this guy if necessary, while me and you find Gilbey and go and sit out at this Brown's place once we know where it is. What's the worst that can happen, maybe we even have a beer while we're sitting on our hands. But once we know what's going down we mobilise the team and clean everything up.'

He looked at John, who shook his head.

'No Patrick, we can't do it. You know we can't. No way you can be anywhere near this Brown's place wherever it is. The whole reason we did this in the first place was to keep the FBI out the way. No, I have to do this. Well me and Gilbey, and trust me, there's nobody you would want with me more than him.'

Patrick considered, worry etched through every pore. He turned away, watching the agents as they searched the pilot. In the end, he agreed.

'Ok. You are right, as much as I hate to say it. I got more crap piled on my head right now than anyone ever, but that's how it goes sometimes I guess. Alright, you fly back but with one of my guys, I will be sending Adams, he is solid, we can depend on him. Not that I'm expecting a lot of problems from Elvis there. So I will be with the team, and we are going to be real close from about seven this evening, waiting for your call. So check in with me often, ok?'

'Yep, got it. And I am sorry Patrick.'

'What the hell are you sorry about? I asked you to do this in the first place! Hell, the best I hoped for is Collis would see it was you and want to rub your nose in it, I thought if he got carried away he might let something slip, at least we could find out where to start looking, maybe. Listen we got so much shit eleven years ago down here it was past crazy. And it got worse. Finally, it calms down and we seem to be ok then next thing we know it all gets dragged up again. It caught us out, the FBI has changed, image is everything. But when the press started all over again we didn't know who was behind it and we looked believe me. Boy, we looked. But we could not find out who was pulling the strings. I never expected anything, I was just real glad it was you doing the asking. You seem to have stirred up a hornet's nest alright, but seems to me we should have known more about the situation in Gray Rock anyway.'

'I think Collis was right. It's a distraction. Something big is going down, or about to, and the press will go crazy for this story. Anything else will be off the front page.'

'Well yeah, but what?'

'No idea. Barlow for Governor?'

'He wouldn't get that. I don't think so anyways.'

John looked at Patrick. The man was in an impossible position. BRP, and therefore Barlow had to be practically untouchable in the eyes of the US administration. And here Patrick was, fighting on the front line.

He sighed.

'Come on, let's go.'

Patrick pulled the rear door open for John and then waved at one of the agents who jogged across, and listened intently to instructions then climbed into the helicopter.

Agent Adams was a big man, young but with a hairline receding fast. He got in the co-pilot's seat and made his feelings clear, although as John climbed in the back he felt it was more for his benefit.

'Fly this helicopter, and don't give me a single reason to believe you are considering any action which might cause me to start getting nervous. Understand?'

The pilot nodded meekly, and went through the start-up procedure.

Checks done, he pressed a button, and there was a loud whine, followed by the slow spin of the rotors, then a rumble getting louder, until the blades rapidly settled into their idle speed. Patrick was standing watching; Adams gave him the thumbs up and strapped himself in. John sat back and watched out the window as they rose steadily into the air. He waved at Patrick, hoping he would see the man again, but the way the day was panning out he really had no idea. He dug out his phone; he needed to speak to Gilbey, they needed to be ready.

Chapter Nineteen

Barlow lifted a bony hand above his head then slammed it down hard on the table. He sat very still, ramrod straight, his big nose quivering, dark spots of red high on his cheeks, bulging eyes fixing on Abel and Hunter alternately.

They were in the 'office' sitting at the long table, Hunter in the small chair on the other side.

Nobody said a word.

Barlow breathed in deeply, in, out, in, out and then spoke very slowly.

'So, just tell me. Humour me. Repeat it. Put it in simple terms. Treat me like I'm a goddamned child. Maybe, and I sure hope so, I am misunderstanding. So much has gone wrong in the past few days I'm becoming confused. It's all becoming a blur of mistakes and ineptitude. So, please. Exactly what the fuck has gone wrong now?'

Abel shrugged and laid his hands on the table looking at Hunter. This wasn't his problem, not even his territory, he had only just found out himself.

Hunter coughed and then uncomfortably offered an explanation.

'Right, well, like I said, I got a call. Gilbey was at the plant. Nosing around. In the security office.'

'Who called?' Barlow snapped.

'Does it matter? One of the guys, saw him and watched where he went.'

'And you fucked it up, again.'

Hunter looked down at his shoes and shook his head. He deserved respect. Barlow should remember who he was. Most people were terrified of him. He could kill the old bastard just like that. And nobody would blame him. But he was so fucking well paid. He counted to ten in his head.

'I sent two men, ok? Two of our men.' He spoke slowly and clearly, as if Barlow really was a young child or a confused old man.

But Barlow just sat glaring back at him.

'And? Well?'

'I can only tell you what I been told, all I know is Gilbey bested them. That's all I got, I wasn't there and I don't know where the fuck they are now. All I got is what I heard, and that don't make a whole lot of sense.'

'Yeah, this is where I get kind of hazy. You are telling me you sent two men, your guys by the way, not ours, yours. Two men, young, fit, trained, or so you say, and don't forget armed, to deal with a man in his seventies. And they lose.'

'There was a second man who came to his rescue is what I'm told. I've already been through this.'

'Yes you have. And who was this second man? Smith? Are you trying to tell me John Smith is back here in my town, when just this morning you said he wouldn't come back?'

'We, well I, don't know it was Smith. My guy didn't really see that much, he couldn't let anyone know he was watching and he had to clear out. But he saw it go down. As you are aware the security office is not overlooked, and their truck was in the way. But there was a second man.'

'Which is likely to have been Smith.'

'I'm telling you, I don't know.'

Hunter looked defiantly back at Barlow, who flared his nostrils and changed tack.

'And what was your guy doing? The one who was so blameless he called you? Where the fuck was he while it all went down? And would one of you care to tell me how it is that Gilbey was allowed anywhere near the plant, let alone in the security office?'

'Listen, my guy works in maintenance, and was on a job. He couldn't stick around. But, it appears Gilbey knows Rob Goodborough.'

'Who in the hell is that?'

'Goodborough is head of security,' Abel told him, waiting for the explosion.

It never came. Barlow sat there opened mouthed, staring at Abel in disbelief.

'So, you failed to mention that we employ a friend of this incredible pain the ass Gilbey, who has been sticking pins in us for the past ten years, as head of security?' Barlow asked incredulously. Hunter sat back, out of the firing line. Now it was Abel's turn.

But Abel was older and wiser, and had been with Barlow a long time. He knew the rules. Deflect everything, if possible onto someone else and if not then back onto the man himself.

'If you recall, when we started recruiting for senior positions you stated that security was vital. In fact you suggested Rob Goodborough. Not by name, but reputation, he has worked for BRP twenty years. I found him and signed him up. You seemed happy, at the time. And of course, back then, I had never even heard of Gilbey, and knew nothing about Goodborough either really, other than your recommendation.'

Barlow pursed his lips.

'Whatever. Dress this shit up how you like. The fact is, you have left us wide open. This Goodborough should have been out on the street once you knew he was friends with Gilbey.

Deflect, deflect, deflect.

'Well, I didn't know. This just came up today, Mr Hunter only advised me about this when he called me about the situation at the plant.'

Barlow snapped back to fixing on Hunter, who immediately started backpedalling.

'I was not aware. All I know is Goodborough is in the National Guard. He would have met Gilbey through being at the base I imagine. But there are thousands of men at Blunt. It never came up until today.'

Barlow sighed, long and deep, then stood up, uncoiling from his chair. Despite his age he stood over six foot four, even taller than Gilbey, but nowhere near as solid. Barlow was thin as a rake. His skinny frame just added to his height. He walked across the room to stand looking out the window. He had to duck slightly to see out.

Abel and Hunter looked at each other; distrust and dislike now. Both men knew they were at the mercy of the other.

'I thought you understood,' Barlow spoke quietly, still looking out the window. 'At last, after all the work, all the dollars I spent, everything we have done, we have an opportunity to break free. We get this deal, and we can sit back and enjoy what we've done. Nobody will be able to fuck with us ever again. It's three days away to getting signed, not even that long really if you factor everything in, and afterward we can just do whatever we want. This town will have a long line of the great and the good waiting to live here. Good, honest white families, and we can grow and grow and be what we set out to do. I thought you knew that. Maybe I wasn't clear.'

'Yes, of course I know,' Abel responded quickly, before Hunter could say anything.

Barlow turned and walked back behind the table and dropped into his chair.

'How did this go so wrong? We discussed it. We knew what had to be done. Thomas told us John Smith was coming here, and would be speaking to Collis. I said, we said, this cannot happen. We do not want any outside interference, and we absolutely do not need the FBI on our doorstep. That's what we said, is my memory correct?'

'Yes you are,' Abel replied earnestly. 'But we knew nothing about this man.'

'That's true. But I did ask for information. We knew he was involved with Collis's original arrest.'

'Yes, Thomas told us that. He told us this Smith is close to the FBI, even though he's a Brit. And I asked for more information, but then Thomas went to ground. I never heard anything.'

'I don't want to start saying I told you so, but I wanted to just take this guy out. Hell, I would have done it as soon as he stepped off the plane in El Paso, or maybe in the car on the way across, one way or another he wouldn't have made it anywhere near here,' Hunter growled at Barlow, wounded after all the attacks.

'And I told you, it was a bad idea. This man works for the FBI, in some manner we don't appreciate or understand. If he was killed anywhere in Texas the FBI would have been breathing down our necks. He told them he would be coming to Gray Rock, which is why Thomas made the call. I don't know why he wanted to come and stay here, there's a lot of places way closer to Howarth but he did. And I knew this could be a problem, and I made it clear that getting anywhere near Collis wasn't to happen.'

Barlow tapped his long fingers on the table and looked around.

'And we didn't deal with it. First Carter, Christ knows what he was thinking. Then you Hunter, with your men. Shit, three men! And then the mess with the girl, and now what happened at the plant with Gilbey and another two men out the picture, and I really think this other man was Smith. We know what he can do.'

'I don't know what happened. I haven't heard anything from the guys that went up there,' Hunter said.

'You know what Mr Hunter? I would have thought you would go yourself. Get your hands dirty, make sure things get done properly. After all, nothing else has been, it's just been one fuck up after another.'

'You know how I work. I don't go into the open. I stay behind the lines,' Hunter replied.

Barlow stared at him witheringly and rubbed his face.

'And where the hell is Cane?'

'No idea,' Abel replied, happily putting someone else in the firing line. 'I know he was at the plant earlier, but no idea where he's got to. I've called him, but his cell is off.'

'Right! So where does this leave us? '

Abel produced his notepad, and pen, and sat waiting expectantly.

'Mr Hunter, let's assume that tonight is going ahead. I can't even bring myself to think this deal won't happen, and tonight is our final opportunity to oil the wheels. You are way down on people, what's your plan?' Barlow's tone was clear; however you reply to this, it better be good.

Hunter knew he was beaten.

'I will be going myself, I got four guys lined up. That will be enough, but I am gonna need a gate man.'

Abel made a note.

'Well that's easy enough, that's ok,' Barlow replied. 'Consider that taken care of.'

Hunter nodded.

'In that case, I say no problem. It's only going to be the two guests tonight, right? Me and four guys will be plenty, plus I guess I can get the van driver to get his hands dirty, he's done it before. That should be plenty.' He spoke clearly, making sure there was no trace of doubt in his voice. 'Good. Right, so we are going to get this done. It is barriers up now gentlemen. Mr Hunter, you must step up, make sure nothing else goes wrong. Mr Abel, how are the other preparations for this evening?'

'All in place, Tiffany has everyone she needs.'

'Right, and the arrangements for our guests?'

'They are being collected from Dallas in an hour or so. It's all in place.'

'Good. In that case, we will get this done, what else do we need to consider?'

'I agree that this has gotten very untidy. But we have plenty on our side. Smith, or Gilbey for that matter know nothing of any substance about any part of our operations. They don't know about our plans. They don't have anything. So let's just stay clear, ok? Our mistakes so far appear to be down to us trying to deal directly, so we don't do it. We stay in the background, out of the way,' Abel said.

'Hmmm, well, there is something in what you say. But I would rather know where they are, especially Smith,' Barlow replied.

'He's not staying in the town,' Hunter told him.

'He's staying somewhere, and close by.'

'Well, I can spread the net, ask further away.'

'Yes, do that, but be subtle. Abel is right, direct action, or trying; well I agree, that seems to have caused all our problems. It sure pains me to admit that, but that's how it is.'

Barlow went quiet, thinking. He rubbed the side of his nose, a sign that Abel recognised. He was calming down.

'I know, for sure, Smith was the other man at the plant today. For certain it was him, no question at all,' he said quietly.

'My guy didn't recognise him, but we don't know that for sure,' Hunter replied.

'We are all to blame for this, we were too confident, I see that now. And we should have been better prepared for trouble. If it wasn't Smith, then who was it? Who the hell dares to stand against us? Gilbey made some noise once, sure. But we soon kept him quiet. Now he's all fired up and running around like he's Superman's granddaddy. I know it was Smith.'

'We don't,' Hunter repeated.

'We do. We allowed this to happen. But it ends right now, hear me? Decision is made, tonight goes ahead, and we are either at the Country Club or the plant over the weekend. It should be reasonably straightforward to keep that secure, right? You can set up a perimeter Mr Hunter, or whatever you call it. Do some military shit. Just make sure nothing else goes wrong.'

Hunter nodded.

'Shall I find Cane?' Abel asked.

Barlow shrugged.

'He wasn't happy about the girl. He's weak, we know that. He's probably somewhere feeling sorry for himself. He seemed more together this morning. Most likely you'll find him at the Country Club sitting at the bar.'

'Maybe,' Abel conceded. 'I'll be up there myself once our guests arrive, I'll make sure he doesn't embarrass himself. Or us.'

Barlow leaned forward on the table and cupped his face in his hands.

'Can I rely on you gentlemen?' he asked.

Both men nodded.

'Then do whatever is needed.'

Gilbey was waiting outside the plant in the pick-up. He drove through back to the security office as soon as he saw the helicopter landing. John walked over to his hire car, gave Adams the key and he whisked the pilot off somewhere to keep him out the way, no communication with anyone.

John climbed into the pick-up cab and sat there. He had called Gilbey as he left San Antonio and let him know what had happened, and now he wasn't sure what to do. The sun had broken through the thick grey clouds and it was hot inside, he found the switch and buzzed the window down then leant his elbow on the sill and breathed in deeply.

'You ok?' Gilbey asked.

John nodded.

'Yeah. It's just, so much has happened. I feel really bad for Patrick, he's my mate in the FBI and he is drowning. Literally. I mean, I never expected any of this. I really thought a night, maybe two in Gray Rock all based around me sitting in Howarth for half an hour or so being ignored by Collis.'

'Yeah, well, blame me. I was the one started blabbing to you in the diner remember?'

'No, I had already had some shit to deal with. I hadn't even got in my motel room when it started.'

'I've been sitting doing nothing waiting for something to happen. I'm serious. Sitting and waiting.'

John breathed out, long and slow and then turned and looked at Gilbey, gave him a grin.

'Right. Enough of me being precious. So, where and what is Brown's?'

Gilbey frowned.

'I don't know! I can't think of anywhere called it. There's three bars here in town, you know Lil's, then there's Pinto in the south, and the Grill Bar in the north. That's it. Two restaurants; one in the south, one in the north and the diner. Nowhere called Brown's. I rang Carrie, because she knows everywhere. She can't think either, she says not in Carline, not Marathon, definitely not Fort Stockton. There's a bunch of small poky places around, some roadhouses, but nothing called that.'

'Shit. Cane just said it's happening tonight; at Brown's. Nothing else.'

'I'm sorry. Maybe it'll come to me. Cane might talk. Meantime, I got these.'

He dug in his pocket and took out a keyring with a couple of keys on it.

'What are those?' John asked.

'Key's to Abel's house. Carrie's got a friend who is the housekeeper. Everybody here is real upset about Rita, and some people are starting to put two and two together. At last. I've asked Carrie a couple of times to see if I can borrow the keys and it seems this time she offered.'

'Is Abel going to be there?'

'Apparently all three of them practically live at the Country Club these days. She says Abel hasn't been at the house properly for weeks, she has nothing to do these days. Run the vacuum and do a bit of dusting, no cooking, nothing.'

'Ok. Be good to get Barlow's keys, no doubt he is the one pulling all the strings.'

'Yeah, well I couldn't tell you if he's even got a housekeeper, or whatever they call it. And if he does, I don't know her.'

'Or him.'

Gilbey looked at him and grinned.

'Or him. My mistake. But look Abel is the one does all the talking, maybe we can find something up there, you never know, it could be useful. Worth a look for sure. Hey, maybe Brown is a person, say 'Meet at Brown's' could be relating to somebody's name, meet at Brown's house I guess.'

'Yeah, that's true. Good point. Common enough name, right?'

'Yep.'

Gilbey started the truck and rolled away, following the road down the hill past the motel and then the diner. John looked carefully, the woman, Mrs Walton was standing in the car park, which was bereft of any vehicles.

'I'm staying at the Radisson,' John said, confident he could trust Gilbey.

'Oh yeah? I never been in that place, what's it like?'

'Fine. Same as every other Radisson in the world, and a lot nicer than the motel. That woman is well in with our friends, it was her tipped off the sheriff when I first got here, and she helped out with whoever and whatever got Rita in my motel room I know it.'

'Definitely. I do not like her one bit, she's on my list for sure.'

'Restaurant ain't called Brown's at the Radisson I suppose?' Gilbey asked with a grin.

'No. It was never going to be that easy.'

Chapter Twenty

John could feel a tightening in his stomach as the afternoon moved on. They drove past the rock, and then turned right at the junction which led to Collis's house, then carried on following the road up.

'Collis got a really bad kicking. He's in intensive care,' John said quietly.

Gilbey tutted.

'Shit. I thought your FBI buddy was pulling him out.'

'Yeah, so did I, in fact so did he. But some internal FBI wires got crossed, and the local agent got involved. He set it up. Patrick already knew not to trust him, so that guy, whoever he is, is up to his neck in this too.'

Gilbey reached the top and then turned into the road with all the big houses, and swung into the drive of the second one. It was a large, grey house, set back far from the road with high pillars on either side of double front doors. There was a triple garage on the left side.

John whistled as they got out the truck.

'Jesus, this place is huge! And he lives here on his own?'

'Barlow's is the one next door, it's even bigger.'

John looked around, Gilbey was right. Barlow's place was colossal. Set even further back and ringed with a high stone wall; gates firmly closed. Jesus. He turned and looked in the other direction down the road.

'That one is Cane's I suppose?'

Gilbey shook his head.

'No, I don't know where he lives now. He was in an apartment on the main street for a while apparently, but that was some time ago. If he's got a house anyplace in this town I don't know about it. Probably been at the Country Club since it opened, before that he was staying with Barlow. I think so. Anyways, it's what people say.'

They walked up the steps to the front doors, and Gilbey slid the key in and turned it, then pushed inside into a big hallway, with a grand sweeping staircase in the centre and shiny pine wood on the floor.

'Have to be methodical,' John said, taking in the enormity of the task.

'Right, let's start upstairs.'

As they climbed up Gilbey bellowed 'Anybody home' at the top of his voice.

No reply. Neither man was particularly concerned should Abel appear. It would be dealt with, one way or another.

There were six bedrooms, four with en suite bathrooms. They were all basically fitted out the same; big bed, wardrobe, chest of drawers. It was like walking through a high-end furniture catalogue, everything matched and there was not a speck of dust or a crease anywhere.

'I'd like to bet nobody ever slept in any one of these,' Gilbey observed as they made their way through.

Looking at everything John would not take that bet.

Every wardrobe, every drawer, every cabinet was empty. The last room they checked was the master bedroom, which was obviously the one Abel used, or normally used before he moved to the Country Club. It stood in the centre with massive picture windows right above the front doors. Here, there were several suits and ironed shirts hanging in the wardrobe. Socks and underwear in the drawers. The bathroom had the usual; toothbrush, toothpaste, soap, shampoo, some questionable medicines on a shelf. But nothing else, they checked carefully then went back downstairs and walked into the living room, which was vast. It covered the whole depth of the house, with massive triple folding glass doors at the back leading onto a garden which was in it's infancy. Not much to see, two large sofas in tasteful dark red, a big TV on the wall. Glass coffee table with a couple of remote controls on it. Again, everything spotlessly clean.

They walked through a dining room which had a table with ten chairs around it, a sideboard completely empty, then into a kitchen with a spectacular modern range cooker built into a wide island. They checked every cupboard. A few had plates and crockery in, some pans, and one cupboard had some pasta and other basic food, like the rest of the house it was immaculate but it looked forgotten, as if it had been only used just once. They wandered out at a bit of a loss, and the last room was a study, right at the front of the house looking out onto the drive. There was an old fashioned solid desk and matching filing cabinet. Which was practically empty, some domestic insurance paperwork, a couple of vehicle pink slips and not much else. No computers, not even a laptop. Big black and white shots, mostly of Abel and Barlow together; always smiling, a couple showed them standing in front of a half-finished building of some sort, one shaking hands outside the plant, another on the pitch at the stadium. But there was one picture, in colour, of Barlow and Abel standing in front of a jeep surrounded by desert. There was another man with them, on one knee in the front, holding a Winchester rifle, also smiling. Short shaved hair, and a green bomber jacket.

John went over to the picture and tapped his finger on the glass.

'I've seen this guy around. He was at the hotel this morning, I reckon he was there looking for me.'

Gilbey looked and frowned.

'That's Paul Hunter. He's their fixer. Makes a lot of people very nervous. Got a lot of big talk alright, he claims to be ex-military, a SEAL, but that's bullshit for sure. Those guys never say nothing. He may have served, but he's a nobody. I've asked around, but no one has ever heard of him. Believe me, if he was a somebody in the military then his name would be ringing bells with the guys I been asking. The word is he runs the Regulators, and that could well be true I suppose. He tried to strong arm me, but just once. In the diner, got heavy, said I was a bad influence, disturbing the peace of the town. That fat prick Carter was with him.'

'What happened?'

Gilbey laughed.

'I explained to him it's real simple. He's fake, but I'm the real thing. What you see is what you get. And if he ever speaks to me again I'll tear his arms off.'

John laughed too.

'What did he do?'

'What could he do? Diner full of people heard me say it. He had nowhere to go, and I would have hurt him bad, and he could see it, all too late I guess. I never had nothing to do with him again, but I keep my eyes open, and I see the reaction to him from other folks. He needs dealing with that's for sure, and I won't lose any sleep if it's me that does it.'

They went through the desk, like everywhere else pretty much empty but in a centre drawer they found a couple of keys on a paper tag and a printed email, which had a picture of John on it, and a basic career resume. John looked at it.

'So, someone's talking, helping them out,' he said, noting the sender address which meant nothing to him.

But Gilbey didn't reply.

John looked up.

Gilbey was staring hard at something. There were two large maps on the wall. One was the state of Texas, with Gray Rock marked in bright green way down in the south west. The other was of the town itself, obviously a blow up of an original old map, but with all the new developments professionally marked in over the top. He saw that Gilbey was smiling and pointing.

'Check this out,' he said.

John walked over.

The map was effectively a checker board, the town itself in the centre, but tiny when it was originally drawn. The whole area surrounding it was covered in clear drawn shapes in various sizes, with names and initials marked in the centre; 'Evans K', 'Garrison H', 'Bartholomew R', the whole map was laid out in the same way. None of the shapes overlapped, some were adjacent, while others stood on their own. The new Gray Rock houses and buildings were boldly drawn in black over the top, with main roads shown. There was a bright red square drawn further south.

'What is it?' John asked, looking closely.

'Must be the old zoning. These are all the old registered oil fields and workings, and the owner's names. Got to be fifty-plus years old I would say. The oil run dry round here by the early eighties, they limped along for a few years after. But look down here, in the red square.'

John looked. The large square was drawn over a bulbous teardrop shape, with the name 'Brown J' right in the middle.

'Brown?' he asked.

'Look carefully, this square has been drawn on the glass. It was done afterward. Recently I'd say. This is Brown's. Has to be.'

'But what's there?'

'Nothing. I mean it's been a good while since I was there. I did some training with the National Guard there about five or so years ago, in the summer, basically war games for Afghanistan. Worked quite well actually, but apart from some rusty old metal lying around from the original rig it's just a big old empty space. Brown was Jay Brown, and he's something of a local legend. I completely forgot about him, I should have thought of this before. People talk about that guy all the goddamn time. I never knew him but Carrie did, she remembers him. He's supposed to be the meanest most miserable man ever drew breath. He didn't live in the town, he had a ranch about another twenty or so miles further south, right close to the border. Died, what, nearly twenty years ago, I guess, but people still talk about him.'

John looked closely at the map.

'So if it's empty maybe it's not here. What about at the old man's ranch? Twenty miles isn't that far, in fact it's nothing at all around here. That would be called Brown's too wouldn't it?

Gilbey shook his head.

'Nah. I can clear that up straight away. You see old man Brown had two sons. Wife left a long time before, but they stayed, worked on the rig by all accounts, least the older one did. Word is the two boys hated each other. Old Brown was a wealthy man, he made a shit load of cash in the boom and milked that spot dry. Now when he died, everything was left to the oldest boy, who was the worker. Brown had given up on the younger, who'd moved away, lived in Corpus Christi, got a bunch of priors, gambling, pimping, money laundering. Ends up in jail, no surprise there. Christ, he was thirty-two or three when he got out. Something like that. Anyways, first thing he does is gets his ass down to the ranch in the middle of the night and sets it on fire. Old wooden building, it went up in seconds. The older boy and his family asleep inside, all perished. Tragedy. Now this was only about six or seven years ago. But the ranch is gone, nothing left but a few burnt timbers and a big old black patch of soot and ashes.'

'Jesus. That's a story. What happened to the younger son?'

'He got lifted. He ran straight over the border into Mexico, started living with some madam down there. Then decides he can be a big time coke dealer, and tries to do a deal with a couple of undercover DEA agents in Laredo. Walked right into it so I hear. No choice but to plead guilty to everything. He might even be in Howarth. No idea.'

'Wow.'

John looked at the map again. Brown J. It was all they had, and Gilbey was right, the square had been drawn later, right onto the glass.

'Ok ... But why there?'

'No idea. Maybe they just want to meet out the way. I don't understand what these fuckers do most of the time anyhow. But happening at Brown's you said. And there it is. Got to be.

It ain't a bar or a restaurant it's just the wilds. And it would be real private out there, I tell you there ain't a soul for miles and miles around.

John nodded.

'Right, so what do we do?'

'Let's take a drive out there and have a look. This town changes real fast. I can't keep up, and like I said, it's been a few years. You never know, there might be a casino there now, maybe a brothel or one of them big ass shopping malls.'

John smiled.

'You never know.'

He reached into the desk and picked up the keys, turning them around in his hand. The tag had faint writing, but he could read 'Brown'.

They looked at each other. John put them in his pocket.

They checked the garage, just for completion's sake. As with the house, it was near enough empty, just an old classic car; a pristine bright red Plymouth Fury, and a more modern Cadillac. No tools, or junk piled up, only the cars, which were both unlocked, and nothing remotely interesting in either one.

There was nothing else to see, that big old house had been searched completely in under an hour. They locked up and left, both men glancing at Barlow's house as they passed.

Barlow was at the plant, sitting up high in the executive boardroom. He was pissed at Cane, nobody knew where he was. He had been at the plant, and by all accounts had done what he was asked, and checked everything was in place for the VIP visit tomorrow. The last anyone knew was a brief conversation with Hunter, and nothing at all since. If he was at the Country Club he was hiding out somewhere, probably with an expensive bottle of red wine. But he would have to explain himself, Barlow didn't like to be ignored.

His mobile rang shrilly, he looked at the display. Abel. Calling so soon after they just met. Jesus Christ. What the fuck had happened now. He could not believe the disaster of the last few days.

'What?' he growled.

'Slight problem. Pilot has gone AWOL, there's been some kind of message he's sick or something.'

'Shit. That's all we need. So, do we have to get a car for Dallas or something? Christ. This won't look good, we're gonna look real amateur.'

'No need, it's all sorted. I called in a favour, got another pilot. So the chopper picked them up, just a little later. They're all settled at the Country Club now, no problem. I just thought you'd want to know.'

Barlow sat back, relieved. At last someone did something right.

'That's good. You did real good, well done. Ok, so you up there too?'

'Yeah, we're having cocktails looking at the eighteenth hole right now. The boys sure did some work this week, it kinda looks like it's gonna be a golf course now. With all the shit we've been dealing with we never noticed.'

Barlow looked at his watch, nearly 5 pm. Everything was as it should be. And the pilot would be out the door come Monday, he'd never liked him anyway, the guy looked like an idiot.

'That's great. Right then, I'll be there in half an hour. Tiffany there yet?'

'Yeah, she's here. They're getting everything ready.'

'Right, well I have to say this is great news. At fucking last. It's almost unexpected after everything. We are nearly home and dry. Nothing can get in our way now. You spoken to Hunter, any sign of Smith? Or Gilbey?'

'Gilbey got spotted a couple of hours ago. The bastard is driving around in one of our fucking trucks! I guess he took it off the boys who were up at the plant earlier. But nothing since and no sign of Smith anywhere.'

'That motherfucker Gilbey. Who saw him?'

'Mrs Walton, at the motel. He drove past.'

'He'll get his. I'm gonna tell Hunter no limits on him, once we get everything done from our side.'

'Yeah, good idea. But let's get it straight first.'

'Agreed.'

Barlow hung up and stood looking out the window. Fucking Gilbey, just rubbing their noses in it now. He was first on the list once the signature was in place. But it seemed like they were out the worst of it now, Gilbey couldn't do anything to hurt them, nor Smith, nobody could.

But he would check.

He called Hunter.

'Hey, I just need to make sure you are all over the security. Our guests are in place at the club.'

'Yeah, I know that Mr Barlow. And I got people in position. Nobody is getting anywhere near it.'

'Abel just told me about Gilbey using one of our trucks, I don't care about that, it's ok for now, it makes no difference. It's of no interest. But nothing on Smith, right?'

'No, nothing. Nobody has seen him.'

'Good, that's all I wanted to hear. And Hunter? No more mistakes. You make sure that's how it stays.'

'Yeah Mr Barlow, I understand. I just got to talk to Carter to make sure he isn't gonna screw anything up and knows exactly what to do.'

'Good idea, tell him exactly what I am expecting. Tell him to earn his money. And if you bump into Cane, you tell him to get his sorry ass front and centre.'

Chapter Twenty-One

The drive out to Brown's took a while. They headed back down the hill, around the rock into the south side, then picked up the meandering road that ran down through the old town, passing through the derelict area John had seen before. Then Gilbey reached the junction and followed the route further south, the pick-up dealing well with all the bumps, potholes and gravel. He drove confidently, used to handling unwieldy military vehicles across far worse than this.

The further south they travelled, the more the terrain changed. Steep inclines followed by identical declines, deep ruts and gullies, eventually they crossed what was effectively a bridge made of graded rubble, that had been piled up so traffic could cross a deep ravine.

'Creek bed,' Gilbey explained. 'Used to be a big old river once upon a time, millions of years since. In fact, this was the border, not that long ago really, until someone here in the states decided the country wasn't quite big enough, so let's get another couple of hundred square miles we don't need. Used to be a wooden bridge here so they tell me, till it fell down. Old man Brown created merry hell with the county, and they gave him this. Least that's the story. They call this ten mile bridge.'

John looked closely at it. He couldn't see where the ten miles came from, it looked a whole lot less than a quarter in his eyes.

Gilbey saw his confusion and smiled.

'Ten miles from the rock or thereabouts anyways. Another three or four to go.'

Shortly after they crossed the bridge, they arrived at a crossroads, which was basically just marked out rough areas of flat ground among the terrain. John had calculated they were travelling roughly southeast, and now Gilbey turned right. The road opened out slightly. Everywhere was parched. The sun had dried out the heavy rain from the previous night but out here it looked like it hadn't seen a drop in centuries. They carried on in a long swooping curve left and then it straightened out, heading downhill. There were a couple more bends, and then straight again. John looked out the windows. It was like being on the moon he reasoned. Then the road turned sharply right and straightened out again. Gilbey hit the brakes, hard. John jolted forward in his seat and looked out trying to spot what had run into the road. An armadillo most likely. But Gilbey was staring ahead. John looked. But there was nothing to see apart from a fence.

Gilbey didn't speak, just rolled forward, then pulled in off the road. He climbed out, so John did too, wondering what it was that Gilbey found so fascinating. He had walked over to the fence and stood in front of it, staring.

'What is it?' John asked.

'This goddamn fence,' Gilbey replied, tapping it hard with his finger.

'What about it?'

'It wasn't here before. Looks pretty new right? And very professional job it is too. Trust me, I seen a lot of fences. And whoever did this, knew what they were doing. This thing means business.'

John studied it. The mesh was thick wire, made from small squares, impossible to climb. It was very high, at least six metres, and topped with razor wire, which was canted in sharply toward the inside. It glinted in the late afternoon sun. He looked along its length. The road was straight here, and the fence ran exactly parallel, a couple of metres set back. They were looking at the corner, and they could see the fence disappear off along the road one way, and into the wilderness the other, exact right angle. There were heavy steel uprights every three metres, and the whole thing was taught and solid.

'When did it get built?' John wondered aloud.

'I don't know. Like I said before, I was last out here, five, maybe more years ago. And it wasn't there then. I mean there's nothing to protect here, and this thing would have cost a fortune.'

They looked through the fence at the inside, but the land was identical in there to the outside. Perplexed, they got back into the truck and drove along the road, following the fence line. A mile and a half further down there was a wide turning and a pair of massive gates, locked with a heavy padlock.

Gilbey looked past the gates at the following fence.

'Tell you what, let's carry on driving down, find the end. Try and work out just how big this is.'

It was another mile and a half, so the gates were dead centre of a three mile length of fence. John whistled.

'Wow, three miles end to end. What do you think; the same off into the distance?'

Gilbey shrugged.

'I guess it's likely. Three miles on every side. Means nine square miles in there. But what the hell for?'

He turned around and drove back to the gates. John climbed out and dug the keys they took from Abel's house out his pockets. He looked at the padlock and inserted a key. It turned freely, the lock opened with a loud snap. They looked at each other.

'Funny if this is their only set,' John commented, and pushed the gate open. Gilbey snorted and drove the truck through. He paused on the other side and John climbed back in. They negotiated between two high banks of rocks and earth in front of them, the gap not much wider than the truck was and followed a straight route forward. There were a lot of tyre tracks visible in the grit. It ran uphill for a stretch and then dropped down the other side, the track basically just a narrow gravel levelled off area of the ground, done simply. In front of them to the left they could see a small building.

'That wasn't there neither,' Gilbey said and steered toward it.

They pulled up and got out. Gilbey checked his watch.

'Ten after five. I guess we shouldn't hang around here, we need to get prepared.'

They looked at the building, which was a block built single storey store room with a sloping corrugated tin roof. It was quite high, with a large steel shutter pulled down on the right side. To the left was a steel door with a small window next to it. John looked in, dark inside, nothing to really see. He took out the keys and unlocked the door.

They walked in. It was just a small rectangular room, empty apart from some shelves on the back wall. Not much on them, a couple of powerful torches, a first aid kit and some shovels. There was door set at the back of the room in the right hand wall. Gilbey opened it and looked in, then ducked out and pressed a switch located next to the door frame. Gloomy lights came on inside the building. He disappeared into the room and then came out.

'Just a backhoe,' he said.

John looked confused. Gilbey shook his head.

'I don't know what you call it in your bullshit language,' he said, so John walked over and went in.

Inside a big digger was parked up, blade on the front and a large shovel on an arm at the back. It looked fairly new, but the tyres and fittings were covered in dirt. Nothing else to see, other than a line of five gallon jerry cans. John popped the cap on one and sniffed.

'Diesel,' he said. 'For the digger.'

They stepped outside and looked at the building again. There was a high steel tower on the roof, which had a ring of powerful spotlights all around it near the top, and a kind of crow's nest built in the centre, really just a simple deck with a low railing. A ladder ran up the side of the tower and there was another leading to it bolted onto the building. John climbed up, and stood on the deck looking around. From here, he could see all four fences. It was a huge area, with mesas, ravines, gullies and steep banks up and down everywhere. No wonder

Gilbey had played his war games here, the place was perfect. He looked down to where Gilbey was standing, shading his eyes as he watched John.

'What do you see?' he called up.

'Just the same as everywhere. The fences are as we thought, perfect square all around. This is a big place, they must be about to build something right?'

'I guess so, yeah. But what, I don't know. They got the contract to build a new prison, I heard about that but it's out to the west a ways, past Lil's. And this is real secure, I can't imagine why if there's nothing here.'

'Could be an environmental thing, you know, protect something. Animals maybe or plants.'

'Nah, I can't see that John. This land goes hundreds of miles identical in both directions, nothing different here. Has to be another build happening, which ain't a surprise I guess. But I got no idea why this has been done, got to be expensive.'

'Must be so they are ready. Maybe it's a requirement? Some legal thing? Another prison?'

John climbed back down and stood next to Gilbey.

'You know just possibly I was right, maybe it is gonna be a casino. Start a new Vegas right here,' he said looking at Gilbey with a smile.

'Maybe. It's weird though, why would they want to meet all the way out here? I mean there's nothing here, nothing to see. It's exactly the same inside the fence as it is outside.'

'Perhaps they want to look at the place.'

'Right, but eleven at night? What the fuck are they gonna look at? Even with those huge goddamn lights switched on there won't be a whole lot to see.'

'I don't know. But what do we do now?'

Gilbey walked over and leant on the truck, scanning all around. They could see through the fence if anyone was coming, but they were alone. All around the building the ground was totally flat unlike the rest of the area, further past were two big rocks close together sticking up out the ground.

'I say, we get back here later. Maybe around nine or so, and hide out. Let's see what happens. They probably won't even turn up, but at least we tried. We can get in behind those rocks, they'll never notice us, even if they put the spotlights on.'

'Yeah, ok.'

'But we need to be ready. I got some stuff to pick up. Let's go eat.'

The locked up the padlock on the way through, they weren't worried about the tyre tracks, they could have been there for forever by the time it got dark.

Chapter Twenty-Two

Carter was on his own in the sheriff's station, bored and tapping aimlessly at the computer on the desk in front of him. A few years ago at least he'd been able to look at porn, but that had all been locked down now so all he had to look at was the county intranet site.

He could be at home, but Hunter had said he needed to talk to him so he had no choice.

Carter was scared of Hunter, in fact Carter was scared of a lot of people. He liked being sheriff because of the power it gave him, but in fact he very rarely did any real work, just what Hunter or the three wise men asked for. But he was always wary, and would avoid anyone who looked as if they could give him any trouble, he had missed that by a mile with John fucking Smith.

The door opened and Hunter walked in, moving fast until he was standing in front of the desk. Carter sat up straight.

'So, you know what to do right?' Hunter barked.

'Yeah, yeah, I got it.'

'And you know the times?'

'Yeah, everything.'

'Good, because you got an important job here. And we can't have no fuck-ups, I don't want no fucking excuses, for once you got to keep all your shit wired tight. Got that?'

Carter winced.

'Yeah, sure I got it. I know what to do. I mean, I never done this before but …'

'But nothing. Just do exactly what we asked and then once it's done forget you done it. As usual.'

'Yeah, sure. It's no problem, I'll be there.'

'Just you fucking remember, your hands are as dirty as all of ours. Don't ever forget that.'

Carter swallowed. He didn't like to be reminded of that, in fact he refused to think about it. But it was there, always. Everything they had done. He had done.

'Yes. Right. I'll be right on time I swear.'

'Right. Just make sure you are. Because if you fuck this ...'

Hunter leaned over the desk until he could smell Carter's foul odour, who moved back and stopped breathing altogether. Hunter deliberately stared hard into the fat man's eyes.

'... up then it's the last thing you will ever do. Don't get fucking comfortable, I know you are a useless lump of shit Carter. Law enforcement my ass.'

With that Hunter whirled around and stalked out of the building.

Carter breathed in and out fast, feeling faint.

He would be glad when the day was over. Maybe tomorrow would be easier.

There was still no sign of Cane, and something was niggling at the back of Abel's brain. He was entertaining their guests, humorous, magnanimous, welcoming. But it troubled him, normally wherever Barlow was Cane wouldn't be too far away, and there had been no word at all.

He led the way into the dining room, smiling. Barlow had invited some of the managers at the plant to come for dinner that Friday evening, and to bring their families. So, for the first time since the club had opened the room was full. It looked completely different, a happy place to be, and with a hubbub of background noise that reinforced the whole setup. A successful restaurant in the beautiful new Country Club, the pinnacle of society at Gray Rock. Barlow had also arranged for extra staff, both on the floor and in the kitchen, and it smelled fantastic.

He headed for their table, occasionally nodding at people

that he faintly recognised and believed he probably should know. Barlow was working the room, shaking hands, and also steadily making his way over. Tiffany looked gorgeous, and had provided an excellent atmosphere to welcome the guests. She had brought along another beauty for the evening called Miranda, and as they sat down they were both very careful to choose their seats alongside the guests. As ever, Tiffany was in complete control, constantly listening, smiling, nodding and touching. Her guest was loving every second, Abel could see that.

He checked his watch; seven-thirty.

After dinner they would retire to a function room, where Tiffany could really do her stuff, and later, it would be time for the evening's main event. All for a signature on some paperwork. But Abel knew, once tonight was over that action would be irrelevant. They would all know a terrible secret, one which would shock the entire world should it ever be known. Abel and Barlow would get what they wanted regardless, no choice. Nobody would ever want the truth to come out. Those concerned would be putty in their hands. Forever.

But where was Cane?

Abel tried to put the thought out of his mind. Now was not the time.

Graciously he accepted the wine poured into his glass by a waiter, and laughed at something inane Miranda said. Barlow caught his eye and tilted his head. Everything was going to plan. There was no need to worry.

They ate at the diner. It was no surprise, but John had only ever eaten breakfast there before. They deliberately talked about nothing, Gilbey with some short stories about his military career and John chipped in with a couple too, but Gilbey's were funnier and more interesting. Carrie brought coffee and looked after them.

But it felt strange, like there was some big, wide, vast unknown in front of them. Something black, implacable. Anything could happen, and nobody was invincible. Of course, it could well be that the pair of them would just end up lying in the dirt for a few hours and see nobody, that was entirely possible, in fact highly likely. They had seen it for themselves, there was nothing at Brown's at all that indicated any kind of wrong doing, only an unexplained fence and a storage building, that were most likely completely innocent. Gilbey had asked around once they were in the diner, most of the people eating in there at this time were working men, and he appeared to know a lot of them. It seemed like the fence went up over three years previously, but there was not one person who knew why or anything about the storage building, and the truth was nobody was really that interested either. Gray Rock had seen nothing other than constant construction for over ten years, no big deal at all, what else was new?

They ate a big meal, John had a burger and apple pie after. Gilbey had a burger too and ice cream. John studied his companion. A big, strong man. In great shape. Seventy-two years old. Amazing. Craggy face, sharp blue eyes, constantly watching, always checking everything and everyone out.

When they finished eating Gilbey suggested John should change. John agreed, he had some black jeans and a dark t-shirt at the hotel. They left the diner and Gilbey dropped him off just after seven. He patted John on the arm.

'I got some things to do. Be ready for eight-thirty,' he said and drove off.

The lobby was empty apart from the same man from the previous night behind the desk. John went up to his room and called Patrick, who was still in San Antonio.

So far Cane had not said very much at all, other than nobody other than him really knew what was going on down in Gray Rock. He had wept frequently, and refused food. He was broken, he despised himself. He had been put under guard in a hotel room in the city, away from anywhere. John talked Patrick through what they had found at Brown's, and their plans, and that that was all they had. As he spoke he realised just how lame it all sounded, they had no specifics, no facts, just a vague idea about an old oilfield based upon a name, and a mysterious fence. But all he could do was relay exactly how he knew it and what they were planning to do.

Patrick didn't say much, John knew what he was thinking, he would probably have felt the same if he was the one listening on the other end of the phone.

Nothing other than speculation. A long shot. Hopeless.

He hung up and lay on the bed, thinking.

Everything hung together so loosely, it was impossible to see any endgame in this. They needed Cane to talk and to answer some questions, and possibly that would come in time. If he was kept away from Barlow, Abel and Gray Rock maybe that could help it along, but it was a waiting game. They had to help him to feel safe, he had looked unhappy when John had first laid eyes on him. And Cane had said it's worse than anyone knew. Worse how? What did that mean?

Whatever way he looked at it, there was definitely something rotten here. The reaction to him just arriving in the town in the first place, and the fact that they had known he was going to be visiting and appeared to be so concerned about it was all wrong from the start; John had never heard of Abel, Barlow or Cane. They had meant nothing to him at all, and Patrick hadn't been aware of them either. They were obviously worried about something being discovered, they really wanted him gone. And Collis had said something was going on, all the reports he was about to be freed were nothing other than a smokescreen. So surely him being at Gray Rock should have been an irrelevance, which just backed up the clear and obvious fact that he was not wanted.

And, they had killed Rita.

Why would they do that? Why murder an innocent young woman? To scare him? That had to be the reason, they must have known he wouldn't be charged with the murder. Or maybe not, maybe they had believed it was enough. Circumstantial for sure, but he was an unknown. They had to have believed he would be tied up and out the way for a significant time. Possibly they had been about to 'find' more evidence against him. Good luck with that if they had been planning on trusting that idiotic sheriff.

His phone rang, shaking him from his thoughts. It was Patrick, calling him back.

'Ok John, here's what I'm going to do. I understand that tonight may be a big old waste of time. But I got to say, we are working through things here. It does kinda feel like we're playing catch up, but I'm not comfortable with you running around in the wilds tonight not knowing what might happen. I got you into this in the first place. I know you got Gilbey, but still.'

'What are you saying Patrick? Don't tell me not to do anything. I'm not put together that way.'

'I know that, and there's no point in me telling you to be careful neither.'

'So?'

'So, I've got a team and we are on our way. We'll set up someplace down in the south, out the way. You holler and I'll be there. As quick as I can. It's the least I can do.'

John considered. There was probably not a lot of point in suggesting otherwise. He had hoped to keep Patrick, in fact the FBI clear until the facts were better known. But in his experience, there was always a bigger picture.

'Right. Well, I can't argue with you on this, but I know how this looks; a big old waste of everyone's time. Ok then Patrick, I'll call you.'

'Yeah, stay in touch, let me know when you are setup.'

'I will, that is if I even get a signal all the way out there.'

Silence for a couple of seconds.

'Good point. I hadn't thought of that. Well, if that looks like the case get to where there is one and let me know, I'll reconsider the options.'

They ended the call, and John walked over and stared out the window. It got dark fast around here, almost like a switch was suddenly flicked. He could see the rock, and beyond that the south side. He was looking at the rear of the buildings in the main street over there and could see nobody out at all, but he knew there was life on the other side. Despite everything that had been done in Gray Rock, and to them, they carried on regardless. They didn't look elsewhere for help. But he would do whatever he could.

He lay back down on the bed and closed his eyes. He wouldn't sleep, just rest. Then he had a thought, he had completely forgotten about the handguns he had hidden at the motel. He jumped up and left the hotel, then jogged down the high street to the road opposite the diner. He turned left and ran up to the motel. There was nobody around, two cars in the car park. Lights on in one room on the first floor. The young guy with the glasses was alone in the office. John moved around the side to under the landing below what had been previously his room, and reached up next to the lamp that shone there.

Both Berettas were still there, cold. The search the PD had done hadn't discovered them. Happier now, John shoved them into his jeans then headed back to the Radisson and got changed.

Chapter Twenty-Three

Gilbey showed up right on time. John was waiting outside the hotel, and watched the truck as it approached and pulled in. Gilbey was looking very serious, and was wearing a black sweatshirt and trousers.

'Let's go to work,' he said and pulled out.

They headed back into the south side again, which as John had anticipated had plenty of people moving around. He wondered what the three wise men must think if they ever ventured over here, the comparison to the north side was poles apart. Here, people were going about their business. He could see them walking around, talking, laughing. They had a lot less than half of what their neighbours to the north possessed, but here they were living.

They followed the route through the town, and passed through the desolate area and onto the road that weaved its way south and east, then over the fake bridge and right at the crossroads. It all looked very different in the dark, the truck's headlights shone a long way into the distance but the landscape to the sides was like outer space as they travelled along.

Once they arrived at the long straight Gilbey drove steadily along; not fast, not slow, just another pick-up truck in the wilds of West Texas, could be a rancher heading to a bar or a cowboy on the way home from one. It seemed to take a long time but eventually they reached the fence. They passed the gates and were pleased to see it was still locked up tight. Gilbey continued on, way past the end of the fence and then turned around one hundred and eighty degrees and hid the truck behind a high ridge not far from the road. John checked his phone and was surprised to see he had a signal.

They got out. It was very dark, what little light there was shone only from the stars and a quarter moon that occasionally flickered through fast moving thick clouds. Gilbey produced a torch and climbed into the truck bed, John got up next to him. There was a low, wide tool box right behind the cab. Gilbey opened it with his foot and shone the torch inside.

So that explains his things he had to do.

Inside the box were two SA80 A2 assault rifles, not new but well maintained, plus an old M40 sniper rifle, and several boxes of ammo for both weapons. John could smell the gun oil. Gilbey lifted out the assault rifles and handed them over to John. It was like being back with an old friend, this was a weapon he knew well. Gilbey passed out a couple of boxes of 5.56 ammo to John and then lifted out the M40 and a carton of 7.62 bullets. He closed the tool box lid quietly and switched off the torch.

'Let's go.'

They jumped from the truck and walked back up the road. Without the headlights, it was very difficult to make anything out at all, they just had to trust their night vision, which improved as they made their way along, until they could make out vague shapes and the road, such as it was, as a pale stripe. Eventually, they arrived at the fence and moved over right next to it, carrying on toward the gates.

Both men were straining to see, waiting for headlights to suddenly appear, but there was nothing, just an eerie silence that was broken by their own crunching footsteps and the occasional rustle from a wild animal out in the scrub. The wind was picking up, what had been a moderate breeze was turning into sharp gusts which blew straight across into their faces.

Gilbey tripped and swore softly, and immediately after John did exactly the same. They didn't want to risk using the torch just in case there was someone out there watching.

They reached the gates, and had some good news. The wind changing was moving the clouds even faster and the moon broke through so immediately the area became lighter, the padlock reflecting clearly. John undid it and pushed the gate open. They walked through and with some difficulty reaching through the gate John was able to lock it back up again.

'That's gonna be a bugger if we have to let ourselves out later,' he whispered.

They turned and looked into the compound. With the moon shining they could see a lot more, so hustled down the track making full use of it before it disappeared again, which it did when they were about halfway to the building.

'Shit,' Gilbey murmured.

'We're ok,' John replied optimistically. 'We just need to keep exactly straight. We should be able to see it in about ten minutes.'

They carried on, John counting off the seconds in his head. He got to six hundred, then seven, but there was no sign of the building.

'Fuck it,' he commented quietly.

They stood still and turned around slowly, willing themselves to see. Then Gilbey thumped him on the arm and physically moved him.

'Look up.'

John did, and high above and behind them he could see the dim reflection back from the spotlights. They had walked right past the building. The made their way back, and then walked around the front and down to the rocks they had spotted earlier, making a camp behind them.

'I was gonna bring night vision goggles, but they aren't always a whole lot of help,' Gilbey said.

John agreed, they could be really useful, but when the action started everything could get very confused very quickly.

John dug out his mobile phone, and cupped his hand over the display and woke it up. To his amazement he could see he had two bars of signal. He called Patrick, clamping the phone hard against his head to minimise the blue glow.

'Patrick? It's me. Checking in, we're in place, and I've got a signal.'

'Right, that's good. Stay in touch, we will be close by real soon.'

They sat there, sheltered from the wind, waiting, then the moon came out again, and they used the time they had when they could see to check the guns over. John produced the Berettas and handed one over, Gilbey nodded approvingly and both men worked a round into the chamber. Then they laid the guns down in front of them, going back to their training days, familiarising themselves with their surroundings by touch and placing them exactly where they could be found in the dark. Gilbey put down the M40 in the centre between the two men.

They sat still, watching, waiting, listening. John checked his watch, just past nine. Cane had said eleven, so there was a long time of doing nothing in front of them, and probably for no result. Sitting there, John suddenly felt ridiculous. Why would anyone come all the way out here at night by choice? There was nothing there, the place was only really one level up from the surrounding desert. The building was just a store room, with a digger in it, and a few tools which were used by builders everywhere. No mystery. And whichever way he looked at it, despite the other man's protestations he had dragged Gilbey into this, there was no tangible proof at all that Barlow and Abel were involved in Rita's murder. Everything was purely circumstantial. In fact, he had reacted exactly as he always did, act first, think later. He shook his head. He was getting too old for this.

'Well, at least it's not cold,' he said ruefully, feeling like he should say something.

'Yep, that's true. It ain't no thing. Hey I've lost count of the hours I've spent doing this crap. You wouldn't believe it. But I bet you can say the same.'

'Oh yeah. All over the fucking place. I've spent days in the snow, and in the desert. Even in water. I've got kinda good at hanging around doing nothing.'

'And me. You know, I was just a boy when I went to 'Nam. Seventeen. Ten weeks short of my eighteenth birthday.'

'Seventeen? Really? Jesus, that is way too young.'

'Well, it's no secret now we were in the shit. We just didn't know it at the time. 1969. Life in the US Marine Corps. You know how they say on TV all that "God, Corps, Country," crap, well I never said that. Hell, I never even heard it apart from lifer assholes. But there is some truth, because it is about your unit, and you get that right from the start. Where your unit go, you go. If your unit fight, you fight. So I never thought about it. I was a kid, on my own, with a whole bunch of others training. Basic ended, I did pretty well doing that shit I have to say, then next thing I'm on a plane. I never flew before, never left the country. But seventeen, and out in the jungle in the middle of the night having no idea what the hell you are doing with an M16 and a bunch of guys who are older but just as scared as you are, that kinda makes you grow up fast you know.'

'It always seems to me that the world never learnt any lessons from Vietnam.'

'You got that right. We spent all those years running around kicking ass, and then it happened to us. Look, the guys on the ground didn't lose that war, it was way bigger than that. The whole thing was a fuck up. You ask any Vietnam Vet and they'll tell you the same, and they will also tell you what we should have been doing. Most are gonna tell you we shouldn't have been there in the first place. But it was a long time ago, and you would think that the politicians by now would know their history and never want to go back there again.'

'I went to Vietnam a few years ago. Beautiful country.'

'It sure is. I went back, 1990 I think. We had some ordinance there, a bunch of us went out and collected it and got rid of it. All part of the process, we're all friends now. It's China we're scared of these days.'

'Always somebody.'

'Oh yeah.'

They sat in companionable silence for a while, each man lost in their own thoughts, memories of other times. John snapped back to the present.

'Do you think anyone will actually show here tonight?'

'I don't know. Stranger things have happened. But I know what you're thinking, and yeah, it's unlikely. But we had to do this, right?'

'Yeah, I think we did. Thanks Gilbey.'

'It wasn't right what happened to Rita, she was a good kid. Her mom is a fucking disaster area, local beauty queen, she always believed she was better than everyone else. Got knocked up at nineteen years old, life did not turn out for that lady like she expected. Married the wrong guy, and he ended up paying for it. She had a whole string of affairs, it was a big old mess. But her dad, he was a good man. He stuck with it for Rita. Anyone else would have hightailed it right outta there.'

'Yeah Rita really loved him, that's for sure. She told me all about him.'

John sighed.

'Just don't keep blaming yourself. You know what happened to her, it weren't your fault. These fucking guys don't give a shit about anyone, don't care who gets hurt as long as they get their way,' Gilbey told him.

They sat there, quietly talking, John feeling strangely comfortable. Then, at almost exactly eleven o'clock headlights came into view. Far away, no sign of the vehicle, but the lights shining clearly and getting brighter. Gilbey stood up and leaned on the rock and John joined him, staring out through the fence toward the road.

It took a while, but eventually the lights rounded the corner, closely followed by another set, then another, and then a final pair. Four vehicles, steadily moving ever closer. They could see the lead was an older blue pick-up, picked out clearly by the wash from the headlights behind. Next was a square panel van, not too big, bouncing high on the bumpy road. After that an expensive four wheel drive, possibly a Lincoln Navigator; dark colour, and finally what looked like a sedan, but hard to see properly because all it had to light it was its own headlights reflected back from the Lincoln in front.

The vehicles cruised slowly forward. John held his breath. Would they go past?

They didn't. The pick-up stopped at the gate and the passenger door opened. It was a long way away but through the gap in the high banks at the entrance they could see the internal light come on, and in the bright headlights saw a pale shirt and a man with light colour hair get out. There was a pause, then the pick-up drove in, closely followed by the other vehicles.

They drove down toward the building, pulling up a couple of hundred metres away, in a rough circle with their headlights on, the pick-up closest. John and Gilbey ducked down out of the light, it was possible to see in a narrow gap between the two rocks but hard to avoid being blinded. The fourth car, the sedan they had seen at the rear of the group was not there.

The Lincoln front passenger door opened and a man got out. Cropped grey hair, green bomber jacket. Hunter, holding an MP5.

He walked casually across to the building and unlocked it. They couldn't see the front very clearly from where they were, but they heard the door opening. Next, there was a dull thump and the spotlights came on. Suddenly the whole area around the building was lit up like daytime. They crouched down further.

'Shit,' Gilbey breathed.

'Where's the other car?' John whispered.

They waited for their vision to adjust, and looked again. The cars had now switched off their headlamps, and were parked together roughly at the edge of the lit area, with the exception of the pick-up that had now stopped close to the building. Beyond the bright centre the rest of the compound was now completely black.

Hunter reappeared and walked back to the Lincoln, he banged on the side of the pick up as he passed and the blond haired man they had seen on the CCTV tape got out. He was carrying a shotgun, and climbed into the back of the truck bed. Now, they could see there was a pole standing upright in the back of the pick-up. Both men had seen this before, they knew what went on the top. The blond man bent down and picked up an M60 machine gun, loaded with a bright bandolier of shells, and dropped it onto a mount on the top of the pole. He fumbled with the latch and then swung it around and picked up the shotgun again. The driver of the panel van climbed out, carrying an M16, wearing the same standard polo shirt. He walked around to the back and waited.

John looked around, wondering what the hell was going on, why all the guns? The blond man was standing up with the shotgun held loosely across his chest, watching the other vehicles. There was another man in the pick-up driver seat, same pale grey polo shirt. Hunter reached the Lincoln and opened the rear doors, walking around the car to stand ready at the front, almost to attention. Two men got out, one was short, older, wispy grey hair. The other man was younger, taller, dark hair slicked back. Both men were grinning. The short man reached inside the car and pulled out a rifle, a Ruger Tactical, fitted with a night scope. He wielded it and walked to stand next to Hunter. The taller man joined them, carrying a Barrett 820, expensive. Both good guns, the Barrett regarded as the best sniper rifle in the world. The driver of the Lincoln climbed out, appearing to be unarmed, again wearing the same polo shirt. He leaned on the bonnet and watched everything. Hunter spoke to the two men in front of him, gesturing around and pointing. Both men nodded eagerly, the taller one laughed. Then Hunter turned around and said something to the van driver.

'Who the hell are those guys? What's going on?' Gilbey whispered.

The van driver stepped forward, and undid the rear doors, pulling them open and stepping back. He pointed the M16 inside. Hunter walked forward and started shouting, there were more raised voices, and the driver climbed up inside. The van's rear was facing away from them, and they couldn't clearly hear what was being said so neither John or Gilbey had any idea what was going on. Elsewhere, everybody seemed relaxed, no movement.

Hunter raised the MP5 and pointed it into the van. There was a flurry of movement and then a man appeared, falling forward to end up lying face down in the dirt. A second joined him, then a third. The driver reappeared and pulled them to their feet lining them up down the side of the van, Hunter keeping the MP5 trained on them all the time.

The three men were all Hispanic, varying ages. Wearing t-shirts and jeans, and they were handcuffed. It wasn't possible to see their faces clearly, but it was obvious they were terrified.

The blond man in the pick-up swung the shotgun round so it pointed to them, and then the driver produced a key and started removing the handcuffs.

John and Gilbey stared.

And then they knew. At exactly the same moment they both realised what was going on.

To the men in the cars, this was sport. It was a hunt. The whole reason for building the compound. What the digger was for. Men who wanted to know how it felt to kill another. The two unknown men with their rifles and night scopes. This was well organised. They were here for one reason.

'People keep disappearing.'

'It's happening again.'

'It's worse than anyone knows.'

And John could see it. The lust for power. White supremacy. The total devaluation of human life in the south side of the town, and beyond that. The further south, the less important the people. Anyone who spoke out was spirited away. Disappeared. The Regulators would see to it, and all for this. A sport to impress a select few, maybe some even paid to be here.

Hunter stepped forward and spoke to the three scared men, pointing away from the van. The men shook their heads, the nearest seemed to be weeping. Hunter pointed the MP5 at them. All three raised their hands, pleading.

Hunter grabbed the nearest to him and pulled him forward, and pushed him so he dropped to his knees on the hard ground, then produced a Beretta and without letting go of the MP5 racked a round into the chamber and with his thumb clicked off the safety.

He put the barrel against the man's head, and looked at the other two, talking all the time.

All the men were shaking their heads. Hunter leaned in with the barrel pushing hard, the man was going to topple over.

All the time Hunter was smiling, eyes bright, getting off on the power.

He moved the gun so it was on top of the man's head and braced.

And Gilbey, smooth as silk, like a man maybe fifty years younger, snatched up his SA80 and unfolded himself to above the top of the rock he was crouched behind, flicking the selector to single shot and racking it, swinging the gun up and raising the butt to his shoulder. All in one slick, seamless movement, like a precise ballet move. He sighted, a single heartbeat and pulled the trigger, then began moving out of cover. Hunter's head exploded, he fell backward into the dirt with a crash that seemed as loud as the shot. John was now also standing, and out of his peripheral vision saw the blond man turning, moving the shotgun, and John raised his own rifle and aimed it.

The man's eyes locked on his, and he froze.

John stepped forward.

Then the man glanced at Gilbey and raised the shotgun, John had only one course of action left.

He shot him in the face.

Two down.

The van driver was staring, waving the M16 around, at nothing. The Lincoln driver was waving his hands high in the air. The two men were clearly panicking. Gilbey strode around the rock and stood very still in front of it, with the SA80 fixed at his shoulder.

'Stand very, very still. Even in this light I can shoot the toenails off a frog from here. Don't fucking move.'

He walked forward, slowly.

John followed him, stopping at the pick-up. The driver was staring at him. He raised his hands in the air.

'Get out,' John ordered.

The man practically fell out the door in his haste. John pulled a Beretta out the man's pocket and pushed him across to where all the others were.

Gilbey had now reached the circle. He patted the shoulder of the first man standing next to the van, all three were shaking violently and blinking open mouthed at him.

'It's ok,' Gilbey told them quietly, and then turned to the others, gun sighted.

'All of you, throw down your weapons. I'm not fucking around, I will shoot every one of you dead and won't lose a second's sleep you motherfuckers,' he growled.

The van driver dropped the M16 immediately.

'Kick it over here you asshole,' Gilbey ordered.

The van driver kicked it hard, and it slid across the ground. Gilbey pointed his SA80 at the shorter, older man.

'What the fuck are you waiting for?' he asked.

'Do you have any understanding what you are doing? I am an important man,' the other man blustered, but he threw the Ruger down next to the M16. The taller man walked forward and laid down the Barrett gently, shaking his head.

'Right, line up in front of the Navigator.'

The men did, the older man, the tall man, the two drivers from the van and the car.

John joined them, pushing the pick-up driver into the line. Then he searched all the men carefully. Both the Regulators were carrying Berettas, and the older man was carrying a five shot chrome plated Smith & Wesson revolver, but the tall man had no other weapons. Mobile phones and wallets were added to the pile. All the men looked bemused, shocked, the older one muttering to himself

'Where's the other car?' John asked, dragging the stack of guns and other items further away.

Everyone looked at him, nobody said anything.

Gilbey stepped forward and slammed the butt of his SA80 hard into the stomach of the van driver, making him double up and topple forward.

'Who's next?'

The pick-up driver pointed behind him.

'It's back there! At the gate.'

John set off. He walked low, soon back into darkness, keeping the faintly visible ridgeline of the two high banks before the gates in view. They were tall enough to obscure him, but he had no idea where the driver and any passengers in the car would be. They could be anywhere out there in the dark. He was nearly halfway there when another set of headlights appeared, following the same route. He ducked lower and sped up, making it to the banks just as the lights turned the corner. It was another sedan. He peered over and watched, the new headlights lit up the area and he could now see there was a sheriff's cruiser parked across the gates. The old and tired Impala. This was the sedan they had seen. The car slowed, it was another cruiser, exactly the same. It stopped alongside, so the two drivers were next to each other. The new driver passed something through the window, then drove off. He passed the end of the fence and turned around, and set off back in the direction he had come from. Once the tail lights had vanished John moved forward.

He approached the cruiser from the rear, on the opposite side from the driver. As he got near he could hear music playing quietly. He moved closer, circling the car on the blind side, which was dimly illuminated within by instrument lights.

It was the fat sheriff, eating a box of fried chicken, so it was his dinner that had just been delivered.

He was sitting, staring out the windscreen at nothing and chewing. So he was security. John smiled to himself, he would enjoy this.

He moved back around, slowly, silently, and then yanked the door open and stepped in with the SA80 raised.

'Well, well,' he said.

The sheriff was midway through taking a bite. He jumped high in his seat and then turned his head, his mouth dropping open, half chewed chicken falling out into his lap.

'Out the car fat man,' John told him, stepping back, keeping the gun trained and happy to be doing it.

The sheriff did as he was told, climbing out with difficulty, the box with his dinner tumbling down and its contents falling onto the dirt. He stood by the car, eyes wide, scared. John leaned forward and took the Colt out of its holster, and removed the handcuffs from his belt. He snapped them painfully tight around the sheriff's wrists behind his back and then pushed him hard.

'You alone?'

The sheriff nodded, hope in his eyes.

'Get going.'

He pushed him along repeatedly with his foot, and then followed the sheriff as the fat man stumbled across and between the banks. It was slow progress, the sheriff kept turning around and pleading ignorance, but John said nothing in reply, just kept pushing the man and trudging back toward the building. It was lit up like a fairground ride in the distance.

Chapter Twenty-Four

As he shepherded Carter across to the circle, John called Patrick, and let him know what was happening. It was hard to keep the disbelief out of his own voice as he recounted the events, with great difficulty he attempted to explain how it had all played out. As he was speaking he knew he was struggling to make it sound credible. But it was all true, and right there, in front of him, in front of everyone.

'Look Patrick, Cane said it was worse than anyone knew. He's right, it's a lot worse. So, this is going to be a major investigation down here, I think this whole place will need to be dug up.'

'Er … Right! Jesus Christ! Ok, well, sit tight, I'm on my way,' Patrick told him, he sounded confused and defeated.

Eventually, after a lot of pushing and shoving and even more snivelling they made it back to the circle. Gilbey had changed things around. Now, the remaining Regulators and the two passengers from the Lincoln were sitting on the ground in a line by the side of the van, each one handcuffed to his neighbour by the wrist. The three men from the van were standing next to Gilbey, gratefully drinking from a bottle of water and talking quietly to him, while all the time he kept his gaze fixed on the other men in front of him.

'Look who I found,' John told him, and pushed the sheriff so hard he toppled over and unable to reach out to stop himself hit his head hard on the front bumper of the Lincoln.

'I hate this fat fucking prick, I warned him. I told him I would make him pay,' John said.

Gilbey walked over and hauled the sheriff to his feet, and then promptly pushed him back down again, even harder so this time he hit the ground solidly on the side of his face.

'Yeah, I hate that guy too,' he growled.

He pulled the sheriff to his feet again, which wasn't easy, and then bundled him over to sit at the end of line, where he sat head down, still snivelling.

'FBI are on the way,' John said.

That got an immediate reaction. First, the older man started to insist on seeing the local police, the taller man tried to convince them he had no idea what was going on and the sheriff started whining that he was a law enforcement officer who could explain everything, he had done nothing wrong and he deserved respect.

But Gilbey was staring at the old man, who suddenly realised he was doing it and stopped talking, staring back.

'I know you. Son of a bitch. Hey John, you'll never guess who this fucker is.'

John looked but had no idea. He shrugged.

'This guy, is none other than Judge Gregory Raymer. Chief Justice of the state of Texas.'

'Raymer?' John queried.

'Yep.'

'Jesus, a lot of people are going to have a score to settle with you.'

The judge looked even more rattled.

'I have no idea who you are or what you are talking about. I want to get this cleared up and go home, whatever it is you think you are doing you need to understand exactly who you are dealing with and the trouble you are in.'

'Us?' laughed Gilbey. 'Us? So your hobby is to run around in the dark murdering a bunch of people and we need to be worried. We just stopped it!'

'I don't know anything about that. I was invited to come out here for target practice. I don't know those men.'

'Right, target practice at night. And they just happened to be in a van that you travelled down here with. By accident, presumably,' John added.

'That's why I'm here too. Exactly,' the other man countered rapidly, starting to try to stand up.

Gilbey swung his SA80 around.

'Just sit down and stay the fuck still. All of you just stay like that. Next one who moves loses their fingers.'

'You can't do this. I demand to be freed,' the judge said, lips quivering.

'Demand all the hell you want. The Feds are on their way, and you'll be seeing the court from the other side soon enough,' Gilbey told him.

'Look, 'the tall man began was trying to stand again. He stopped and dropped down when Gilbey aimed his gun at him.

'Just move once more. Just once, and I swear I will put a bullet in every one of your fucking skulls. Try me.'

John looked over at the three Hispanic men, who were just standing, shocked, confused and fearful, looking all around them.

'What's the story?' he asked.

Gilbey looked at him and then nodded back at the men.

'Some guy went over the border, offered them some work. Usual story I think. They've been locked in that van for three days. Nothing in there but a bucket.'

'Jesus.'

But Gilbey had thought of something. He moved forward and grabbed up the sheriff, and pushed him across, back into the centre.

'Was this the man?' he asked, looking carefully at the reaction from the three men.

The oldest nodded immediately.

'Yes. That's him,' he said in a weak voice. 'He came, he was wearing his uniform. It was him.'

'This just gets fucking worse,' Gilbey hissed. 'You piece of shit.'

He punched the sheriff straight in the face, sending him backwards. He fell down and rolled onto his side, moaning, his nose trickling blood.

John put his hand on Gilbey's arm, preventing him from going in for the kill.

'Leave it,' he said quietly.

He looked at the three men, who were still gratefully passing around the bottle of water. He nudged the Lincoln driver with his foot.

'You got any food in that thing?' he asked, gesturing across at the big shiny car.

The man looked up at him, and nodded.

Gilbey walked over and undid the handcuffs on the man's wrist.

'Get up.'

John marched him across to the car and watched him carefully, always keeping the rifle aimed. The man pressed a button and the boot door opened, rising up on its own. He pulled out a wicker box.

John took it and lifted the lid. Inside were chicken pieces, salad, crisps, fruit and small bottles of white wine. There were plates, glasses and napkins

'Nice,' he said. 'Give it to them.'

The driver stiffly walked across and placed the box at the feet of the three men without meeting anyone's eye, and then went and sat back down again, a pretence of defiance that John could see right through. The cuffs went back on.

The three men tentatively rooted through the box and ate, staying silent and keeping close to Gilbey.

Chapter Twenty-Five

Ray Tilling was a Regulator. In fact, technically, he was the last one, as the others were either seriously injured and recovering elsewhere, lined up incapacitated against the side of a van, or dead.

Tilling enjoyed being a Regulator, it appealed to him. He liked the sense that people were scared, enjoyed suddenly turning up at someone's house and making threats, meting out justice of some kind or another. It was about respect, and soon he would be getting plenty of that, at last, there hadn't been much of it so far in his life. And he had particularly enjoyed the fun they had with Rita Geller, that was a bonus for sure.

But now, he was confused, and he was lost.

This was his third hunt, and he had been ordered to do exactly what he had the last time they were out. Hunter was along with them for this one, which was a first, and unexpected. Tilling was wary of Hunter, and this could be the opportunity to get on his good side. It was about time, Tilling was fed up with always being regarded as dim, someone who always needed extra help, the butt of the jokes. He had travelled out to Brown's in the pick-up, and had jumped out just inside the gates and then ran across, following the fence down to where there was a big round rock at the base, and then turning ninety degrees heading toward the centre for a bunker that had been dug out, especially for him.

Tilling was a safety, he was there for two reasons. At a previous hunt, in fact it had been the first one that he had worked, one of the prey had overpowered one of the guests and made off with his AK47. He had bolted for the fence after loosing off a few shots. Luckily, nobody had been hit, and the gun just had the standard thirty round magazine, which the guy emptied with wild shots within the next two minutes. But it had been problematic, the hunt had descended into chaos, people shooting at shadows, it was a miracle one of their own hadn't been killed. Eventually they had flushed him out as he tried to hide in a corner and it was dealt with, although the guest's wounded pride took longer. So, the new strategy was to have someone behind enemy lines as it were, somebody who could respond quickly and flank any problematic prey. His job was also to clean up, occasionally a hunter may suddenly get cold feet about finishing one of the prey off, and it would be Tilling's job to get it done. Not that it had happened so far. All that had occurred in the last hunt unfortunately, was that he had spent hours in the bunker on his own listening to excited shouts and watching sporadic bursts of gunfire.

Tilling carried an MP5, and had a backpack with five full clips in it. Plus he had his Beretta in a holster on his belt. He was longing to use either gun, he had an itch desperate to scratch. It was agreed his job was dangerous, after all he was out in the open while untrained, excitable men were shooting high power rifles at anything that moved, so he wore a Kevlar vest, and had a radio which linked him to the master of the hunt, which today was Hunter. He had night vison goggles strapped to his head. And best of all, because it was dangerous, he got extra in his wage packet. He was an important man, doing an important job.

But tonight wasn't working out so well. The worst part of it initially was finding the goddamn bunker in the dark. Once he was there and inside he was reasonably safe, with the goggles on he could see anything moving a long way off. But tonight, he was still looking for the bunker. There was a long berm, which ran almost straight across for many metres, and was deep in places. The bunker was at the east end of this. He had worked out the best way to find it in the daytime, and at the last hunt once he had hit the berm the bunker had been easy to find. But tonight, after what felt like hours of walking, he just couldn't seem to find even the berm. He guessed he must have wandered off the centre line that he should have taken, and had now finally made the decision to turn around, intending to make his way back to the fence and start again. It would take a long time, and he would get all sorts of shit about it, he knew. And if anyone came his way he was biting the dirt, and fast, he would lay very still until he was on his own again.

Fuck it, at last he had been given some responsibility, and he would probably lose it now if anybody discovered what an asshole he was being.

But as he warily made his way toward the fence he realised, nobody had to know! He could just say he was in the bunker, how would anyone ever find out he was wandering around the place lost? Pleased with himself, he checked in on the radio, to no response. He sniggered silently, he was much smarter that anyone gave him credit for.

He wondered how it was progressing, apart from two shots early on there had been nothing since, but he knew that sometimes the guests would take some time to get moving. In the distance he could see the spotlights on top of the tower, but he tried not to look at them too much as it spoiled his visibility. He decided that he would move closer to it, while all the time heading toward where he knew the gates were, as that way he should be able to get a better fix on his direction; the last thing he needed right now was to be wandering around in circles in the dark or to blunder in on everyone as they were setting up.

He moved the goggles up and away from his face then walked along steadily, watching his steps as best as he could and straining his ears to listen, moving closer to the building meant it was more possible he could run into someone, from either side. The wind was becoming more and more of a problem, it was building up in loud gusts that seemed to blow in from different directions.

He kept moving, as fast as he could while avoiding falling over on the difficult terrain, his head down. He checked his progress repeatedly, and realised that he had strayed too close to the centre again. Behind him and away to his left he could make out the vehicles in the remaining light from the spot lamps. He shook his head, embarrassed. What the hell was wrong with him tonight? He couldn't even walk in a straight line.

He looked over, something didn't look right to him. He realised what it was, the pick-up was still there. Normally that would be roving around the perimeter, but it was parked up.

He wondered what was happening, and dropped down the goggles.

Now, the area was a sea of green, he could see the warm engines in the vehicles, but he could also see people, and what he was looking at didn't make a whole lot of sense. They were concentrated in one area, with a one group that appeared to be sitting or kneeling, and another standing.

He dug out the radio and keyed the button.

'Ray to Hunter, can I get a sit rep please? Er ... over.'

He stood there, watching. No response, nothing at all.

'Er ... Hunter? It's Ray here, just checking in, wondering what's happening can you let me know? Over.'

Again nothing. Tilling had no idea what to do, his tall frame still, hair blowing everywhere in the wind, head moving around slowly. If the shit had gone down, then at least he was out in the open. His best bet would be to get the hell out. He took the Beretta out his pocket and walked forward, then stumbled and fell, dropping the gun in the dirt. Swearing softly to himself he used the display screen on the radio to find it and put it back in his pocket, shaking his head.

Suddenly his dream job didn't feel so great. He was out here, on his own, and no contact on the radio. Anything could have happened and he would have no idea. Tilling was not at all sure what to do next.

He realised he had no choice, he needed to try and work out what was going on. He put the radio back in his pocket and moved toward the centre, if he couldn't get anyone on the radio he better find out for himself. If it looked like everything had gone to shit for whatever reason he was well hidden and should be able to get clear, at the very least hide out somewhere.

Gilbey was reassuring the Hispanic men that they had nothing to worry about but he needed them to stay right where they were for now when he suddenly snatched up his rifle and peered out through the sight into the wilderness of the compound. John raised his too and followed the direction.

'What is it?' he asked.

'I saw something out there, something blue, lit up. Some ways off, could be a cell phone maybe but it was there for sure. I seen it.'

John turned back to the Regulators.

'You got someone out there?'

The men looked at each other, then shook their heads.

'You understand, if you're lying, then we'll just waste you where you are. Because it makes no difference to us at all. I'd just as soon shoot the whole damn lot of you anyways, including the fucking judge,' Gilbey growled, without taking his eye off the scope.

John crouched down by the van.

'So?'

The Regulators were nervous, he could see that. Scared. They were in it now, that much was for sure. Whatever happened, they wouldn't be going home. The Lincoln and the pick-up drivers were younger, probably thirty at most, in fact they looked similar, maybe related. The van driver was bigger, older, with a hard face and mean eyes, he was avoiding looking at John, his eyes were fixed on some point way in the distance.

John decided he didn't like him.

He got the handcuffs key off Gilbey and unlocked the man's wrist, then stood him up.

'What's your name?' John asked.

'Paul. Paul Gibbs.'

'Well Paul, I don't like you. I don't like any of you idiots. So, you're going to have to help.'

'I don't think so.'

Gibbs was staring at him hard. He was taller, and had long arms. Tough guy.

John placed the SA80 carefully on the ground near Gilbey, and then turned and stood in front of Gibbs.

'You'll do it,' he told him.

Gibbs glanced over at Gilbey and then back at John, his eyes narrowed and he swung a big fist. He had some tactics, lead in with the left while preparing the real damage with the right. But John could see it coming, the way Gibbs was shaping up, so he ducked down from the left and moved sharply around to the side and then let go with his own right, a solid, crashing punch straight to Gibb's face.

Gibbs staggered backwards, shaking his head.

John moved forward, opening his arms out wide.

'Come on,' he invited.

Gibbs tried to rush him, still reeling from the punch and John sidestepped and punched again, this time straight onto the other man's nose, and then another, equally hard into the kidneys. Gibbs fell forward on all fours, breathing hard. John kicked him solidly in the ribs, sending him onto his side. Gibbs rolled over onto his back groaning.

'Job done?' Gilbey asked, still staring off the other way.

'I think so,' John replied, and hauled Gibbs to his feet, where he stood shakily.

'Well Paul, here's what we are going to do. Me and Gilbey think there's another one of you idiots out there somewhere, probably armed, probably intent on getting away if he's worked out you are all fucked. He ain't gonna be trying to save your arse, and you know that. Right now, he's too far out to do us any damage. So, you are going to start walking, straight that way. Once the guy starts shooting, we'll see where the muzzle flashes are, and deal with it. Good plan, right?'

'That's a great fucking plan,' Gilbey said with a grin, still focussing his rifle outward.

Beaten, Gibbs stepped forward then halted sharply and turned.

'Wait ...'

John looked hard at him.

'Yeah wait. You just realised it. He's gonna start shooting at anybody, because by now he's realised there's a problem and it's dark out there. He's gonna want to get the hell out of here, and I can't say I blame him. What he doesn't know is the FBI are on their way, so whatever happens now you guys are all fucked.'

Gibbs looked out into the open, and gulped.

'Shit! Ok, ok. Fucking hell. There is a guy out there. I don't know him real well, he's name's Ray. He's the clean-up guy.'

'Where?'

'Out there. I don't know, there's a bunker, but I've never been there. I guess he's there.'

'How does he keep in touch?'

'Radio. Hunter's got one. Or did, anyway.'

John picked up his rifle and pushed Gibbs over to Hunter's body. Together they searched it. No radio. Gibbs looked at the other Regulators questioningly.

'In the car,' the Lincoln driver said.

At that point, headlights came into view, way in the distance but heading their way and moving fast.

At last, John thought.

John opened the Lincoln's passenger door and found a radio on the dashboard. He threw it to Gibbs.

'Over to you. Probably best he comes in.'

Gibbs turned the radio over in his hands. He keyed the talk button uncertainly.

'Er … Ray? This is Paul, you should get your ass over here. We got some deep shit.'

No reply.

He looked at John and shrugged. John sat him back down and snapped the cuffs on him, and walked over to Gilbey.

'He'll go for the gates.'

'Definitely.'

The headlights were getting closer, impossible to see how many there were.

John jogged over to the pick-up and started it, then threw it around in a tight circle and headed off back up the track toward the gates, full beam and lights on the roof shining out brightly in front of him, the whole area now lit up.

He saw him less than five minutes later, moving across to his left, ducking and moving but clearly silhouetted against the blackness behind him. John drove past and then turned sharply, so his headlights were aiming right at the man and then stuck the pick-up in park and leapt out with the SA80 raised high, walking right between the car lights, impossible to see from the other direction.

Through the scope he could clearly see the man right in front of him moving one way then another, wanting to run but unsure which way. John fired a warning shot, which kicked up the dirt right at the man's feet.

'Stand still!' he commanded.

The man continued to move, so he fired again, same place, a big dust cloud.

'I said stand still!'

Finally, the man got the message. John walked closer.

'Throw your weapons out in front of you, and also the backpack. I won't ask a second time.'

The man did exactly as he was asked, the MP5, the Beretta, then the backpack and held his hands high in the air.

John walked past them and grabbed the man, and herded him back toward the pick-up. By now the vehicles were at the gates, it looked like five or six. He picked up the guns and the backpack and shoved the man forward. He put both rifles in the back and cocked the Beretta, aiming at the man's head.

'You drive,' he said.

They got in and the man turned around slowly and headed back. He stopped at the edge of the circle. John dragged him out and pushed him into the line, just as the first cars reached them.

Chapter Twenty-Six

The Country Club had several function rooms, all in the residence wing, which was a grand, gleaming white five-storey Georgian looking building with massive windows and a flat roof. The finest room was called The Club, and had a curved sweeping wall of windows that overlooked the grounds and further out down the hill, the lights of the town could be seen.

Barlow was sitting in a comfortable armchair, rolling an unlit cigar between his thumb and forefinger, Abel was standing at the window staring into the night.

'Sit down for Christ's sakes,' Barlow told him. 'Jesus relax, will you? Have a cigar.'

'Yeah, you know, I'm just keen for them to get back.'

'They won't be long, it will be a quick one tonight, and you know that, so stop worrying.'

Abel turned and Barlow slid a glass of brandy across the side table toward him.

'Thanks.'

Abel drank it down and picked up a cigar from the box. Outside the skinny trees they had planted all along the driveway were bending sharply in the strong wind.

Barlow clipped the end off the cigar and with a chunky lighter sitting on the table lit it, and then puffed away in a thick cloud of blue smoke. It smelt good, so Abel lit his, and then poured himself another brandy. He didn't know why he was so nervous, but it had been niggling away at him all night, in fact he admitted to himself that he had been uneasy all day. He would be very relieved when everyone was back and they could all go to bed. Tomorrow was another day, and then nobody could get in their way. He passed a hand over his face, he was tired. Once this was done he was going to take a vacation, Barlow would moan about it but he needed some time and space away.

Maybe he could visit southern Italy, or Spain. He sat down heavily and then sprang back up out the chair, as the first headlights could be seen at the top of the drive.

'Thank God,' he breathed, turning around and smiling.

Barlow just nodded, as if he had known this was the precise moment they would return all along.

Abel happily poured himself another brandy, then looked back out the window and froze. He had expected to see two, or possibly three vehicles if Sheriff Carter had obstinately decided to come for a nightcap, but he could see four separate sets of headlights now and they were moving fast. He walked over to the window and looked down as the first two cars pulled up.

Two dark sedans. Big shiny cars. Radio aerials visible on the boot. Two more vehicles were slowing and stopping behind them. Car doors opening, men streaming all over the place.

'Er …' he started, his mouth opening and closing.

Barlow pulled himself up out of his chair and stared out the window.

'What the hell!' he snarled.

'You …' Abel started again, and then stopped. He turned around slowly on the spot, then moved into the centre of the room, his hand over his mouth. He looked around, and then pushing past Barlow walked from the room in short, jerky steps, out into the reception area for the conference rooms. The lift to the ground or up to the residence floors was to his left. The door to the stairway was next to it.

He pushed through and walked up the stairs, blinking rapidly, shallow breaths, mouth hanging open. He reached the top floor and then walked up a final set that ran straight with a solid door on the top. He opened it, and stepped onto the roof.

The strong wind blew him forward, and he lurched across the roof to the front, where he could look down over a low wall that ran all the way around, amazed by all the activity. He stood very still watching everything, then reached into his jacket pocket and pulled out his notepad, and his trusty, expensive pen. He looked at it lovingly, and held it up. Then he wrote something on the notepad, and clutching it in his hand climbed onto the wall, then stepped off.

John looked at his watch wearily, ten past six. Dawn was finally breaking; the first proper rays of sunlight stretching out across the compound. He looked around, whichever direction he turned there were people working.

Patrick had arrived, listened carefully, and swept into immediate action. He had bought seven agents with him, but within three hours had over thirty on the ground. Two helicopters had arrived, then more vehicles, the state police, an hour ago Frank Slater had turned up.

For the first time ever, Patrick wasn't wearing a suit. He was dressed in dark jeans, sweatshirt and jacket, emblazoned with the letters F.B.I. across the back in yellow. All the other agents were dressed similarly. Now, there were generators running, and spotlights everywhere. The Regulators had been taken away in one van, handcuffed, silent and subdued.

The first big news was when Patrick looked at the two men that were there. He recognised Raymer, but he stared in amazement at the other man.

'Jesus,' he stated, unable to look away.

'What?' John asked.

Patrick shook his head and pointed.

'So, we've got a judge, and also the planning director for Homeland Security. Meet James Waldron.'

'Fuck!' Gilbey blurted out.

'Indeed,' Patrick agreed. 'I think this will take some explaining Mr Waldron.'

Waldron started to blabber a series of excuses, but Patrick cut him off, and he and Raymer were taken away and driven off in separate vehicles, the judge loudly protesting his innocence.

The search had begun in earnest, more and more agents and state police arriving.

An hour later John and Gilbey were sitting on the ground with their backs against the front wall of the building. Gilbey had collected their pick-up and it was sitting forlornly over by the gates, it was light enough that they could see everywhere now.

Patrick walked across and dropped to the ground in front of them.

'I'm sorry, but I'm going to need you to come in. Both of you.'

John agreed, he had expected this. Gilbey didn't look happy.

'Come in where?' he asked.

'Austin. I'm sorry, but I got no choice. This is massive, we already found two bodies. This whole place will have to be dug up, we got to get searching, identification, plus all the forensics. Raymer and Waldron won't go quietly. We've arrested Barlow, who is also making a lot of noise. So now we've got to put it all together, and this is beyond serious. I've got you two, and the three men that were abducted. But we should be able to get it tidy, and fast. Listen, I'll get rooms in the Four Seasons, I'll treat you guys like kings. But I'm gonna need all the help I can get.'

'I know that, it's no problem for me,' John replied, looking at Gilbey.

The big man sighed, and nodded.

'Fine. But Carrie comes with me. She loves Austin.'

Patrick chuckled.

'Ok. Hell, I'll pay for a romantic dinner. Least I can do.'

Another helicopter flew in, and hovered kicking up a massive cloud of dust before settling. More agents, plus a man in a suit who was looking around everywhere shocked.

'That's my cue,' Patrick said standing up.

He started to walk toward the helicopter and then stopped and turned back.

'By the way, there's a couple of things you should probably know, I said we had Barlow; he has been taken in, he's going to be held at Travis, along with the Regulators, or whatever it is they call themselves.'

'Travis?' John asked.

'Prison near to Austin, there's a few around but that one has the best access for us in the jail.'

'What about Abel?' Gilbey asked.

'That's the other thing. He jumped off the roof at the Country Club, so no trial for him.'

'Shit.'

'Left a note, they found it on him. Just said "I'm sorry", that was it.'

Patrick turned back and walked quickly across to meet the man in the suit.

'Abel. Man, what a fucking chickenshit.' Gilbey spat into the dirt.

But John wasn't all that surprised. Cane had completely disintegrated, right in front of his eyes, and he guessed that Abel had done the exact same thing once realisation had hit home. Barlow was the one that was behind everything, and he would go down fighting. He would be the prize.

Chapter Twenty-Seven

By the time everything was in place in Austin, it was after five.

A conference had been arranged for five-thirty in the FBI office in Austin, which was a big brick and glass building. John and Gilbey had packed some clothes and then been flown into Austin by helicopter, Gilbey as amazed by the experience of travelling in such style as John had been the previous day. They had been whisked straight off to the Four Seasons, a grand building overlooking the Colorado river. They had both got a couple of hours' sleep, and met for a very late lunch/early dinner. Carrie was coming in that evening, she was excited by all the fuss.

It had been decided that John should be at the conference, but Gilbey could miss it, as it was all about procedure at this stage, so John was picked up from the hotel and taken to the FBI headquarters, which were way out to the north.

Patrick had also been able to get a some sleep, he was staying in a Holiday Inn not far from the headquarters, and was back in the usual suit with crisp shirt and tie. They sat down with a cup of coffee while Patrick filled him in.

'Ok, so the guy you saw in the suit getting out the helicopter? That's Jack Carpenter, he's regional director for the state. He's an old hand and a good guy. He can be volatile, and he will not take any shit from anyone, but I'd rather have him at the top than a lot of others.'

'Right, well, I'm happy if you are.'

'Not so good, is the DA is in on it now. Name of Philip Reed. He insisted. Technically it's FBI jurisdiction but as ever we got to play the political game. We've also got the PD involved, and your old friend Frank Slater.'

'Slater's ok, I think he's a good enough cop. What's the problem with the DA?'

Patrick raised his eyebrows.

'Not sure where to start ... He's an old buddy of Raymer's, which is not ideal. And we know he has met Barlow on a few occasions. But there is nothing to tie him to Gray Rock. Look, I got no choice in this, but trust me, I am checking this guy out. And If I get even the slightest whiff of anything I am pulling him, Texas or no Texas.'

He looked at his watch.

'Come on, let's go up.'

The conference room was on the top floor, with big windows all around.

Jack Carpenter was already there, wearily sitting at the head of the table in a crumpled suit. He stood up when they came in and Patrick introduced them.

Carpenter nodded to him and smiled grimly.

'It's good to meet you John. I'd like to be saying thank you for bringing this to us, but, well, as you can imagine, hell, I just don't know what the hell to say to you.'

John raised a hand.

'I get it.'

They sat down, and John was introduced to another man sitting opposite, a big, dark-skinned Hispanic agent called Carl Munoz.

'Carl is one of the section heads here,' Patrick explained. 'Jack has asked him to get involved.'

Frank Slater walked in, and John shook his hand.

'I knew you were going to be trouble, I just knew it,' he said with a wry smile as he sat down.

There were another couple of agents whose names John immediately forgot, plus a lieutenant from the Austin PD. Then in walked Philip Reed, the DA. He was wearing a light grey suit, pink shirt and had blow-dried hair. He looked around and headed straight for Carpenter, who stood up and shook his hand.

'Hey Philip, this is Patrick Skelton, he is one of our senior investigators out of Washington, and the gentleman to his left is John Smith, who's involvement I believe has been explained to you.'

Reed shook Patrick's hand, and then took hold of John's and looked at him shrewdly.

'Mr Smith, you're a long way from home, I understand you are at the heart of all this.'

'No, not really. I kind of got dragged into it. And I didn't expect anything like all this shit.'

'Hmmm, well.'

Reed shrugged and sat down. He had an assistant with him, the only person who did, a young blonde girl who sat down next to him and opened a big folder.

An agent was busy handing around cups of coffee. Carpenter coughed.

'Right. So, we got ourselves a situation. To bring everyone onto the same page, this afternoon we had agents at Travis take initial statements.'

Small stacks of printed sheets were passed around.

'Now at this stage, we got only slight co-operation, two of these Regulators, one named Raymond Tilling, the other Paul Gibbs, well, they seem the most likely to talk and we are hopeful they will be helpful. The other two are in denial. Raymer, Barlow, and Waldron, all refused to say anything at all, other than Raymer and Barlow's insistence they are innocent. They all demanded an attorney, no real surprise.'

'Judge Raymer,' Reed said pointedly.

'What?' Carpenter asked irritably.

'Judge Raymer. It's his correct title. I think he deserves it.'

Carpenter fixed with Reed with a stare of cold steel.

'What he deserves Philip, is to be made to run around in that goddam burial ground while a bunch of his assholes buddies chase him with hand grenades. That's what he deserves.

And don't start thinking you are going to change my mind, or anyone else in the agencies mind neither. He is guilty, and he is going to pay. We need you of all people to do your damn job, forget about all the days you had lunch on him or played golf with the man. This is a solid case. Carter is being held at State, but had a medical episode this morning, and is in the hospital building; his situation is said to be serious. He has also shown a willingness to talk. So, I don't want to hear one goddamn word defending Barlow or Raymer, I don't care that we're in Texas.'

Well said, thought John, admiration for Carpenter growing.

Reed coloured and went to speak, but decided to say nothing.

'Next thing,' Carpenter continued, 'Is Patrick will be the lead on this. He is in charge. He will report to me and I will assist where necessary but he has the experience and he has the knowledge to make sure we stay on track.'

'Now wait a minute,' Reed interjected. 'This is a Texas matter and …'

'I don't care Philip. It just happens to have occurred here in Texas. I cannot keep hearing this bullshit. It needs investigating properly and Patrick is by far and away the best person to do it. So, you'll have to learn to live with it Mr District Attorney because I am not changing my mind. '

Hear, hear thought John inwardly smiling.

Again, Reed said nothing, while his assistant scribbled away furiously.

Carpenter looked hard at him, and then continued.

'Tomorrow, is day one. Raymer, Waldron and Barlow will be brought here for formal questioning in the morning. Austin PD will be assisted by Patrick and Carl and will have full documentation.'

'What about bail?' Reed asked.

Carpenter shrugged.

'I'm not a judge, and I don't work for the PD or the justice department Philip, but I would imagine that the flight risk would be high, wouldn't you? And yes, I do know this isn't a money issue, no amount couldn't be met by Mr Barlow. I am recommending no bail, as is Lieutenant Jackson. We have already entered that and their attorneys are aware.'

He nodded to the police lieutenant who was sitting further down the table who nodded back.

'Finally, at this time five bodies have been recovered from the scene. There are only IDs on two. Both gunshot victims. One of those is Paul Hunter, who is a known close associate of Barlow and the other is one Andrew Walters who worked in some capacity for Hunter, and we have documented testimony surrounding their shootings and these are not considered suspicious. However at this time there have been three other bodies that have been unearthed. So far, they all appear to have suffered death by firearms and the basic forensic at the scene so far is at least one of the bodies has been in the ground there over two years. The corpses discovered have yet to be identified and the search is continuing. There is also considerable forensic evidence at the scene, we can place Mr Hunter and Mr Walters there, and also Mr William Harold Barlow.'

Reed sat up straight.

'Barlow?'

'Yes. His fingerprints are on the door to the storeroom. He already stated he knew nothing about Brown's field, but we can place him there. Good work actually.'

'What about this Hunter and er … Walters?' Reed asked.

'If you read your notes, you will see they are both part of the Gray Rock organisation, known as the Regulators, and were shot and killed at Brown's. It has been deemed a legal killing; protecting the three men who had been abducted and kept by force.'

'And where are these abducted men? Can they provide evidence?'

'They have already provided detailed statements, and have identified Carter as being the man responsible for their abduction, which has not been contested. He travelled over the border driving the van they were held in. He was in uniform and was credible; he told the men they were needed as labourers for a road being built. It's clear this is something he has done previously, like I said he has told us that he will give a statement.'

Reed looked at the notes his assistant had in front of her.

'And Mr Cane?' he asked.

Carpenter sat back and looked steadily at Reed.

'Tell me, do you know him too?'

Reed cleared his throat.

'No, well not really. I attended a presentation at the plant by BRP and he was there. I was introduced but we didn't speak.'

Carpenter held his gaze.

'The man has a lot to say. He could bring all this down on his own. I say again Philip, whatever your relationship is it is important you keep your distance from all of these men.'

Reed looked uneasy but said nothing.

Then, the meeting went around the table, people asking questions, plenty getting written down. John had nothing to say, he just listened, and looked forward to tomorrow. He spoke to Carpenter afterward, asking about Sheriff Carter, unable to shift the animosity he felt.

'Heart attack,' Carpenter told him simply.

John remembered the fat man, huge gut hanging over his belt, waddling around breathlessly and eating the big bucket of fried chicken in the car. He tried to feel some compassion but it was impossible. There was no real surprise in what had happened to Carter, and a lot of people would say he had got what he deserved.

Chapter Twenty-Eight

Day One

John and Gilbey sat in a room at headquarters. They were at a table, and on the wall in front of them was a large monitor. There were a couple of other agents in the room, and Jack Carpenter was constantly moving in and out. Philip Reed and his assistant were present for a lot of the time, whenever there was something actually happening. They were watching Gregory Raymer being interviewed. He wasn't saying very much, he appeared to view the whole process as a disdainful waste of time, yawning a lot and sneering disinterestedly at the camera. In the room with him was his attorney, also aloof, plus a beefy police detective sergeant called Canning, Patrick, and also Carl Munoz. Canning was patiently asking questions, that Raymer would occasionally answer vaguely, insisting that his invitation to Gray Rock was for dinner, and he had been invited to do some target practice afterward. For fun, he added, smugly. The interview dragged on, Patrick also asking questions, until he terminated it, and told Raymer that he would be going back to Travis, which clearly angered the old judge. He stopped as he was being led out the door and hurled a torrent of abuse at Patrick, who just smiled back at him.

Next in was Waldron, same cast present, just a different attorney. He was not as comfortable as Raymer, frequently changing his story, but sticking to the target practice version which he had unfortunately heard Raymer spouting at Brown's, then at the end throwing in he thought he could maybe shoot an armadillo. But he was stuttering and unconvincing, even his own attorney was clearly uncomfortable. John could not believe he would be able to last.

Then finally, the one that John wanted to see. In walked Barlow. He looked very different. Still wearing a suit, but without a tie and no shiny shoes, just the same pair of paper bootees as worn by the others. He looked ruffled and unhappy. His attorney was an overweight, fastidious man who was pedantic in his attempts to control the interview. Barlow insisted he was not aware of any building, or fence at Brown's field, had never even been there, and knew nothing about any shooting expeditions. Yes, he had dinner with the judge, but they were old friends and socialised frequently. He had met Mr Waldron for the first time, who was just visiting the state. He had committed no crime. Then he leant toward his interrogators and spoke in a conspiring whisper, fixing an overly sincere expression on his face. Since his shocking detainment the previous night he had given everything a lot of thought he told them. It was possible, he believed, that Dennis Abel had been party to the events, he had been acting very secretively recently and had been a close friend of Paul Hunter, who was a lover of guns and violence, and a man that he only knew vaguely. Yes, it was with his deep regret to tell them that his old friend Dennis was to blame for everything along with Hunter, both their deaths were a tragic loss, but he had to speak out. Crimes had been committed. He wanted no part in anything illegal.

Then he sat back smugly.

So Barlow knew Hunter was dead, John thought. He wondered how that had got out.

Patrick did not mention the fingerprint that had been discovered at Brown's, eventually he tired of dealing with the attorney and terminated the interview.

Everybody met again at the end of the day. They had heard better news from the agents at the prison. It looked like they would be able to get full testimony from both Tilling and

Gibbs who were looking to shift as much of the blame as possible, and Carter was also making a lot of noise, when he wasn't on the ventilator.

John mentioned the fact that somehow Barlow had found out Hunter was dead, while he said it he stared at Reed, but it turned out to be inconsequential. The district attorney was not at fault. Barlow's attorney had demanded full disclosure, and in the initial police documents there had been copies of the FBI reports.

Jack Carpenter seemed reasonably pleased, but frustrated.

'Ok, so same drill tomorrow. We are in court for the arraignment hearing first thing and then on with the questioning. We will be keeping everyone at Travis,' he looked at Reed, expecting confrontation.

But Reed was different. He had watched the interviews, his job was to prosecute, whatever his previous standing was with Raymer, or with Barlow, things had moved on. He had to make a choice, and he had opted for the safe one. Do the right thing, do his job.

'I agree,' he said, 'and I will be in the court. I have already supplied papers from my office.'

Carpenter nodded, satisfied.

Day Two

The courtroom wasn't busy, it had been closed to the press and public. John and Gilbey were both there, along with several agents. But there had been big news, already. Carter was now seriously ill, and had broken down in the night and asked to speak. Completely of his own doing, with no threats or persuasion of any kind he had given a full statement, or as close to one as they could expect with the condition he was in. He had been asked to find Mexicans, preferably men, along the border who would be looking to work in the US. He denied knowing what that work was, but unconvincingly, in the end admitting that he knew the work wasn't real. He stated that he had driven down into Mexico to a border town called Orida, where he had known there would be people looking for work. He said that he had done this previously, but wouldn't admit to how many times. He had been asked to bring them to the airport at Gray Rock, which he had done, and had used the van because as a sheriff he wouldn't be stopped. He said he had explained that to the men he picked up. He left the van at the airport as requested. Then, on Friday afternoon, he had been asked to watch over the gate that same night, as there was going to be a special VIP event at Brown's. It had not been explained to him what the event was. He said Abel had asked him to find the men and also watch the gate, not Barlow but was vague and did not provide any details. He admitted to being suspicious when he saw the van was there when he followed everyone to Brown's. He didn't know if Barlow knew about what was going on or not. He had recognised Judge Raymer, but had never seen Waldron before and wasn't introduced.

So they had a part of the story, full of bullshit about Barlow's involvement but because Abel was dead it was clean and simple to pin it on him. They were confident that in time Carter would soon complete everything, provided he stayed alive.

In court, Philip Reed stood up, and despite all their original misgivings, he did his job. It turned out that different to appearances Reed was actually a good man and knew what he was doing. John, Gilbey and Patrick all enjoyed the look on both Barlow's and Raymer's face when Reed categorically stated bail must be denied. These men were all rich, and all powerful in their own worlds. Flight was not a possibility should they be bailed, it was definite. Reed had pages of evidence from both the PD and the FBI, which he had submitted to the court. The process didn't take very long. The judge, a woman, agreed. Bail was denied. The three men were to be detained at Travis and Carter at State for the duration of the investigation. None of the Regulators had applied for bail. The attorneys all talked a lot, raised voices, arms being waved around, but the judge just looked down at them placidly until they ran out of steam. Raymer looked furious while Barlow especially was clearly shocked.

And so, the interviews started again.

This time John shook Reed's hand when he walked into the monitor room.

Raymer was angry. Immediately he went on the attack. Canning, Munoz and Patrick sat there watching, smiling, enjoying the show, as did John and Gilbey. Eventually, the attorney could see where this would lead and calmed it down. A copy of Carter's statement was laid on the table, and read out slowly by Canning.

'So, at no point did you wonder what the van was there for, and you didn't question the fact that three handcuffed men were thrown from it?' Patrick asked.

Raymer blustered, he hadn't seen the men in the van, he had been sitting in the car.

Patrick produced John's, Gilbey's and the three Mexican men's statements, which recounted the events where the van was opened and where everybody's positions were at the time.

Raymer tried to change tack, but was starting to contradict himself, the damage was done.

Then Canning asked about Hunter's movements, again referring to the statements, which had led to Gilbey taking action, forcibly stopping everything by shooting Hunter before he killed one of the men. Gilbey and Smith had made themselves known and disarmed everyone present, then the FBI was called.

Raymer stood up, defiant.

'I am a judge, the most senior in the state of Texas. I will not spend another minute in this room listening to this. I HAVE DONE NOTHING WRONG!'

'Apart from knowingly joining in on the hunting and potentially the eventual murdering of three innocent men, who were all abducted and held against their will, facts which despite all the bullshit we have been forced to listen to is undeniable,' Canning replied.

'The judge …' his attorney started jumping out of his seat but was brusquely interrupted by Patrick.

'Don't call him that. He is no longer to be treated with any respect. It makes me sick to my stomach. Sit down and shut up. We don't need to listen any more lies. Your client is guilty, and every one of us in this room knows it, including you.'

The attorney blinked and said nothing and Raymer turned bright red but clammed up too, visibly shaken.

End of interview.

There was a break in proceedings, Patrick was confident but wary.

Barlow was next, he did nothing but blame Abel. Everything was down to him, Cane had run off because of it.

'No, no,' Patrick told him gently. 'Mr Cane is here, he's with us.'

Barlow looked startled, then immediately started accusing Cane of being a cold, manipulative liar and having a hold over Abel.

Patrick said nothing, and then explained very slowly exactly how Cane came to be helping them. Again, Barlow looked shocked.

He recovered, once more denying any knowledge, but visibly a desperately worried man now. His high forehead a sheen of sweat and constant fidgeting with his hands.

He wanted to speak privately with his attorney.

End of interview.

Finally, Waldron, who was asked the same questions as Raymer. He sweated, stuttered and stammered and suddenly vomited down himself.

End of interview.

Patrick walked into the monitor room afterward.

'Getting there,' John told him.

Patrick nodded.

'Let's go and see Cane.'

It was decided Gilbey would sit this out, it was important that Cane did not feel intimidated. Patrick drove, Cane was at the Hyatt hotel. He parked underneath and then travelled up in the lift, using a room key to activate it. Cane was high up on the top floor, as they walked toward the room they saw a police officer outside the door.

'How's he doing?' Patrick asked, showing ID.

'Better. He's eaten something today,' the cop said.

They walked in. Cane was sitting in a chair under a blanket watching the TV. He looked up when the two men walked in, and sat up straight, switching off the television.

'It's about time. I got something to say,' he told them simply.

Patrick set a Dictaphone down on the table and they took their seats.

Day Three

There was a conference at eight in the morning. This time, a real sense of excitement filled the room, a buzz that had not been there before. Canning gave John a high five hard enough it hurt when he walked in the room.

More good news. Raymer's fingerprints had been found on one of the shovels at Brown's; a clear set.

Another body and a lot of spent cartridges, of various calibres had been unearthed, the search was slow going.

They had found out where Waldron had acquired the Barrett rifle. He had obtained it from the Homeland Security armoury in Washington. He was senior enough that it wasn't questioned, it was unloaded after all. He had acquired a box of ammo with almost ridiculous simplicity through a supplier that had an eye on building their relationship with the government.

Raymer's Ruger proved to be unlicensed. It had been a gift to him from a retiring chief of police several years earlier and was taken during a raid on a drug dealer in San Marcos, Raymer had decided to keep it as a trophy.

Everybody present had read Cane's statement, which was simple but descriptive and to the point.

Chapter Twenty-Nine

Statement of William Franklin Cane

Gray Rock was the product of two men's desire to build white America. Barlow had been the main protagonist but had seen a kindred spirit in Abel when they had first met and they had started One Race along with many other rich, white American businessmen, as a voice to get their opinions heard. They had discussed building a town for white people even back then and had spoken of it many times.

My involvement started properly in the early nineties. Barlow was already incredibly rich but wanted more and I became his banker. I had been working in banking for many years and knew the system very well. I was appointed BRP relationship manager, and I also took on Barlow's personal affairs. BRP was making millions, but Barlow was obsessed with his own fortune and I helped and advised him on maximising his payments from the business. I developed a scheme which is still in use today, I was exceptional with moving money around, so it was impossible to trace. BRP grew fast, and so did the profits, and Barlow's own wealth. I did so well that Barlow gave me a job as CFO at BRP, and then everything really started to happen. Barlow and Abel had already decided on Texas as the location for their Utopia, and Gray Rock looked good. I had heard all about their dreams for the town but was not fully aware of the progress being made. I moved down to Dallas and started living the life there. It was like a dream. I was earning amazing money,

287

and I had everything, we all felt untouchable. But Barlow had a weakness, which I knew nothing about but Abel did and stayed well away from. I admit fully that Barlow had power over me and one day insisted I come along with him to a party, I was invited to the house in Highland Park. There was no conversation as such, I was just advised I should come along, it would be in my interests, I would meet many rich and powerful men. I wasn't told what happened in that house and once I realised what it was I was sick, I wanted to run away, but the place was raided that night and everyone was taken into police custody. I hadn't done anything more than walk in through the door so I didn't ask for an attorney, but one had turned up anyway. The attorney wasted no time, he told me that it was a conspiracy, Barlow was innocent he had never been before there either. It was a setup. I didn't believe him, I said Barlow had invited me, he had said it was a regular party but I had realised what really went on so it was spelled out exactly what was expected of me, what to say and what to do, and if I did exactly as instructed I would be rewarded. If not, then anything could happen. I was told there were others involved who were not so understanding. I am just a banker, and was afraid more of that threat than I was the police, so I said nothing, and took all the blame. Then, one day in the jail, Seaton came to see me and spoke to me and Greaves about information that was going to be given, and that the two of us should do the same. He told me that a lot of men, Barlow included had been released the same night. I thought about it and decided that Seaton was right. He would ask to talk to the police tomorrow. That same afternoon Barlow visited the prison for the first time. He asked me and asked me if I was going to keep quiet, that it was in my interests, that I would be very rich. I told him that I didn't know, I had done nothing wrong and was looking at a long sentence. The very next morning both the other men were found dead.

And I stayed quiet.

BRP was a massive organisation, making huge profits. They had several factories in locations all over the world. Barlow is president, but has no day to day involvement other than that of a kind of busybody elderly relative, and the actual management tolerate him sticking his oar in, mostly because of history and it is harmless. They have no idea of the cash being rinsed out of the business every single day. But then Barlow discovered, coincidentally completely by accident that planning was underway to build a new super factory. In Mexico. He was furious, but then he remembered Gray Rock, and the plans he had been making. He realised that this would be perfect. A new plant, and a new town. Cheap labour already there. So he spoke earnestly to the BRP team, and they listened.

What choice did they have, Barlow was president, and held the controlling interest.

It was agreed.

And with the plant plans confirmed, Gray Rock was started in earnest. There had already been some construction, but not really anything serious. The town was eventually built from BRP money, without anyone in the company; managers, employees, or shareholders, having any idea. Abel was in charge of construction, and at any one time there were over a hundred teams, all working away. The big houses were completed first, and then around the high street area, and then the plant. The airport was built on top of the old airfield, and the hospital, which were part of the infrastructure demands of the plant. The town continued to grow.

Meanwhile I was nearing the end of my sentence. I had been diagnosed with what was eventually discovered to be a benign melanoma on my tongue. I spent several weeks in hospital, and because of my spotless record the decision had been made to release me. I left the hospital and returned to the prison to serve my remaining days. The week before I was due to get out I had a visit from a guard, it wasn't one that I had ever seen before. The guard told me to get to Gray Rock, Barlow wanted to take care of me.

Gray Rock? I had never heard of the place. Barlow and Abel would discuss 'their town' but I had always believed it was just a dream.

The guard told me not to worry about it, I would be collected from the prison on my release, which I was, whisked away in a limousine and flown to Gray Rock in a helicopter.

I changed my name, to avoid any potential embarrassment with BRP, because at the time I still believed I would be back working there.

Barlow was very pleased to see me, because despite of all the glory in this fantastic new town there was an issue arising. Money. They wanted white families. The temptation was to sell the houses cheaply, but they had discovered this caused a serious problem. They were trying to paint the picture of the perfect life, a town with big dreams and no crime, but it didn't stand up if the property values were so low. I was happy to be back so I rolled my sleeves up. The cash was there, and ABC Finance was born, offering amazing mortgage deals and unguaranteed loans at spectacular rates. Banking had changed a lot while I was away, but mostly the technology and I picked it up quickly. I was back doing what I did best, and everyone was happy.

But it went to Barlow's head, he wanted more. He cultivated his friendship with Judge Raymer and the justice department, and secured the deal to build the prison. Raymer was a frequent visitor to Gray Rock.

I found out about the hunts, which had started a good few years ago, although thankfully I had never had any involvement. I was never asked, because Barlow knew I would never want to go. I was introduced to Paul Hunter, who was apparently an ex-Special Forces soldier and a 'security advisor' to Barlow and Abel. The hunts had begun when originally Barlow, Hunter, and any selected interested others, which apparently sometimes included Abel would drive off toward the border at night and sit and wait, more often than not targets would appear. It was a common occurrence for people to believe they could cross over, despite the patrols. But the risk of official discovery was becoming greater as the border was more tightly controlled. The compound had been built especially as it was a tidier, safer solution. People with connections that Barlow needed were invited and given the full works, while others would pay. I made my disapproval very clear, but by then they had become an institution. From that point the hunts were never discussed in front of me, I was aware of work at Brown's which I believed was acquired for the new project.

At this point Cane was asked what the big new secret was. 'Ah,' Cane replied.

Homeland Security.

The department had grown hugely over the past decade, and it had been decided to give them a new home of their own; somewhere with space to grow and develop. 9/11 had changed the world, and the threat was greater than ever. They went out across the country looking for locations, talking to justice departments as part of the due diligence. Judge Raymer found out about it and spoke to Barlow, who realised immediately what it would do for the town. So, they did what they do best; they got ready with the money. Anything could be bought, anything. Even better, it turned out that James Waldron was a name they knew, he had been originally a supporter of One Race. Everything started to fit together. Barlow made Waldron a good offer. A nice, big house in the town where he would be working, and of course a large financial consideration to suit. Waldron went away and painted a pretty picture for the department, here was a big state, with willing and supportive partners. There was a huge amount of space, they would have everything they wanted; headquarters, training, infrastructure and also, detention. And right on the border with Mexico.

It was agreed. There was a party at the Country Club. I met Waldron for the first time, and I congratulated everyone on what appeared to me to be a major coup for the town.

And Barlow was now a very happy man. Nobody could get in his way now. He had been paranoid about external intrusion for years, and hated the FBI and even the police, believing them to be weak and always working with the minorities. Having Homeland Security in the town would mean they could never be touched.

The only problem was announcing it, the normal channels for any operation like this had been effectively short-circuited. Judge Raymer came up with freeing Anthony Collis, fill the press with this story and the new Homeland Security project could be nestled in the centre pages.

I am very sorry for the helicopter incident, I have been at breaking point for some time, alone and deep into something which was terrible and becoming worse every day. Then suddenly I had felt wanted again and had been keen to sustain it. I had known a long time that money was not the reason to be alive.

But I knew it was the end for me when I was told about Rita's murder. Up to that point all the hunting and the other things the Regulators were doing were remote, I was told very little and never asked. Hunter had proudly told me and Abel all about it, and Barlow had been pleased. I had liked Rita, and the real horror of everything that was going on and how weak I had become was truly hammered home the moment John Smith had reached out and taken my own gun from me.

I could not live this life a second more.

****

Patrick got the recording put into writing and returned to the Hyatt so Cane could sign it, then released copies to everyone concerned.

Carpenter sat the whole team down around the table and tried his best to make sure the day's business was done calmly.

'You all have done excellent work. None of this has been easy, and we are not even a fifth of the way through digging the ground at Brown's oilfield yet. Last night Carter was moved into the county hospital ICU, and the prognosis is he won't be coming out. We won't be able to speak to him again, but I believe, and I think in fact as we all do that we should have enough now. We will be bringing the remaining Regulators, or whoever the hell they are in for formal interviewing today and we believe that there will be no holes left by tonight.'

He looked around at everyone.

'All I ask is that you keep doing your jobs like you have been, and don't change anything in the way you guys are dealing with this. We're at the end stage. And we can all feel it.'

'Let's all make sure nothing goes wrong.'

The interviews started, later than they had on the previous days. Waldron's was first. His attorney had already read Cane's statement and had spent a long time going through it with his client.

The attorney solemnly read out a statement. Waldron admitted to everything, including to having extreme views, but denied he was racist. Barlow had invited him to the hunt, but it was the first time, he had never killed anyone and had not intended to do so. He had believed he was doing the best for his job with Homeland Security and for that he needed to keep Barlow close. When he had been invited he didn't fully understand what it was they were going to be doing, Barlow had basically said it would be a fun weekend, good food and drink and entertainment. There would be some hunting, bring along a good gun. Hints had been dropped about hunting at night and it was obvious the judge had been before, but at no point did anyone say specifically what they would be hunting. When the men had been pulled from the van he had realised, but he would never have shot anyone.

Patrick prodded and probed, surely there had to be more? After all, they were down there at eleven at night in the middle of nowhere?

Waldron swallowed helplessly.

After dinner there had been a small party, he believed the woman he had been with had been paid but he had a good time. Afterward Barlow had told him the fun would really start. And yes, he had made a comment which at the time had sounded like a joke. He had said nobody cared about a couple fewer beaners.

Waldron wept constantly throughout the proceedings.

Strike one. Confession taken. End of interview.

While Waldron was being interviewed, the agents at Travis made a breakthrough. Ray Tilling had followed Gibbs' and Cane's leads, without any prompting. The agents were at the prison for the round of interviews before the formal ones would begin and he had just walked in and told them he was going to come clean. Tilling was one of the newer Regulators, and was ashamed (now, anyway) to admit he had been on a couple of hunts. He liked it because they were paid extra. From what he had been told Judge Raymer had been on several of these, but he had never seen Waldron before. Hunter ran the Regulators but Tilling believed that he wasn't regularly there at a hunt. Barlow was the big dog (his own words) he called all the shots. Abel did the organising, and Cane, well, nobody really knew what Cane did, but it was said he was never at a hunt. Gibbs didn't know exactly how many people had been murdered at Brown's, he thought probably about ten, but it could be more, he was seen as the new guy, and told very little. They had been instructed to bury the bodies, and used the backhoe. He had been told that the hunts were normally one man as the target, sometimes two. As far as he knew there had never been three before that night. His statement was signed and placed as evidence.

Next up Raymer. Again, Cane's statement had been disclosed and the attorney and his client had locked themselves away for several hours.

Raymer admitted to making mistakes in his choice of relationships, but then rallied, claiming that he had been blinded by Barlow, who was rich and manipulative and he and Abel were to blame for everything. He had no idea what the hunt was and had absolutely never taken part in anything like it before, he had been asked if he wanted to go shooting out of the blue over dinner. It had sounded like it would be a lot of fun. Raymer wore a sincere and concerned expression, one which he had no doubt used many times in the past.

But not this time.

'Manipulative,' Canning said quietly. 'Sure have heard that word a lot in here.'

Without ceremony Patrick produced the forensic reports, and the judge's fingerprints on the handle of a shovel locked inside the storeroom at Brown's. The attorney was visibly startled, Raymer squirmed, Canning turned up the pressure and referred to Cane's disclosure that the judge was a frequent visitor. Raymer denied this, talking breathlessly, it was a conspiracy, they were trying to destroy him, it was all lies. He did not know Cane, but Barlow had told him repeatedly the man couldn't be trusted, he believed he had been set up, but why, he didn't know. But there was no room for manoeuvre, not now. Patiently, Patrick referred back to the fingerprint again, there it was, in black and white, what then was the explanation? More squirming, and more anger. He suddenly vaguely remembered doing some garden work at Barlow's house, but he had no idea why the shovel should be at Brown's. Then a knock on the door, and an agent walked in handing a sheet of paper to Patrick, who read it, and then looked up and smiled. Tilling's statement. He handed it over to the attorney, who also read it, and paled even further.

Immediately he requested a break, while he had the chance to speak to his client. Patrick went upstairs and walked into the monitor room. Everyone there already knew the news about Tilling's statement.

'What do you think?' he asked John, who smiled back at him.

'I think you've got him.'

It took some time, but eventually the interview resumed. Raymer was defeated, a wreck. Along with all the other evidence Cane's, Gibb's and Tilling's' statements left him nowhere to go. The attorney said that they were prepared to admit that Judge Raymer had been present at the hunts, but had never actively taken part.

'Too little, too late,' Patrick told them.

The attorney nodded, and then said Judge Raymer would disclose completely his involvement if mitigating factors could be considered.

Strike two. There were no mitigating factors. Confession taken. End of interview.

And finally, Barlow.

The man sitting at the table was scarcely recognisable as the same man John had first met just a few days ago. He looked even thinner, but was now haggard, his clothes all creased. His attorney stated that his client was unwell, which Barlow promptly blew by shouting angrily that he should not be kept at a prison and ranting that he deserved respect.

They sat still watching him, waiting and then patiently, Patrick and Canning went through every statement, taking their time, concentrating on Cane's, Carter's, Tillings' and Gibbs' words, detailing Raymer's confession and itemising every damning shred of evidence, unrelenting in their pursuit and finally, eventually, Barlow gave up.

He slumped back in his chair, fidgeting, pulling on his long nose.

'You are guilty, you may as well start telling the truth,' Patrick told him.

Barlow reacted angrily, it was all lies, he had done nothing wrong.

He had done everything wrong, Canning told him. He brought back segregation, which had been outlawed over fifty years previously. He had tried to build a ghetto, and when that hadn't worked had opted for his own form of racial cleansing.

Patrick looked directly into Barlow's eyes.

'What did you think? Nobody would notice? You've spent years and years setting this up, building white America. You started that bullshit One Race, what was that about?'

Barlow looked back defiantly.

'You won't ever understand, you're blinkered, like all the politicians and the journalists who attacked us, when we were doing good. Making lives better, are you telling me you don't want the best for your kids?'

'Yeah, I want everything for my kids. I'm no different from any parent. But I don't believe spreading racist crap is going to achieve anything. All you did was get a bunch of idiots fired up, for a couple of years maybe, before it was all forgotten.'

'It isn't forgotten. Blame the goddamn banks if you want to, it's their fault we had so many people left with nothing when that industry crashed and burned. We were the voice for them, and there are still believers today, more than you know.'

'You're living ten years in the past Mr Barlow. And you've just got worse and worse, from shooting dead anybody you can spot crossing the border to organising a hunt so others twisted just like you can enjoy themselves. Anthony Collis survived the sudden attack in Howarth by the way. And he is talking, so we know your connection to the murders in Europe all those years ago. We know exactly what you have done, everything. And I can make you a solemn promise, you are not walking away. This will end today. We have everything we need, you know we do and so does your attorney. All we are doing right now is delaying the inevitable. But we're ok with that, the result is going to be the same.'

His attorney started to whisper in Barlow's ear, but it was clear he wasn't listening. The anger was written all over him. He pulled his head away and frowned at his attorney who shut up and looked at Patrick.

There was nothing he could do, it was over. Everybody knew what his client had done. Raymer and Waldron had finally admitted to everything.

Barlow shook his head from side to side, mumbling away to himself, then stopped and stared hard at the camera.

He stood up straight, to his full height, towering over everyone.

'So, I guess you win,' he said. 'Congratulations. But there will never be another like me.'

Patrick also stood up, nowhere near as tall but still magnificent.

'You're wrong. There will never be another Elvis, that's for damn sure. Lots of people have tried, so many big stars, but none like him. But you, well there will be another you tomorrow, and the day after, and the day after that. Because rich, greedy bigots are a fact of life, thousands, right across the globe. You are nothing special Mr Barlow, and nobody will remember you this time next year. Get used to prison, you won't ever be getting out.'

Chapter Thirty

John left the next day. He had a long breakfast with Gilbey and Patrick, and then they said goodbye. They all promised to keep in touch, Patrick asking that next time maybe they could just go and have a beer or something. Just do something goddamn normal for Christ's sakes. Carrie hugged him and emotionally told him that Gilbey had promised to take her to London. Then he flew to New York, where he stayed for over three weeks, enjoying time with his daughter. He even got on well with her mother for a change, no fights, no recriminations.

The he was back at home, down on the south coast, repairing the leaking roof on his garage.

Patrick sent several messages over the coming months.

Carter never made it out it out of the hospital. The news of all the charges filtered down and he had a second, more serious heart attack, almost immediately followed by a third, which killed him.

Another who would not face any charges.

Anthony Collis miraculously survived, and John realised he was pleased about it. He would never walk normally again and had lost the use altogether of his left hand. He released a long and detailed statement and agreed to appear as a witness for the prosecution at the trial. Patrick was true to his word, he got Collis transferred to a low security detention centre in Kansas, which apparently was essentially nothing more than a rest home with locked gates, and he got a few years off his sentence for assisting the FBI.

James Waldron attempted suicide while in the jail, the court date set for less than a month away. He survived, but it was close. Homeland Security revoked the Gray Rock plan and launched an internal investigation into how it was ever accepted without the proper authority.

John had been called to give evidence, so flew into Austin. Patrick put him and Gilbey up in the Four Seasons again.

The trial started, there was a huge media and public interest. Barlow was hit by an egg as he was led from the transport into the court for the first day (John laughed when Patrick told him all about it later). It went on for over three weeks in the end, but the judge clearly knew there was only one way to deal with everything. The fact that Raymer was one of his peers, had probably been someone that most judges in the state looked up to was not lost on him. He stated clearly that this was shameful and damaging to the state of Texas. He would ensure that justice was done. He looked directly at Raymer as he spoke.

But ultimately there was no defence, none at all. All the men were guilty. The defence had attempted unsuccessfully to get John and Gilbey on the stand for the shootings but the testimony was too strong, Gibbs took the stand, as did Tilling and they gave a detailed account of everything that had happened on that night, plus they also described other hunts that they had worked on.

Collis was able to disclose the real hatred that Barlow had of immigrants, who in his eyes was anybody not white.

In total thirteen bodies were recovered from Brown's, ten men, two women and a sixteen year old male youth. Eleven were eventually identified, both of the women were mothers to several children. All were Mexican, there was a lot of anger, and the police presence at the courtroom was massive.

There were no twists or turns, no last minute shocks or surprises. Only a lot of rhetoric and blame shifting from the defence. Philip Reed was impressive again, John had to admit he had been very wrong about him. Waldron was the only one to show any remorse, there was no doubt Barlow had coerced him into taking part in the hunt, control was power, and Waldron would have never been able to change anything regarding the Homeland Security project, in fact he would never be able to do anything without permission again, he just hadn't realised it. The rewards in front of him were too great. The big house in Gray Rock. There was also the matter of the million and a half dollars sitting in an offshore account.

Raymer tried a different tack. He had hired an expensive legal team who persistently claimed coercion, that Raymer was an upstanding citizen who had been tricked.

Of course, it went nowhere. The evidence was too strong.

Barlow barely spoke at all. Finally, the reality of the situation had sunk in and there was nothing he could say. BRP issued a statement that there were pursuing an action over the millions and millions of dollars that had been stolen from the company by their previous president.

They were all found guilty.

Waldron, Raymer and the Regulators were all given long sentences, although there was no evidence that they had ever actually killed anyone. Tilling admitted his involvement in Rita Geller's murder but stated he did not kill her, the other man with him was Andrew Walters, the blond shot by John in the pick-up, and he was supposedly responsible. It was not possible to prove it either way.

Barlow was given the death sentence, it seemed Raymer narrowly avoided it out of deference for his long years as a judge.

Cane was allowed to go free. There was still the case of fraud to answer, but the judge accepted that he was effectively doing the job he was instructed to, and he had not made a single dollar out of any of the transactions and had already served ten years in prison unnecessarily.

In summing up, the judge thanked the jury, and stated that he hoped to never have to preside over such a horrific case again.

John said goodbye for the last time, went home, and back to work. There were always problems to solve.

Several months later Patrick emailed him three photographs, which he had received from the agent that was now closest to Gray Rock. The first one showed an event sponsored by the plant, crowds of people all around the square by the rock, a long line of barbecues, and a bar, everyone laughing and smiling. A mix of races and ages, all together in one place. And a big group of soldiers all enjoying a beer. The second was a picture of a sheriff walking out of the town hall. A young, black man. The final one was of people leaving a church, the old tired, wooden one on the south side. Most of the congregation were Hispanic and black, but there were several white faces in the crowd too.

There was also a copy of an article. Texas state education authority had looked at Gray Rock's schools and had been unable to work out why there were two big high schools, and also why the new one with all the facilities on the north side was only a third occupied. It had taken the decision to make that the Gray Rock High School, and to change the use of the southern building to a special education centre. There was a photograph of the new High School football team, a collection of sixteen and seventeen year old boys. Black, white and Hispanic, all wearing their uniforms and smiling. They had just won their first ever game 17–6, the first victory for any sporting event in the school's history.

There was a short note at the bottom from Patrick, which just read 'You did a good thing, you asshole.'